2016

ONCE CRAVED

(A RILEY PAIGE MYSTERY—BOOK 3)

BLAKE PIERCE

Heritage Point HOA
44 Heritage Point Blvd
Barnegat, NJ 08005

ISBN: 978-1-63291-560-3

Prologue

Janine thought she saw something dark in the water down near the shoreline. It was big and black, and it seemed to move a little in the gently lapping water.

She took a hit off the marijuana pipe and handed it back to her boyfriend. Could that be a really big fish? Or some other kind of creature?

Janine shook herself a little, telling herself not to let her imagination run away with her. Getting scared would ruin her high. Nimbo Lake was a huge artificial reservoir stocked for fishing just like lots of other Arizona lakes. There'd never been tales of Nessie monsters around here.

She heard Colby say, "Wow, the lake's on fire!"

Janine turned to look at her boyfriend. His freckled face and red hair glowed in the late afternoon sunlight. He had just taken a hit off the pipe and was staring across the water with an expression of idiotic awe.

Janine giggled. "You're just lit, dude," she said. "In every way."

"Yeah, so is the lake," Colby said.

Janine turned and looked out over Nimbo Lake. Even though her own high hadn't quite kicked in yet, the sight was stunning. The late afternoon sun set the canyon wall ablaze in reds and golds. The water reflected the colors like a big smooth mirror.

She remembered that *nimbo* was Spanish for halo. The name totally fit.

She took back the pipe and inhaled deeply, feeling the welcome burn down her throat. She'd be good and high any minute now. It was going to be fun.

Still, what *was* that black shape down in the water?

Just a trick of the light, Janine told herself.

Whatever it was, it was best to ignore it, not get creeped out by it, or scared. Everything else was so perfect. This was their favorite spot, hers and Colby's—so beautiful, tucked into one of the coves on the lake, away from the campgrounds, away from everything, everybody.

She and Colby usually came here on weekends, but today they had cut school and just taken off. The late summer weather was too good to pass up. It was way cooler and nicer up here than back in Phoenix. Colby's old car was parked off the dirt road behind them.

As she looked out over the lake, the buzz came on—the feeling of a really great impending high. The lake seemed almost too intensely gorgeous to look at. So she looked at Colby. He looked intensely gorgeous too. She grabbed hold of him and kissed him. He kissed her back. He tasted fabulous. Everything about him looked and felt fabulous.

She pulled her lips away from his and looked into his eyes and said breathlessly, "Nimbo means halo, did you know that?"

"Wow," he said. "Wow."

He sounded like that was the most amazing thing he'd ever heard in his life. He looked and sounded so funny, saying that, like it was religious or something. Janine started to laugh, and Colby laughed too. In another couple of seconds, they were completely tangled up in each other's arms, groping and pawing.

Janine managed to disentangle herself.

"What's the matter?" Colby asked.

"Nothing," Janine said.

In a flash, she pulled off her halter top. Colby's eyes widened.

"What are you doing?" he asked.

"What do you think I'm doing?"

She began to struggle with his T-shirt, trying to pull it off of him.

"Wait a minute," Colby said. "Right here?"

"Why not right here? It's better than the back seat of your car. Nobody's looking."

"But maybe a boat …"

Janine laughed. "If there's a boat, so what? Who cares?"

Colby was cooperating now, helping her get him out of his T-shirt. They were both clumsy with excitement, which only added to the thrill. Janine couldn't imagine why they hadn't done this here before. It wasn't like this was the first time they'd smoked pot here.

But Janine kept picturing that shape down in the water. It was *something*, and until she knew what it was, it would keep nagging at her and ruin everything.

Panting, she rose to her feet.

"Come on," she said. "Let's go check something."

"What?" Colby asked.

"I dunno. Just come on."

She took Colby's hand and they stumbled down the rough slope toward the shore. Janine's buzz was starting to turn sour now. She hated when that happened. The sooner she found out that this whole thing was harmless, the sooner she could get back to feeling good.

Still, she was starting to wish her high hadn't come on so fast and so strong.

With every step, the object came into clearer view. It was made out of black plastic, and here and there bubbles of it broke through the water's surface. And there was something small and white right alongside of it.

Just a yard away from the water, Janine could see that it was a big black garbage bag. It was open at the end, and out of the opening poked the shape of a hand, unnaturally pale.

A mannequin, maybe, Janine thought.

She bent down toward the water to get a closer look. The fingernails were painted garishly red in contrast to the paleness. A terrible realization ripped through Janine's body like an electrical current.

The hand was real. It was a woman's hand. The bag contained a dead body.

Janine started screaming. She heard Colby scream too.

And she knew that they wouldn't be able to stop screaming for a long time.

Chapter One

Riley knew that the slides she was about to show would shock her FBI Academy students. Some of them probably weren't going to be able to take it. She scanned the eager young faces watching her from the half-circle of tiered desks.

Let's see how they react, she thought. *This could be important for them.*

Of course, Riley knew that in the whole range of criminal offenses, serial murder was rare. Still, these young people had to learn everything there was to learn. They aspired to be FBI field agents and they'd soon find that most local law officers had no experience with serial cases. And Special Agent Riley Paige was an authority on serial murder.

She clicked the remote. The first images to appear on the large flat-screen were anything but violent. They were five charcoal portraits of women, ranging in age from young to middle age. All the women were attractive and smiling, and the portraits had been done with skill and loving artistry.

As Riley clicked, she said, "These five drawings were made eight years ago by an artist named Derrick Caldwell. Every summer, he made lots of money drawing portraits of tourists on the Dunes Beach Boardwalk here in Virginia. These women were among his very last clients."

After the last of the five portraits, Riley clicked again. The next photograph was a hideous image of an open chest freezer filled with dismembered female body parts. She heard her students gasp.

"This is what became of those women," Riley said. "While he was drawing them, Derrick Caldwell became convinced, to use his own words, that they 'were too beautiful to live.' So he stalked them one by one, killed them, dismembered them, and kept them in his freezer."

Riley clicked again, and the images that came up next were more shocking still. They were photographs taken by the medical examiner's team after they'd reassembled the bodies.

Riley said, "Caldwell actually 'shuffled' the body parts, so that the women were dehumanized beyond recognition."

Riley turned toward the classroom. One male student was rushing toward the exit, clutching his stomach. Others looked on the verge of throwing up. A few were in tears. Only a handful appeared to be unperturbed.

4

Paradoxically, Riley felt pretty sure that the unruffled students would be the ones who wouldn't survive academy training. To them, these were just pictures, not real at all. They wouldn't be able to handle true horror whenever they had to face it firsthand. They wouldn't be able to handle the personal aftershocks, the post-traumatic stress that they could suffer. Visions of a flaming torch still slipped into her consciousness from time to time, but her PTSD was decreasing. She was healing. But she was sure that anybody first had to feel something before they could recover from it.

"And now," Riley said, "I'm going to make a couple of statements, and you're going to tell me if they're myth or fact. Here's the first. 'Most serial murderers kill for sexual reasons.' Myth or fact?"

Hands shot up among the students. Riley pointed to an especially eager-looking student in the first row.

"Fact?" the student asked.

"Yes, fact," Riley said. "Although there can be other reasons, a sexual component is the most frequent. This can take various forms, sometimes rather bizarre. Derrick Caldwell is a classic example. The medical examiner determined that he committed acts of necrophilia on the victims before he dismembered them."

Riley saw that most of her students were typing notes into their laptops. She continued, "Now here's another statement. 'Serial killers inflict increasing violence on their victims as they continue to kill.'"

Hands went up again. This time Riley pointed to a student a few rows back.

"Fact?" the student said.

"Myth," Riley said. "Although I've certainly seen some exceptions, most cases show no such change over time. Derrick Caldwell's level of violence stayed consistent while he was killing. But he was reckless, hardly an evil mastermind. He got greedy. He took his victims within a period of a month and a half. By drawing that kind of attention, he made his capture all but inevitable."

She glanced at the clock and saw that her hour was up.

"That's all for today," she said. "But there are many mistaken assumptions about serial killers and a lot of myths still circulate. The Behavioral Analysis Unit has collected and analyzed the data, and I have worked serial cases in locations all over the country. We still have a lot of information to cover."

The class broke up, and Riley started packing up her materials to go home. Three or four students clustered around her desk to ask questions.

A male student asked, "Agent Paige, weren't you involved in the Derrick Caldwell case?"

"Yes, I was," Riley said. "That's a story for another time."

It was also a story that she wasn't eager to tell, but she didn't say so.

A young woman asked, "Was Caldwell ever executed for his crimes?"

"Not yet," Riley said.

Trying not to be rude, Riley brushed past the students toward the exit. Caldwell's impending execution wasn't something she felt comfortable discussing. The truth was, she expected it to be scheduled for any day now. As his principal captor, she had a standing invitation to witness his death. She hadn't decided yet whether or not she'd go.

Riley felt good as she walked out of the building into a pleasant September afternoon. She was, after all, still on leave.

She'd suffered from PTSD ever since a maniacal killer had held her captive. She'd escaped and eventually taken down her tormentor. But she hadn't gone on leave even then. She'd continued straight on to finish another case. It was a grisly business in Upstate New York that had ended with the killer committing suicide right in front of her by slashing his own throat.

That moment still haunted her. When her supervisor, Brent Meredith, approached her with another case, she'd declined to accept it. At Meredith's suggestion, she'd agreed to teach a class at the Quantico FBI Academy instead.

As she got into her car and started to drive home, Riley thought about what a wise choice it had been. Finally, her life had a sense of peace, of calm.

And yet, as she drove, a creeping, familiar feeling began to set in, one that made her heart begin to pound in the middle of a clear blue day. It was a heightened sense of anticipation, she realized, of something ominous to come.

And try as she might to envision herself in this calm forever, she knew, she just knew, it wouldn't last.

Chapter Two

Riley felt a twinge of dread as she felt the buzzing in her handbag. She stopped outside the front door of her new townhouse and pulled out her phone. Her heart skipped a beat.

It was a message from Brent Meredith.

Call me.

Riley worried. Her boss might merely be checking in to see how she was doing. He did that a lot these days. On the other hand, he might want her to return to work. What would she do then?

I'll say no, of course, Riley told herself.

That might not be easy, though. She liked her boss, and she knew he could be very persuasive. It was a decision she didn't want to have to make, so she put the phone away.

When she opened her front door and stepped into the bright, clean space of her new home, Riley's momentary anxiety vanished. Everything seemed so right since she'd moved here.

A pleasant voice called out.

"¿Quién es?"

"Soy yo," Riley called back. "I'm home, Gabriela."

The stout, middle-aged Guatemalan woman stepped out of the kitchen, drying her hands with a towel. It was good to see Gabriela's smiling face. She'd been the family housekeeper for years, long before Riley had gotten divorced from Ryan. Riley was grateful that Gabriela had agreed to move in with her and her daughter.

"How was your day?" Gabriela asked.

"It was great," Riley said.

"¡Qué bueno!"

Gabriela disappeared back into the kitchen. The smell of a wonderful dinner wafted through the house. She heard Gabriela start to sing in Spanish.

Riley stood in her living room, relishing her surroundings. She and her daughter had moved here only recently. The little ranch-style house they had lived in when her marriage dissolved had been too isolated for safety. Besides, Riley had felt an urgent need for a change, both for herself and April. Now that her divorce was final and Ryan was being generous with child support, it was time to make a whole new life.

There were still a few finishing touches to take care of. Some of the furniture was rather old and out of place in such a pristine

7

environment. She'd have to find replacements. One of the walls looked rather empty, and Riley had run out of pictures to hang there. She made a mental note to go shopping with April this coming weekend. That idea made Riley feel comfortably normal, a woman with a nice family life rather than an agent tracking down some deviant murderer.

Now she wondered—where *was* April?

She stopped to listen. No music was emanating from April's room upstairs. Then she heard her daughter scream.

April's voice was coming from the backyard. Riley gasped and rushed through her dining area and out onto the large back deck. When she saw April's face and torso pop into view above the fence between yards, it took Riley a moment to realize what was happening. Then she relaxed and laughed at herself. Her automatic panic had been an overreaction. But it had been instinctive. All too recently, Riley had rescued April from the clutches of a madman who had targeted her for revenge on her mother.

April disappeared from view and then popped up again squealing with pleasure. She was jumping on the neighbor's trampoline. She'd made friends with the girl who lived there, a teenager who was about April's age and even went to the same high school.

"Be careful!" Riley called out to April.

"I'm fine, Mom!" April called back breathlessly.

Riley laughed again. It was an unfamiliar sound, springing from feelings she had almost forgotten. She wanted to get used to laughing again.

She also wanted to get used to the joyful expression on her daughter's face. It seemed like only yesterday when April had been terribly rebellious and sullen, even for a teenager. Riley could hardly blame April. Riley knew that she had left a lot to be desired as a mother. She was doing everything she could to change that.

That was one thing she especially liked about being on leave from field work, with its long, unpredictable hours often in faraway locations. Now her schedule meshed with April's, and Riley dreaded the likelihood that this would someday have to change.

Best to enjoy it while I can, she thought.

Riley went back into the house just in time to hear the front doorbell ring.

She called out, "I'll get it, Gabriela."

She opened the door and was surprised to find herself facing a smiling man she hadn't seen before.

"Hi," he said, a bit shyly. "I'm Blaine Hildreth, from next door. Your daughter is over there now with my daughter, Crystal." He held out a box to Riley and added, "Welcome to the neighborhood. I've brought you a small housewarming gift."

"Oh," Riley said. She was startled at the unaccustomed cordiality. It took her a moment to say, "Please, come on in."

She accepted the box awkwardly and offered him a seat in a living room chair. Riley sat down on the sofa, holding the gift box in her lap. Blaine Hildreth was looking at her expectantly.

"This is so kind of you," she said, opening up the package. It held a mixed set of colorful coffee mugs, two of them decorated with butterflies and the other two with flowers.

"They're lovely," Riley said. "Would you like some coffee?"

"I'd love some," Blaine said.

Riley called out to Gabriela, who came in from the kitchen.

"Gabriela, could you bring us some coffee in these?" she said, handing her two of the mugs. "Blaine, how do you like yours?"

"Black will be fine."

Gabriela took the mugs into the kitchen.

"My name is Riley Paige," she said to Blaine. "Thanks for stopping by. And thank you for the gift."

"You're welcome," Blaine said.

Gabriela returned with two mugs of delicious hot coffee, then went back to work in the kitchen. Somewhat to her embarrassment, Riley found herself sizing up her male neighbor. Now that she was single, she couldn't resist. She hoped he didn't notice.

Oh, well, she thought. *Maybe he's doing the same with me.*

First, she observed that he wasn't wearing a wedding ring. Widowed or divorced, she figured.

Second, she estimated that he was about her age, maybe a little younger, perhaps in his late thirties.

Finally, he was good-looking—or at least reasonably so. His hairline was receding, which wasn't a strike against him. And he seemed to be lean and fit.

"So, what do you do?" Riley asked.

Blaine shrugged. "I own a restaurant. Do you know Blaine's Grill downtown?"

Riley was pleasantly impressed. Blaine's Grill was one of the nicest casual lunch places here in Fredericksburg. She'd heard that it was terrific for dinner, but hadn't had a chance to try it.

"I've been there," she said.

"Well, that's mine," Blaine said. "And you?"

Riley took a long breath. It was never easy to tell a total stranger what she did for a living. Men especially were sometimes intimidated.

"I'm with the FBI," she said. "I'm—a field agent."

Blaine's eyes widened.

"Really?" he said.

"Well, on leave at the moment. I'm teaching at the academy."

Blaine leaned toward her with growing interest.

"Wow. I'm sure you've got some real stories. I'd love to hear one."

Riley laughed a bit nervously. She wondered if she'd ever be able to tell anybody outside of the Bureau about some of the things she had seen. It would be even harder to talk about some of things she had done.

"I don't think so," she said a bit sharply. Riley could see Blaine stiffen, and she realized that her tone was rather rude.

He ducked his head and said, "I apologize. I certainly didn't mean to make you feel uncomfortable."

They chatted for a few moments after that, but Riley was aware that her new neighbor was being more reserved. After he politely said goodbye and left, Riley closed the door behind him and sighed. She was not making herself approachable, she realized. The woman starting a new life was still the same old Riley.

But she told herself that it hardly mattered at the moment. A rebound relationship was the very last thing she needed right now. Her life required some serious sorting out, and she was just beginning to make progress in that direction.

Still, it had been nice to spend a few minutes talking to an attractive man, and a relief to finally have neighbors—and pleasant ones at that.

*

When Riley and April sat down at the table for dinner, April couldn't keep her hands off her smartphone.

"Please stop texting," Riley said. "It's supper time."

"In a minute, Mom," April said. She kept right on texting.

Riley was only mildly irritated by April's display of teen behavior. The truth was, it definitely had an upside. Riley was doing great at school this year and making new friends. As far as Riley was concerned, they were a much better bunch of kids than April had hung out with before. Riley guessed that April was now texting with a boy she was interested in. So far, though, April hadn't mentioned him.

April did stop texting when Gabriela came in from the kitchen with a tray of chiles rellenos. As she set the steaming, lusciously stuffed bell peppers on the kitchen table, April giggled mischievously.

"Picante enough, Gabriela?" she asked.

"Sí," Gabriela said, also giggling.

It was a running joke among the three of them. Ryan had disliked foods that were too spicy. Actually, he couldn't eat them at all. As far as April and Riley were concerned, hotter was better. Gabriela no longer had to hold back—or at least not as much as she used to. Riley doubted whether even she or April could handle Gabriela's original Guatemalan recipes.

When Gabriela finished setting out the food for all three of them, she said to Riley, "The gentleman is *guapo,* no?"

Riley felt herself blush. "Handsome? I hadn't noticed, Gabriela."

Gabriela let out a burst of laughter. She sat down to eat with them and started to hum a little tune. Riley guessed that it was a Guatemalan love song. April stared at her mother.

"What gentleman, Mom?" she asked.

"Oh, our neighbor came by a little while ago—"

April interrupted excitedly. "Omigod! Was it Crystal's dad? It was, wasn't it! Isn't he gorgeous?"

"And I think he is single." Gabriela said.

"OK, back off," Riley said with a laugh. "Give me some room to live. I don't need the two of you trying to fix me up with the guy next door."

They all dug into the stuffed peppers, and dinner was almost finished when Riley felt her phone buzz in her pocket.

Damn it, she thought. *I shouldn't have brought it to the table.*

The buzzing continued. She couldn't very well not answer it. Since she'd gotten home, Brent Meredith had left two more text messages, and she'd kept telling herself that she'd call him later. She couldn't put it off anymore. She excused herself from the table and answered the phone.

"Riley, I'm sorry to bother you like this," her boss said. "But I really need your help."

Riley was startled to hear Meredith call her by her first name. That was rare. Although she felt quite close to him, he usually addressed her as Agent Paige. He was normally businesslike, sometimes to the point of being brusque.

"What is it, sir?" Riley asked.

Meredith fell silent for a moment. Riley wondered why he was being reticent. Her spirits sank. She felt sure that this was precisely the news she'd been dreading.

"Riley, I'm asking a personal favor," he said, sounding much less commanding than usual. "I've been asked to look into a murder in Phoenix."

Riley was surprised. "A single murder?" she asked. "Why would that require the FBI?"

"I've got an old friend at the field office in Phoenix," Meredith said. "Garrett Holbrook. We went to the academy together. His sister Nancy was the victim."

"I'm so sorry," Riley said. "But the local police …"

There was a rare note of entreaty in Meredith's voice.

"Garrett really wants our help. She was a prostitute. She just disappeared and then her body turned up in a lake. He wants us to look into it as the work of a serial killer."

The request seemed odd to Riley. Prostitutes often did disappear without getting killed. Sometimes they decided to do their work somewhere else. Or just quit.

"Does he have any reason to think so?" she asked.

"I don't know, Meredith said. "Maybe he wants to think that in order to get us involved. But it's true, as you know, that prostitutes are frequent targets of serials."

Riley knew that this was true. Prostitutes' lifestyles made them high-risk. They were visible and accessible, alone with strangers, often drug dependent.

Meredith continued, "He called me personally. I promised him I'd send my very best people to Phoenix. And of course—that includes you."

Riley was touched. Meredith wasn't making it easy to say no.

"Please try to understand, sir," she said. "I just can't take on anything new."

Riley felt vaguely dishonest. *Can't or won't?* she asked herself. After she had been captured and tortured by a serial killer, everyone had insisted she take a leave from work. She'd tried to do that, but found herself desperately needing to be back on the job. Now she wondered what that desperation had really been all about. She had been reckless and self-destructive and had a hell of a time getting her life under control. When she had finally killed Peterson, her tormentor, she had thought everything would be fine. But he still haunted her, and she was having new problems over the resolution of her last case.

After a pause, she added, "I need more time off the field. I'm still technically on leave and I'm really trying to put my life together."

A long silence followed. It didn't sound as though Meredith was going to argue, much less pull rank on her. But he wasn't going to say he was OK with it, either. He wouldn't let up the pressure.

She heard Meredith heave a long, sad sigh. "Garrett had been estranged from Nancy for years. Now what happened to her is eating him up inside. I guess there's a lesson there, isn't there? Don't take anyone in your life for granted. Always reach out."

Riley almost dropped the phone. Meredith's words hit a nerve that hadn't been touched for a long time. Riley had lost contact with her own older sister years ago. They were estranged and she hadn't even wondered about Wendy for a long time. She had no idea what her own sister was doing now.

After another pause, Meredith said, "Promise me you'll think it over."

"I will," Riley said.

They ended the call.

She felt terrible. Meredith had seen her through some awful times and he'd never shown such vulnerability toward her before. She hated to let him down. And she'd just promised him to think it over.

And no matter how desperately she wanted to, Riley wasn't sure she could say no.

Chapter Three

The man sat in his car in the parking lot, watching the whore as she approached along the street. "Chiffon," she called herself. Obviously not her real name. And he was sure there was a lot more about her that he didn't know.

I could make her tell me, he thought. *But not here. Not today.*

He wouldn't kill her here today either. No, not right here so near her regular workplace—the so-called "Kinetic Custom Gym." From where he sat, he could see the decrepit exercise machinery through the storefront windows—three treadmills, a rowing machine, and a couple of weight machines, none of them working. As far as he knew, nobody ever came here to actually exercise.

Not in a socially acceptable manner anyway, he thought with a smirk.

He didn't come around to this place much—not since he'd taken that brunette who had worked here years ago. Of course, he hadn't killed her here. He'd lured her off to a motel room for "extra services" and with the promise of a lot more money.

It hadn't been premeditated murder even then. The plastic bag over her head was only meant to add a fantasy element of danger. But once it was done, he'd been surprised at how deeply satisfied he'd felt. It had been an epicurean pleasure, distinctive even in his lifetime of pleasures.

Still, in his trysts since then, he'd exercised more care and restraint. Or at least he had until last week, when the same game went deadly again with that escort—what was her name?

Oh, yes, he remembered. *Nanette.*

He'd suspected at the time that Nanette might not be her real name. Now he'd never find out. In his heart, he knew that her death was not an accident. Not really. He'd meant to do it. And his conscience was unsullied. He was ready to do it again.

The one who called herself Chiffon was approaching about a half a block away, clad in a yellow tube top and a barely existent skirt, tottering toward the gym on impossibly high heels while talking on her cell phone.

He really wanted to know if Chiffon was her real name. Their one previous professional encounter had been a failure—her fault, he was sure, not his. Something about her had put him off.

He'd known perfectly well that she was older than she claimed to be. It was more than just her body—even teenage whores had stretch marks from childbirth. And it wasn't the lines in her face. Whores aged faster than any kind of women he knew.

He couldn't put his finger on it. But there was plenty about her that perplexed him. She displayed a certain kind of faux-girlish enthusiasm that wasn't the mark of a true professional—not even a novice.

She giggled too much, like a child playing a game. She was too eager. And most oddly, he suspected that she actually liked her job.

A whore who really enjoys sex, he thought, watching her come nearer. *Who ever heard of such a thing?*

Frankly, it turned him off.

Well, at least he was sure that she wasn't an undercover cop. He would have picked up on that in a split second.

When she got close enough to see him, he honked his car horn. She stopped talking on the phone for a moment and looked his way, shielding her eyes from the morning sunlight. When she saw who it was she waved and smiled—a smile that looked, for all the world, completely sincere.

Then she walked around back of the gym toward the "service" entrance. He realized that she probably had an appointment to keep inside the brothel. No matter, he would hire her some other day when he was in the mood for a specific kind of pleasure. Meanwhile, there were plenty of other hookers around.

He remembered how they'd left things last time. She'd been cheerful and good-natured and apologetic.

"Come back anytime," she'd told him. *"It will go better next time. We'll hit it off together. Things will get really exciting."*

"Oh, Chiffon," he murmured aloud to himself. "You've got no idea."

Chapter Four

Gunfire rang out around Riley. To her left, she heard the noisy cracks of pistols. To her right, she heard heavier weaponry—blasts from assault rifles and staccato sprays from submachine guns.

In the midst of the clamor, she drew her Glock handgun from her hip holster, dropped to a prone position, and fired off six rounds. She rose into a kneeling position and fired three rounds. She deftly and quickly reloaded, then stood and fired six rounds, and finally knelt and fired three more rounds with her left hand.

She stood up and holstered her weapon, then stepped back from the firing line and pulled off her earmuffs and eye protectors. The target with the bottle-shaped outline was twenty-five yards away. Even from this distance, she could see that she had clustered all her shots nicely together. In neighboring lanes, the FBI Academy trainees kept up their practice under the guidance of their instructor.

It had been a while since Riley had fired a weapon, even though she was always armed on the job. She'd reserved this lane at the FBI Academy firing range for a little target practice and, as always, there was something satisfying about the gun's powerful recoil, the raw force of it.

She heard a voice behind her.

"Kind of old-school, aren't you?"

She turned and saw Special Agent Bill Jeffreys standing nearby, grinning. She smiled back. Riley knew exactly what he meant by "old-school." A few years ago, the FBI had changed the live-fire rules for pistol qualification. Firing from a prone position had been part of the old drill, but it was no longer required. Now more emphasis was put on firing at targets from up close, between three and seven yards. That was supplemented by the virtual reality installation where agents were immersed in scenarios involving armed confrontations in close quarters. And trainees also went through the notorious Hogan's Alley, a ten-acre mocked-up town where they fought off imitation terrorists with paintball guns.

"Sometimes I like to go old-school," she said. "I figure that someday I might actually have to use deadly force at a distance."

From her own experience, Riley knew that the real thing was almost always up close and personal, and often unexpected. In fact, she'd actually had to fight hand to hand in two recent cases. She'd killed one attacker with his own knife and another with a random rock.

"Do you think anything prepares these kids for the real thing?" Bill asked, nodding toward the trainees who were now finished and leaving the firing range.

"Not really," Riley said. "In VR your brain does accept the scenario as real, but there's no imminent danger, no pain, no rage to control. Something inside always knows there's no chance of being killed."

"Right," Bill said. "They'll have to find out what it's really like just like we did a lot of years ago."

Riley glanced sideways at him as they moved farther away from the firing line.

Like her, he was forty years old with touches of gray in his dark hair. She wondered what it meant that she found herself mentally comparing him to her leaner, slighter male neighbor.

What was his name? she asked herself. *Oh, yeah—Blaine.*

Blaine was good-looking, but she wasn't sure whether he gave Bill a run for his money. Bill was big, solid, and quite attractive.

"What brings you here?" she asked.

"I heard you'd be here," he said.

Riley squinted at him uneasily. This probably wasn't just a friendly visit. From his expression, she detected that he wasn't ready to tell her what he wanted just yet.

Bill said, "If you want to do the whole drill, I'll keep time for you."

"I'd appreciate that," Riley said.

They moved off to a separate section of the shooting range, where she wouldn't be at risk of being hit by stray bullets from the trainees.

While Bill operated a timer, Riley breezed through all the stages of the FBI pistol qualification course, firing at the target from three yards, then five, then seven, then fifteen. The fifth and last stage was the only part that she found the least bit challenging— firing from behind a barricade at twenty-five yards.

When she was through, Riley took off her headgear. She and Bill walked up to the target and checked her work. All the impact marks were clustered nicely together.

"A hundred percent—a perfect score," Bill said.

"It had better be," Riley said. She'd hate it if she were getting rusty.

Bill pointed toward the earthen backstop beyond the target.

"Kind of surreal, huh?" he said.

Several white-tailed deer were contentedly grazing on top of the hill. They'd actually gathered there while she'd been shooting. They were within easy range, even with her pistol. But they weren't the least bit bothered by all the thousands of bullets slamming into targets just below the high ridge they walked on.

"Yes," she said, "and beautiful."

Around this time of year, the deer were a common sight here at the range. It was hunting season, and somehow they knew that they would be safe here. In fact, the grounds of the FBI Academy had become a sort of wildlife haven for lots of animals, including foxes, wild turkeys, and groundhogs.

"A couple of days ago, one of my students saw a bear in the parking lot," Riley said.

Riley took a few steps toward the backstop. The deer raised their heads, stared at her, and trotted away. They weren't afraid of gunfire, but they didn't want people getting too close.

"How do you suppose they know?" Bill asked. "That it's safe here, I mean. Don't all gunshots sound alike?"

Riley simply shook her head. It was a mystery to her. Her father had taken her hunting when she was little. To him, deer were simply resources—food and hide. It hadn't bothered her to kill them all those years ago. But that had changed.

It seemed odd, now that she thought about it. She had no trouble using deadly force against a human being when it was necessary. She could kill a man in a heartbeat. But to kill one of these trusting creatures now seemed unthinkable.

Riley and Bill walked off to a nearby rest area and sat down together on a bench. Whatever it was he came to talk about here, he still seemed reticent.

"How are you doing on your own?" she asked in a gentle voice.

She knew it was a delicate question and she saw him wince. His wife had recently left him after years of tension between his job and home life. Bill had been worried about the prospect of losing touch with his young sons. Now he was living in an apartment in the town of Quantico and spending time with his boys on weekends.

"I don't know, Riley," he said. "I don't know if I'll ever get used to it."

He was clearly lonely and depressed. She had been through enough of that herself during her own recent separation and then divorce. She also knew that the time after a separation was particularly fragile. Even if the relationship hadn't been very good, you found yourself out in a world of strangers, missing years of familiarity, never knowing quite what to do with yourself.

Bill touched her arm. His voice a bit thick with emotion, he said, "Sometimes I think that all I've got left to depend on in life is … you."

For a moment Riley felt like hugging him. When they had worked as partners, Bill had come to her rescue plenty of times, both physically and emotionally. But she knew she had to be careful. And she knew that people could be pretty crazy at times like this. She had actually phoned Bill one drunken night and proposed that they begin an affair. Now the situations were reversed. She could sense his impending dependence on her, now that she was just beginning to feel free and strong enough to be on her own.

"We were good partners," she said. It was lame, but she couldn't think of anything else to say.

Bill took a long, deep breath.

"That's what I came out here to talk to you about," he said. "Meredith told me he'd called you about the Phoenix case. I'm working on it. I need a partner."

Riley felt just a trace of irritation. Bill's visit was starting to seem like a bit of an ambush.

"I told Meredith I'd think about it," she said.

"And now *I'm* asking you," Bill said.

A silence fell between them.

"What about Lucy Vargas?" Riley asked.

Agent Vargas was a rookie who had worked closely with Bill and Riley on their most recent case. They both were impressed with her work.

"Her ankle hasn't healed," Bill said. "She won't be back in the field for another month at least."

Riley felt foolish for asking. When she, Bill, and Lucy had closed in on Eugene Fisk, the so-called "chain killer," Lucy had taken a fall and broken her ankle and almost gotten killed. Of course she couldn't go back to work so soon.

"I don't know, Bill," Riley said. "This break away from work is doing me a lot of good. I've been thinking about just teaching from now on. All I can tell you is what I told Meredith."

"That you'll think about it."

"Right."

Bill let out a grunt of discontentment.

"Could we at least get together and talk it over?" he asked. "Maybe tomorrow?"

Riley fell silent again for a moment.

"Not tomorrow," she said. "Tomorrow I have to watch a man die."

Chapter Five

Riley looked through the window into the room where Derrick Caldwell would soon die. She was sitting beside Gail Bassett, the mother of Kelly Sue Bassett, Caldwell's final victim. The man had killed five women before Riley had stopped him.

Riley had wavered about accepting Gail's invitation to the execution. She'd only seen one other, that time as a volunteer witness sitting among reporters, lawyers, law enforcement officers, spiritual advisors, and the jury foreman. Now she and Gail were among nine relatives of women that Caldwell had murdered, all of them crowded together in a tight space, sitting on plastic chairs.

Gail, a small sixty-year-old woman with a delicate, birdlike face, had kept up contact with Riley over the years. By the time of the execution her husband had died, and she had written Riley that she had no one to see her through the momentous event. So Riley had agreed to join her.

The death chamber was right there on the other side of the window. The only furniture in the room was the execution gurney, a cross-shaped table. A blue plastic curtain hung at the head of the gurney. Riley knew that the IV lines and lethal chemicals were behind that curtain.

A red telephone on the wall connected with the governor's office. It would only ring in case of a last-minute decision for clemency. No one expected that to happen this time. A clock over the door to the room was the only other visible decor.

In Virginia, convicted offenders could choose between the electric chair and lethal injection, but the chemicals were far more often chosen. If the prisoner made no choice, injection was assigned.

Riley was almost surprised that Caldwell hadn't opted for the electric chair. He was an unrepentant monster who seemed to welcome his own death.

The clock read 8:55 when the door opened. Riley heard a wordless murmur in the room as several members of the execution team ushered Caldwell into the chamber. Two guards flanked him, gripping each arm, and another followed right behind him. A well-dressed man came in after all the rest—the prison warden.

Caldwell was wearing blue pants, a blue work shirt, and sandals with no socks. He was handcuffed and shackled. Riley hadn't seen him for years. During his brief stint as a serial killer he'd had unruly long hair and a shaggy beard, a bohemian look befitting a sidewalk artist. Now he was clean-shaven and ordinary looking.

Although he didn't put up a struggle, he looked frightened.

Good, Riley thought.

He looked at the gurney, then glanced quickly away. He seemed to be trying not to look at the blue plastic curtain at the head of the gurney. For a moment, he stared into the viewing room window. He suddenly seemed calmer and more collected.

"I wish he could see us," Gail murmured.

They were shielded from his view behind one-way glass and Riley didn't share Gail's wish. Caldwell had already looked at her much too closely for her liking. To capture him, she'd gone undercover. She'd pretended to be a tourist on the Dunes Beach Boardwalk and hired him to draw her portrait. As he worked, he'd showered her with flowery flattery, telling her that she was the most beautiful woman he'd drawn in a long time.

She knew right then that she was his next intended victim. That night she'd served as bait to draw him out, letting him stalk her along the beach. When he had tried to attack her, backup agents had no trouble catching him.

His capture had been pretty nondescript. The discovery of how he had carved up his victims and kept them in his freezer had been another matter. Standing there when the freezer was opened was one of the most harrowing moments of Riley's career. She still felt pity for the victims' families—Gail among them—for having to identify their dismembered wives, daughters, sisters …

"Too beautiful to live," he had called them.

It chilled Riley deeply that she had been one of the women he had seen that way. She'd never thought of herself as beautiful, and men—even her ex-husband, Ryan—seldom told her that she was. Caldwell was a stark and horrible exception.

What did it mean, she wondered, that a pathological monster had found her so perfectly lovely? Had he recognized something inside her that was as monstrous as he? For a couple of years after his trial and conviction, she'd had nightmares about his admiring eyes, his honeyed words, and his freezer full of body parts.

The execution team got Caldwell up onto the execution gurney, removed the cuffs and shackles, took off his sandals, and strapped him into place. They fastened him down with leather bands—two across his chest, two to hold his legs, two around his ankles, and two around his wrists. His bare feet were turned toward the window. It was hard to see his face.

Suddenly, the curtains closed over the viewing room windows. Riley understood that this was to conceal the phase of the execution where something was most likely to go wrong—say, the team might have trouble finding a suitable vein. Still, she found it peculiar. The people in both viewing rooms were about to watch Caldwell die, but they were not allowed to witness the mundane insertion of the needles. The curtains swayed a little, apparently brushed by one of the team members moving around on the other side.

When the curtains opened again, the IV lines were in place, running from the prisoner's arms through holes in the blue plastic curtains. Some members of the execution team had retreated behind those curtains, where they would administer the lethal drugs.

One man held the red telephone receiver, ready to receive a call that would surely never come. Another spoke to Caldwell, his words a barely audible crackle over the poor sound system. He was asking Caldwell whether he had any last words.

By contrast, Caldwell's response came through with startling clarity.

"Is Agent Paige here?" he asked.

His words gave Riley a jolt.

The official didn't reply. It wasn't a question that Caldwell had any right to have answered.

After a tense silence, Caldwell spoke again.

"Tell Agent Paige that I wish my art could have done justice to her."

Although Riley couldn't see his face clearly, she thought she heard him chuckle.

"That's all," he said. "I'm ready."

Riley was flooded by rage, horror, and confusion. This was the last thing she had expected. Derrick Caldwell had chosen to make his last living moments all about *her*. And sitting here behind this unbreakable shield of glass, she was helpless to do anything about it.

She had brought him to justice, but in the end, he had achieved a weird, sick kind of revenge.

She felt Gail's small hand gripping her own.

Good God, Riley thought. *She's comforting* me.

Riley fought down a wave of nausea.

Caldwell said one more thing.

"Will I feel it when it begins?"

Again, he received no reply. Riley could see fluid moving through the transparent IV tubes. Caldwell took several deep

23

breaths and appeared to fall asleep. His left foot twitched a couple of times, then fell still.

After a moment, one of the guards pinched both feet and got no reaction. It seemed a peculiar sort of gesture. But Riley realized that the guard was checking to make sure the sedative was working and that Caldwell was fully unconscious.

The guard called out something inaudible to the people behind the curtain. Riley saw a renewed flow of fluid through the IV tubes. She knew that a second drug was in the process of stopping his lungs. In a little while, a third drug would stop his heart.

As Caldwell's breathing slowed, Riley found herself thinking about what she was watching. How was this different from the times she had used lethal force herself? In the line of duty, she had killed several killers.

But this was not like any of those other deaths. By comparison, it was bizarrely controlled, clean, clinical, immaculate. It seemed inexplicably wrong. Irrationally, Riley found herself thinking …

I shouldn't have let it come to this.

She knew she was wrong, that she had carried out Caldwell's apprehension professionally and by the book. But even so she thought …

I should have killed him myself.

Gail held Riley's hand steadily for ten long minutes. Finally, the official beside Caldwell said something that Riley couldn't hear.

The warden stepped out from behind the curtain and spoke in a clear enough voice to be understood by all the witnesses.

"The sentence was successfully carried out at 9:07 a.m."

Then the curtains closed across the window again. The witnesses had seen all that they were meant to see. Guards came into the room and urged everybody to leave as quickly as possible.

As the group spilled out into the hallway, Gail took hold of Riley's hand again.

"I'm sorry he said what he said," Gail told her.

Riley was startled. How could Gail be worried about Riley's feelings at a time like this, when justice had finally been done to her own daughter's killer?

"How are you, Gail?" she asked as they walked briskly toward the exit.

Gail walked along in silence for a moment. Her expression seemed completely blank.

"It's done," she finally said, her voice numb and cold. "It's done."

In an instant they stepped out into the morning daylight. Riley could see two crowds of people across the street, each roped away from the other and tightly controlled by police. On one side were people who had gathered to cheer on the execution, wielding hateful signs, some of them profane and obscene. They were understandably jubilant. On the other side were anti–death penalty protesters with their own signs. They'd been out here all night holding a candlelight vigil. They were much more subdued.

Riley found that she couldn't muster sympathy for either group. These people were here for themselves, to make a public show of their outrage and righteousness, acting out of sheer self-indulgence. As far as she was concerned, they had no business being here—not among people whose pain and grief were all too real.

Between the entrance and the crowds was a swarm of reporters, with media trucks nearby. As Riley waded among them, one woman rushed up to her with a microphone and a cameraman behind her.

"Agent Paige? Are you Agent Paige?" she said.

Riley didn't reply. She tried to go past the reporter.

The reporter stayed with her doggedly. "We've heard that Caldwell mentioned you in his last words. Do you care to comment?"

Other reporters closed in on her, asking the same question. Riley gritted her teeth and pushed on through the throng. At last she broke free from them.

As she hurried toward her car, she found herself thinking about Meredith and Bill. Both of them had implored her to take on a new case. And she was avoiding giving either of them any kind of an answer.

Why? she wondered.

She had just run away from reporters. Was she running away from Bill and Meredith as well? Was she running away from who she really was? From all that she had to do?

*

Riley was grateful to be home. The death she had witnessed that morning still left her with an empty feeling, and the drive back to Fredericksburg had been tiring. But when she opened the door of her townhouse, something didn't seem right.

It was unnaturally silent. April should be home from school by now. Where was Gabriela? Riley went into the kitchen and found it empty. A note was on the kitchen table.

Me voy a la tienda, it read. Gabriela had gone to the store.

Riley gripped the back of a chair as a wave of panic swept over her. Another time that Gabriela had gone to the store, April had been kidnapped from her father's house.

Darkness, a glimpse of flame.

Riley turned and ran to the foot of the stairs.

"April," she screamed.

There was no answer.

Riley raced up the staircase. Nobody was in either of the bedrooms. Nobody was in her small office.

Riley's heart was pounding, even though her mind was telling her that she was being foolish. Her body wasn't listening to her mind.

She raced back downstairs and out onto the back deck.

"April," she screamed.

But no one was playing in the yard next door and no kids were in sight.

She stopped herself from letting out another scream. She didn't want these neighbors convinced that she was truly crazy. Not so soon.

She fumbled at her pocket and pulled out her cell phone. She texted a message to April.

She received no reply.

Riley went back inside and sat down on the couch. She held her head in her hands.

She was back in the crawlspace, lying on the dirt in the darkness.

But the small light was moving toward her. She could see his cruel face in the glow of the flames. But she didn't know whether the killer was coming for her or for April.

Riley forced herself to separate the vision from her present reality.

Peterson is dead, she told herself emphatically. *He will never torture either of us again.*

She sat up on the sofa and tried to focus on here and now. Today she was here in her new home, in her new life. Gabriela had gone to the store. April was surely somewhere nearby.

Her breathing slowed, but she couldn't make herself get up. She was afraid she'd go outside and yell again.

After what seemed like a long time, Riley heard the front door opening.

April walked through the door, singing.

Now Riley could get to her feet. "Where the hell have you been?"

April looked shocked.

"What's your problem, Mom?"

"Where were you? Why didn't you answer my text?"

"Sorry, I had my phone on mute. Mom, I was just over at Cece's house. Just across the street. When we got off the school bus, her mom offered us ice cream."

"How was I supposed to know where you were?"

"I didn't think you'd be home yet."

Riley heard herself yelling, but couldn't make herself stop. "I don't care what you thought. You weren't thinking. You have to always let me know …"

The tears running down April's face finally stopped her.

Riley caught her breath, rushed forward, and hugged her daughter. At first April's body was stiff with anger, but Riley could feel her relax slowly. She realized that tears were running down her own face too.

"I'm sorry," Riley said. "I'm sorry. It's just that we went through so much … so much awfulness."

"But it's all over now," April said. "Mom, it's all over."

They both sat down on the couch. It was a new couch, bought when they had moved here. She had bought it for her new life.

"I know that it's all over," Riley said. "I know that Peterson is dead. I'm trying to get used to that."

"Mom, everything is so much better now. You don't have to worry about me every minute. And I'm not some stupid little kid. I'm fifteen."

"And you're very smart," Riley said. "I know. I'll just have to keep reminding myself. I love you, April," she said. "That's why I get so crazy sometimes."

"I love you too, Mom," April said. "Just don't worry so much."

Riley was delighted to see her daughter smile again. April had been kidnapped, held captive, and threatened with that flame. She seemed to be back to being a perfectly normal teenager even if her mother hadn't yet regained her stability.

Still, Riley couldn't help but wonder whether dark memories still lurked somewhere in her daughter's mind, waiting to erupt.

As for herself, she knew that she needed to talk to somebody about her own fears and recurring nightmares. It would have to be soon.

Chapter Six

Riley fidgeted in her chair as she tried to think of what she wanted to tell Mike Nevins. She felt unsettled and edgy.

"Take your time," the forensic psychiatrist said, craning forward in his office chair and gazing at her with concern.

Riley chuckled ruefully. "That's the trouble," she said. "I don't have time. I've been dragging my feet. I've got a decision to make. I've put it off too long already. Have you ever known me to be this indecisive?"

Mike didn't reply. He just smiled and pressed his fingertips together.

Riley was used to this kind of silence from Mike. The dapper, rather fussy man had been many things to her over the years—a friend, a therapist, even at times a sort of mentor. These days she usually called on him to get his insight into the dark mind of a criminal. But this visit was different. She had called him last night after getting home from the execution, and had driven to his DC office this morning.

"So what are your choices, exactly?" he finally asked.

"Well, I guess I've got to decide what I'm going to do with the rest of my life—teach or be a field agent. Or figure out something else entirely."

Mike laughed a little. "Hold on a minute. Let's not try to plan your whole future today. Let's stick to right now. Meredith and Jeffreys want you to take a case. Just one case. It's not either/or. Nobody says you've got to give up teaching. And all you've got to do is say yes or no this once. So what's the problem?"

It was Riley's turn to fall silent. She didn't know what the problem was. That was why she was here.

"I take it you're scared of something," Mike said.

Riley gulped hard. That was it. She was scared. She'd been refusing to admit it, even to herself. But now Mike was going to make her talk about it.

"So what are you scared of?" Mike asked. "You said you were having some nightmares."

Riley still said nothing.

"This has to be part of your PTSD problem," Mike said. "Do you still have the flashbacks?"

Riley had been expecting the question. After all, Mike had done more than anybody to get her through the trauma of an especially horrible experience.

She leaned her head back on the chair and closed her eyes. For a moment she was in Peterson's dark cage again, and he was threatening her with a propane flame. For months after Peterson had held her captive, that memory had constantly forced its way into her mind.

But then she had tracked down Peterson and killed him herself. In fact, she had beaten him to a lifeless pulp.

If that's not closure, I don't know what is, she thought.

Now the memories seemed impersonal, as though she was watching someone else's story unfold.

"I'm better," Riley said. "They're shorter and much less often."

"How about your daughter?"

The question cut Riley like a knife. She felt an echo of the horror she'd experienced when Peterson had taken April captive. She could still hear April's cries for help ringing through her brain.

"I guess I'm not over that," she said. "I wake up afraid that she's been taken again. I have to go to her bedroom and make sure that she's there and she's all right and sleeping."

"Is that why you don't want to take another case?"

Riley shuddered deeply. "I don't want to put her through anything like that again."

"That doesn't answer my question."

"No, I don't suppose it does," Riley said.

Another silence fell.

"I've got a feeling there's something more," Mike said. "What else gives you nightmares? What else wakes you up at night?"

With a jolt, a lurking terror surfaced in her mind.

Yes, there *was* something more.

Even with her eyes wide open, she could see his face—Eugene Fisk's babyish, grotesquely innocent-looking face with its small, beady eyes. Riley had looked deeply into those eyes during their fatal confrontation.

The killer had held Lucy Vargas with a razor at her throat. At that moment, Riley probed her most terrible fears. She'd talked about the chains—those chains that he believed were talking to him, forcing him to commit murder after murder, chaining up women and slitting their throats.

"The chains don't want you to take this woman," Riley had told him. *"She isn't what they need. You know what the chains want you to do instead."*

His eyes glistening with tears, he'd nodded in agreement. Then he'd inflicted the same death upon himself that he had inflicted upon his victims.

He slit his own throat right before Riley's eyes.

And now, sitting here in Mike Nevins's office, Riley almost choked on her own horror.

"I killed Eugene," she said with a gasp.

"The chain killer, you mean. Well, he wasn't the first man you killed."

It was true—she'd used deadly force a number of times. But with Eugene, it had been very different. She'd thought about his death quite often, but she'd never talked to anybody about it before now.

"I didn't use a gun, or a rock, or my fists," she said. "I killed him with understanding, with empathy. My own mind is a deadly weapon. I'd never known that before. It terrifies me, Mike."

Mike nodded sympathetically. "You know what Nietzsche said about looking too long into an abyss," he said.

"The abyss also looks into you," Riley said, finishing the familiar saying. "But I've done a lot more than look into an abyss. I've practically lived there. I've almost gotten comfortable there. It's like a second home. It scares me to death, Mike. One of these days I might go into that abyss and never come back out. And who knows who I might hurt—or kill."

"Well, then," Mike said, leaning back in his chair. "Maybe we're getting somewhere."

Riley wasn't so sure. And she didn't feel any closer to making a decision.

*

When Riley walked through her front door a while later, April came galloping down the stairs to meet her.

"Oh, Mom, you've got to help me! Come on!"

Riley followed April up the stairs to her bedroom. An open suitcase was open on her bed and clothes were scattered all around it.

"I don't know what to pack!" April said. "I've never had to do this before!"

31

Smiling at her daughter's mixed panic and exhilaration, Riley set right to work helping her get her things together. April was leaving tomorrow morning on a school field trip—a week in nearby Washington, DC. She'd be going with a group of advanced American History students and their teachers.

When Riley had signed the forms and paid the extra fees for the trip, she'd had some qualms about it. Peterson had held April captive in Washington, and although that had been far off on the edge of the city, Riley worried that the trip might dredge up the trauma. But April seemed to be doing extremely well both academically and emotionally. And the trip was a wonderful opportunity.

As she and April teased each other lightheartedly about what to pack, Riley realized that she was having fun. That abyss that she and Mike had talked about a little while ago seemed far away. She still had a life outside of that abyss. It was a good life, and whatever she decided to do, she was determined to keep it.

While they were sorting things, Gabriela stepped into the room.

"Señora Riley, my cab will be here *pronto,* any minute," she said, smiling. "I'm packed and ready. My things are at the door."

Riley had almost forgotten that Gabriela was leaving. Since April was going to be away, Gabriela had asked for time off to visit relatives in Tennessee. Riley had cheerfully agreed.

Riley hugged Gabriela and said, *"Buen viaje."*

Gabriela's smile fading a little, she added, *"Me preocupo."*

"You're worried?" Riley asked in surprise. "What are you worried about, Gabriela?"

"You," Gabriela said. "You will be all alone in this new house."

Riley laughed a little. "Don't worry, I can take care of myself."

"But you have not been *sola* since so many bad things have happened," Gabriela said. "I worry."

Gabriela's words gave Riley a slight turn. What she was saying was true. Ever since the ordeal with Peterson, at least April had always been around. Could a dark and frightening void open up in her new home? Was the abyss yawning even now?

"I'll be fine," Riley said. "Go have a good time with your family."

Gabriela grinned and handed Riley an envelope. "This was in the mailbox," she said.

Gabriela hugged April, then hugged Riley again, and went downstairs to wait for her cab.

"What is it, Mom?" April asked.

"I don't know," Riley said. "It wasn't mailed."

She tore the envelope open and found a plastic card inside. Decorative letters on the card proclaimed "Blaine's Grill." Below that she read aloud, "Dinner for two."

"I guess it's a gift card from our neighbor," Riley said. "That's nice of him. You and I can go there for dinner when we get back."

"Mom!" April snorted. "He doesn't mean you and me."

"Why not?"

"He's inviting you out to dinner."

"Oh! Do you really think so? It doesn't say that here."

April shook her head. "Don't be stupid. The man wants to date you. Crystal told me her dad likes you. And he's really cute."

Riley could feel her face flushing red. She couldn't remember the last time someone had asked her on a date. She had been married to Ryan for so many years. Since their divorce she had been focused on getting settled in her new home and decisions to be made about her job.

"You're blushing, Mom," April said.

"Let's get your stuff packed," Riley grumbled. "I'll have to think about all this later."

They both went back to sorting through clothes. After a few minutes of silence, April said, "I'm kind of worried about you, Mom. Like Gabriela said …"

"I'll be fine," Riley said.

"Will you?"

Folding a blouse, Riley wasn't sure what to answer. Surely she'd recently faced worse nightmares than an empty house— murderous psychopaths obsessed with chains, dolls, and blowtorches among them. But might a host of inner demons break loose when she was alone? Suddenly, a week began to feel like a long time. And the prospect of deciding whether or not to date the man who lived next door seemed scary in its own way.

I'll handle it, Riley thought.

Besides, she still had another option. And it was about time to make a decision once and for all.

"I've been asked to work on a case," Riley told April. "I'd have to go to Arizona right away."

April stopped folding her clothes and looked at Riley.

"So you're going to go, aren't you?" she asked.

"I don't know, April," Riley said.

"What's there to know? It's your job, right?"

Riley looked into her daughter's eyes. The hard times between them really did seem to be over. Ever since they'd both survived the horrors inflicted by Peterson, they'd been linked by a new bond.

"I've been thinking about not going back to field work," Riley said.

April's eyes widened with surprise.

"What? Mom, taking down bad guys is what you do best."

"I'm good at teaching, too," Riley said. "I'm *very* good at it. And I love it. I really do."

April shrugged with incomprehension. "Well, go ahead and teach. Nobody's stopping you. But don't stop kicking ass. That's just as important."

Riley shook her head. "I don't know, April. After all I put you through—"

April looked and sounded incredulous. "After all *you* put me through? What are you talking about? *You* didn't put me through anything. I got caught by a psychopath named Peterson. If he hadn't taken me, he'd have taken someone else. Don't you start blaming yourself."

After a pause, April said, "Sit down, Mom. We've got to talk."

Riley smiled and sat down on the bed. April was sounding just like a mother herself.

Maybe a little parental lecture is just what I need, Riley thought.

April sat down next to Riley.

"Did I ever tell you about my friend Angie Fletcher?" April said.

"I don't think so."

"Well, we used to be tight for a while but she changed schools. She was really smart, just one year ahead of me, fifteen years old. I heard that she started buying drugs from this guy everybody called Trip. She got really, really into heroin. And when she ran out of money, Trip put her to work as a hooker. Trained her personally, made her move in with him. Her mom's so screwed up, she barely noticed Angie was gone. Trip even advertised her on his website, made her get a tattoo swearing she was his forever."

Riley was shocked. "What happened to her?"

"Well, Trip eventually got busted, and Angie wound up in a drug rehab center. That was just this summer while we were in Upstate New York. I don't know what happened to her after that. All I know is that she's just sixteen now and her life is ruined."

"I'm so sorry to hear that," Riley said.

April groaned with impatience.

"You really don't get it, do you, Mom? *You've* got nothing to be sorry for. You've spent your whole life stopping this kind of thing. And you've put away all kinds of guys like Trip—some of them forever. But if you stop doing what you do best, who's going to take over for you? Somebody as good at it as you? I doubt it, Mom. I really doubt it."

Riley fell silent for a moment. Then with a smile, she squeezed April's hand tightly.

"I think I've got a phone call to make," she said.

Chapter Seven

As the FBI jet lifted off from Quantico, Riley felt sure that she was on her way to face yet another monster. She was deeply uneasy at the thought. She had been hoping to stay away from killers for a while, but taking this job had finally seemed like the right thing to do. Meredith had been clearly relieved when she'd said she would go.

That morning, April had left on her field trip, and now Riley and Bill were on their way to Phoenix. Outside the airplane window the afternoon had turned dark, and rain streaked across the glass. Riley stayed strapped into her seat until the plane had made its way through rough-and-tumble gray clouds and into clearer air above. Then a cushiony surface spread out beneath them, hiding the earth where people were probably scurrying about to stay dry. And, Riley thought, going about their everyday pleasures or horrors or whatever lay in between.

As soon as the ride smoothed out, Riley turned to Bill and asked, "What have you got to show me?"

Bill flipped open his laptop on the table in front of them. He brought up a photo of a large black garbage bag barely submerged in shallow water. A dead white hand could be seen poking out of the bag's opening.

Bill explained, "The body of Nancy Holbrook was found in an artificial lake in the reservoir system outside of Phoenix. She was a thirty-year-old escort with an expensive service. In other words, a pricey prostitute."

"Did she drown?" Riley asked.

"No. Asphyxiation seems to have been the cause of death. Then she was stuffed into a heavy-duty garbage bag and dumped into the lake. The garbage bag was weighted with large rocks."

Riley studied the photo closely. A lot of questions were already forming in her mind.

"Did the killer leave any physical evidence?" she asked. "Prints, fibers, DNA?"

"Not a thing."

Riley shook her head. "I don't get it. The disposal of the body, I mean. Why didn't the killer go to just a little more trouble? A freshwater lake is perfect for getting rid of a body. Corpses sink and decompose fast in fresh water. Sure, they might resurface later on because of bloating and gases. But enough rocks in the bag would solve that problem. Why leave her in shallow water?"

"I guess it's up to us to figure that out," Bill said.

Bill brought up several other photos of the crime scene, but they didn't tell Riley much.

"So what do you think?" she said. "Are we dealing with a serial or aren't we?"

Bill's knitted his brow in thought.

"I don't know," he said. "Really, we're just looking at a single murdered prostitute. Sure, other prostitutes have disappeared in Phoenix. But that's nothing new. That happens routinely in every major city in the country."

The word "routinely" struck an uncomfortable chord with Riley. How could the ongoing disappearance of a certain class of women be considered "routine"? Still, she knew that what Bill was saying was true.

"When Meredith phoned, he made it sound urgent," she said. "And now he's even giving us the VIP treatment, flying us directly there on a BAU jet." She thought back for a moment. "His exact words were that his friend *wanted us to look into it as the work of a serial killer.* But you sound like nobody's sure it is a serial."

Bill shrugged. "It might not be. But Meredith seems to be really close to Nancy Holbrook's brother, Garrett Holbrook."

"Yeah," Riley said. "He told me they went to the academy together. But this whole thing is unusual."

Bill didn't argue. Riley leaned back in her seat and considered the situation. It seemed pretty obvious that Meredith was bending FBI rules as a favor to a friend. That wasn't typical of Meredith at all.

But this didn't make her think any less of her boss. Actually, she really admired his devotion to his friend. She wondered ...

Is there anybody I'd bend the rules for? Bill, maybe?

He'd been more than a partner over the years, and more than even a friend. Even so, Riley wasn't sure. And that made her wonder—just how close did she feel to any of her coworkers these days, including Bill?

But there didn't seem much point in thinking about it now. Riley closed her eyes and went to sleep.

*

It was a bright sunny day when they landed in Phoenix.

As they got off the jet, Bill nudged her and said, "Wow, great weather. Maybe at least we'll get a little vacation out of this trip."

Somehow, Riley doubted that it was going to be a lot of fun. It had been a long time since she'd taken a real vacation. Her last attempt at an outing in New York with April had been cut short by the usual murder and mayhem that was such a big part of her life.

One of these days, I need to get some real rest, she thought.

A young local agent met them at the plane and drove them to the Phoenix FBI field office, a striking new modern building. As he pulled the car into the Bureau parking lot, he commented, "Cool design, isn't it? Even won some kind of award. Can you guess what it's supposed to look like?"

Riley looked over the facade. It was all straight, long rectangles and narrow vertical windows. Everything was carefully placed and the pattern seemed familiar. She stopped and stared at it for a moment.

"DNA sequencing?" she asked.

"Yep," the agent said. "But I'll bet you can't guess what the rock maze over there looks like from above."

But they walked into the building before Riley or Bill could hazard a guess. Inside, Riley saw the DNA motif repeated in the sharply patterned floor tiles. The agent led them among severe-looking horizontal walls and partitions until they reached the office of Special Agent in Charge Elgin Morley, then left them there.

Riley and Bill introduced themselves to Morley, a small, bookish man in his fifties with a thick black mustache and round glasses. Another man was awaiting them in the office. He was in his forties, tall, gaunt, and slightly hunched. Riley thought he looked tired and depressed.

Morley said, "Agents Paige and Jeffreys, I'd like you to meet Agent Garrett Holbrook. His sister was the victim who was found in Nimbo Lake."

Hands were shaken all around, and the four agents sat down to talk.

"Thank you for coming," Holbrook said. "This whole thing has been pretty overwhelming."

"Tell us about your sister," Riley said.

"I can't tell you much," Holbrook said. "I can't say I knew her very well. She was my half-sister. My dad was a philandering jerk, left my mom and had children with three different women. Nancy was fifteen years younger than me. We barely had contact over the years."

He stared blankly at the floor for a moment, his fingers picking absent-mindedly at the arm of his chair. Then without looking up he said, "The last I heard from her, she was doing office work and taking classes at a community college. That was a few years ago. I was shocked to find out what had become of her. I had no idea."

Then he fell silent. Riley thought he looked like he was leaving something unsaid, but she told herself that maybe that was really all the man knew. After all, what could Riley say about her own older sister if anyone asked her? She and Wendy had been out of contact for so long that they might as well not be sisters at all.

Even so, she sensed something more than grief in Holbrook's demeanor. It struck her as odd.

Morley suggested that Riley and Bill go with him to Forensic Pathology, where they could take a look at the body. Holbrook nodded and said that he'd be in his office.

As they followed the Agent in Charge down the hall, Bill asked, "Agent Morley, what reason is there for thinking we're dealing with a serial killer?"

Morley shook his head. "I'm not sure we've got much of a reason," he said. "But when Garrett found out about Nancy's death, he refused to leave it alone. He's one of our best agents, and I've tried to accommodate him. He tried to get his own investigation underway, but didn't get anywhere. The truth is, he hasn't been himself this whole while."

Riley had certainly noticed that Garrett seemed to be terribly unsettled. Perhaps a little more so than a seasoned agent would usually be, even over a relative's death. He'd made it clear that they weren't close.

Morley led Riley and Bill into the building's Forensic Pathology area, where he introduced them to its team chief, Dr. Rachel Fowler. The pathologist pulled open the refrigerated unit where Nancy Holbrook's body was being kept.

Riley winced a little at the familiar odor of decomposition, even though the smell hadn't gotten very strong yet. She saw that the woman had been short of stature and very thin.

"She hadn't been in the water long," Fowler said. "The skin was just beginning to wrinkle when she was found."

Dr. Fowler pointed to her wrists.

"You can see rope burns. It looks like she was bound when she was killed."

Riley noticed raised marks on the crook of the corpse's arm.

"These look like track marks," Riley said.

"Right. She was using heroin. My guess was that she was slipping into serious addiction."

It looked to Riley like the woman had been anorexic, and that seemed consistent with Fowler's addiction theory.

"That kind of addiction seems out of place for a high-class escort," Bill said. "How do we know that's what she was?"

Fowler produced a laminated business card in a plastic evidence bag. It had a provocative photo of the dead woman on it. The name on the card was simply "Nanette," and the business was called "Ishtar Escorts."

"This card was on her when she was found," Fowler explained. "The police got in touch with Ishtar Escorts and found out her real name, and that soon led to identifying her as Agent Holbrook's half-sister."

"Any idea how she was asphyxiated?" Riley asked.

"There's some bruising around her neck," Fowler said. "The killer might have held a plastic bag over her head."

Riley looked closely at the marks. Was this some kind of a sex game gone wrong, or a deliberate act of murder? She couldn't yet tell.

"What did she have on when she was found?" Riley asked.

Fowler opened up a box that contained the victim's clothing. She had been wearing a pink dress with a low neckline—barely respectable, Riley observed, but definitely a notch above a streetwalker's typical trashy attire. It was the dress of a woman who wanted to look both very sexy and suitably attired for nightclubs.

Nestled on top of the dress was a clear plastic bag of jewelry.

"May I have a look?" Riley asked Fowler.

"Go right ahead."

Riley took out the bag and looked at the contents. Most of it was fairly tasteful costume jewelry—a beaded necklace and bracelets and simple earrings. But one item stood out among the rest. It was a slender gold ring with a diamond setting. She picked it up and showed it to Bill.

"Real?" Bill asked.

"Yes," Fowler replied. "Real gold and a real diamond."

"The killer didn't bother to steal it," Bill commented. "So this wasn't about money."

Riley turned to Morley. "I'd like to see where the body was found," she said. "Right now, while it's still light."

Morley looked a bit puzzled.

40

"We can get you there by helicopter," he said. "But I don't know what you expect to find. Cops and agents have been all over the site."

"Trust her," Bill said knowingly. "She'll find out something."

Chapter Eight

The broad surface of Nimbo Lake looked still and tranquil as the helicopter approached it.

But looks can fool you, Riley reminded herself. She knew well that calm surfaces could guard dark secrets.

The helicopter descended, then wobbled as it hovered in search of a place to land. Riley felt a little queasy from the unsteady movement. She didn't much like helicopters. She looked at Bill, who was sitting next to her. She thought he looked equally uneasy.

But when she glanced over at Agent Holbrook, his face seemed blank to her. He had barely said a word during the half-hour flight from Phoenix. Riley didn't yet know what to make of him. She was used to reading people easily—sometimes too easily for her own comfort. But Holbrook still struck her as an enigma.

The helicopter finally touched down, and all three FBI agents stepped out onto solid ground, ducking through the churning air under the still-spinning blades. The road where the chopper had landed was nothing more than parallel tire tracks through the desert weeds.

Riley observed that the road didn't look heavily used. Even so, it appeared that enough vehicles had passed over it during the past week to conceal any tracks left by whatever the killer had been driving.

The noisy helicopter engine died down, making it easier to talk as Riley and Bill followed Holbrook on foot.

"Tell us what you can about this lake," Riley said to Holbrook.

"It's one of a series of reservoirs created by dams along the Acacia River," Holbrook said. "This is the smallest of the artificial lakes. It's stocked with fish, and it's a popular recreation spot, but the public areas are on the other side of the lake. The body was discovered by a couple of teenagers stoned on pot. I'll show you where."

Holbrook led them off the road to a stone ridge overlooking the lake.

"The kids were right where we're standing," he said. He pointed down to the edge of the lake. "They looked down there and saw it. They said that it just looked like a dark shape in the water."

"What time of day were the kids here?" Riley asked.

"A little earlier than it is right now," Holbrook said. "They had cut school and gotten stoned."

Riley took in the whole scene. The sun was low, and the tops of the red rock cliffs across the lake were ablaze with light. There were a couple of boats out on the water. The sheer drop from the ridge down to the water wasn't far—a mere ten feet, maybe.

Holbrook pointed to a place nearby where the slope wasn't as steep.

"The kids climbed down over there to get a closer look," he said. "That's when they found out what it really was."

Poor kids, Riley thought. It had been some two decades since she'd tried marijuana back in college. Even so, she could well imagine the heightened horror of making such a discovery while under the influence.

"Do you want to climb down there for a closer look?" Bill asked Riley.

"No, it's a good view from here," Riley said.

Her gut told her that she was right where she needed to be. After all, the killer surely hadn't lugged the body down the same slope where the kids had gone down.

No, she thought. *He stood right here.*

It even looked like the sparse vegetation was still broken down a little where she was standing.

She took a few breaths, trying to slip into his point of view. He'd undoubtedly come here at night. But was it a clear night or a cloudy one? Well, in Arizona at this time of year, the chances were that the night was clear. And she recalled that the moon would have been bright about a week ago. In the starlight and moonlight, he could have seen what he was doing pretty well—possibly even without a flashlight.

She imagined him putting the body down right here. But then what had he done next? Obviously he had rolled the body off the ledge. It had fallen straight down into the shallow water.

But something about this scenario struck Riley as wrong. She wondered again, as she had on the plane, how he could have been so careless.

True, from up here on the ledge, he probably couldn't have seen that the body hadn't sunk very far. The kids had described the bag as *"a dark shape in the water."* From this height, the submerged bag had likely been invisible even on a bright night. He'd assumed that the body had sunk, as newly dead bodies do in fresh water, especially when weighted down with stones.

But why did he suppose that the water was deep right here?

She peered down into the clear water. In the late afternoon light, she could easily see the submerged ledge where the body had landed. It was a small horizontal area, nothing more than the top of a boulder. Around it, the water was black and deep.

She looked around the lake. Sheer cliffs jutted up everywhere out of the water. She could see that Nimbo Lake had been a deep canyon before the dam had filled it with water. She saw only a few places where one could walk along the shoreline. The cliff sides dropped straight down into the depths.

To her right and left, Riley saw ridges that were similar to the one where they were standing, rising to about the same height. The water beneath those cliffs was dark, showing no signs of the kind of ledge that lay below right here.

She felt a tingle of comprehension.

"He's done this before," she told Bill and Holbrook. "There's another body in this lake."

*

On the helicopter ride back to the FBI Phoenix Division headquarters, Holbrook said, "So you think this is a serial case after all?"

"Yes, I do," Riley said.

Holbrook said, "I wasn't positive. Mostly I was eager to get someone good on the case. But what did you see that made up your mind?"

"There are other ledges that look just like the one he pushed this body over," she explained. "He used one of those other drop-offs before, and that body sank just like it was supposed to. But maybe he couldn't find the same spot this time. Or maybe he thought this *was* the same spot. Anyway, he expected the same result this time. He was wrong."

Bill said, "I told you she'd find something there."

"Divers will need to search this lake," Riley added.

"That will take some doing," Holbrook said.

"It's got to be done anyway. There's another body down there somewhere. You can count on it. I don't know how long it's been there, but it's there."

She paused, mentally assessing what all this said about the killer's personality. He was competent and capable. This wasn't a pathetic loser, like Eugene Fisk. He was more like Peterson, the killer who had captured and tormented both her and April. He was

44

shrewd and poised, and he thoroughly enjoyed killing—a sociopath rather than a psychopath. Above all else, he was confident.

Maybe too confident for his own good, Riley thought.

It might well prove to be his downfall.

She said, "The guy we're looking for isn't some criminal lowlife. My guess is he's an ordinary citizen, reasonably well-educated, maybe with a wife and family. Nobody who knows him thinks he's a killer."

Riley watched Holbrook's face as they talked. Although she now knew something about the case she hadn't known before, Holbrook still struck her as utterly impenetrable.

The helicopter circled over the FBI building. Twilight had fallen and the area below was well lighted.

"Look there," Bill said, pointing out the window.

Riley looked down where he pointed. She was surprised to see that from here the rock garden looked like a gigantic fingerprint. It spread out beneath them like a welcome sign. Some offbeat landscaper had decided that this image arranged out of stone was better suited for the new FBI building than a planted garden would have been. Hundreds of substantial stones had been carefully placed in curving rows to create the ridged illusion.

"Wow," Riley said to Bill. "Whose fingerprint do you suppose they used? Someone legendary, I guess. Dillinger, maybe?"

"Or maybe John Wayne Gacy. Or Jeffrey Dahmer."

Riley thought it a strange spectacle. On the ground, no one would ever guess that the arrangement of stones was anything more than a meaningless maze.

It struck her almost as a sign and a warning. This case was going to demand that she view things from a new and unsettling perspective. She was about to probe regions of darkness that not even she had imagined.

Chapter Nine

The man enjoyed watching streetwalkers. He liked how they grouped on the corner and pranced up and down the sidewalks, mostly in pairs. He found them to be much feistier than call girls and escorts, prone to easily losing their temper.

For example, right now, he saw one cursing a bunch of uncouth young guys in a slow-moving vehicle for taking her picture. The man didn't blame her one bit. After all, she was here to do business, not to serve as scenery.

Where's their respect? he thought with a smirk. *Kids these days.*

Now the guys were laughing at her and yelling obscenities. But they couldn't match her colorful retorts, some of them in Spanish. He liked her style.

He was slumming tonight, parked along a row of cheap motels where streetwalkers gathered. The other girls were less vivacious than the one who had done the cursing. Their attempts at sexiness looked awkward by comparison, and their come-ons were crude. As he watched, one hiked up her skirt to show her skimpy underpants to the driver of a slowly passing car. The driver didn't stop.

He kept his eye on the girl who had first drawn his attention. She was stomping around indignantly, complaining to the other girls.

The man knew he could have her if he wanted her. She could be his next victim. All he had to do to get her attention was to drive along the curb toward her.

But no, he wouldn't do that. He never did that. He'd never approach a hooker on the street. It was up to her to approach him. It was the same even with whores he met through a service or a brothel. He'd get them to meet him alone somewhere separately without ever asking directly. It would seem like their idea.

With some luck, the feisty girl would notice his expensive car and trot right on over. His car was wonderful bait. So was the fact that he dressed well.

But however the night ended, he had to be more careful than last time. He'd been sloppy, dropping her body over that ledge and expecting her to sink.

And such a stir she had created! An FBI agent's sister! And they'd called in big guns from Quantico. He didn't like it. He

46

wasn't out for publicity or fame. All he wanted to do was indulge his cravings.

And didn't he have every right? What healthy adult man didn't have his cravings?

Now they were going to send divers down in the lake to look for bodies. He knew what they might find there, even after some three years. He didn't like that at all.

It wasn't just out of concern for himself. Oddly, he felt bad for the lake. Having divers probe and poke into its every submerged nook and cranny struck him as rather obscene and invasive, an inexcusable violation. After all, the lake hadn't done anything wrong. Why should it be harassed?

Anyway, he wasn't worried. There was no way they were going to trace either victim back to him. It simply wasn't going to happen. He was through with that lake, though. He hadn't yet decided where to deposit his next victim, but he was sure he would come to a decision before the night was over.

Now the vivacious girl was looking at his car. She started walking toward him, with lots of sass in her step.

He rolled down the passenger window and she poked her head in. She was a dark-skinned Latina, heavily made-up with thick lip liner, colorful eye shadow, and fierce arched eyebrows that seemed to be tattoos. Her earrings were big gold-painted crucifixes.

"Nice car," she said.

He smiled.

"What's a nice girl like you doing out so late?" he asked. "Isn't it past your bedtime?"

"Maybe you'd like to tuck me in," she said, smiling.

Her teeth struck him as remarkably clean and straight. Indeed, she looked remarkably healthy. That was pretty rare out here on the streets, where most of the girls were "tweakers," in various stages of meth addiction.

"I like your style," he said. "Very *chola.*"

Her smile broadened. He could see that she took being called a Latina gangbanger as a compliment.

"What's your name?" he asked.

"Socorro."

Ah, "socorro," he thought. *Spanish for "help."*

"I'll bet you give great *socorro,*" he said in a leering tone.

Her deep brown eyes leered right back. "You look like maybe you could use some *socorro* right now."

"Maybe I could," he said.

But before they could start settling terms, a car pulled into the space right behind him. He heard a man call out from the driver window.

"*¡Socorro!*" he yelled. "*¡Vente!*"

The girl drew herself up with a rather lame show of indignation.

"*¿Porqué?*" she yelled back.

"*Vente aquí, ¡puta!*"

The man detected a trace of fear in the girl's eyes. It couldn't be because the man in the car had called her a whore. He guessed that the man was her pimp, checking on her to see how much cash she had brought in so far tonight.

"*¡Pinche Pablo!*" She muttered the all-purpose insult under her breath. Then she walked toward the car.

The man sat there, wondering if she was going to come back, still wanting to do business with him. Either way, he didn't like it. Waiting around was not his style.

His interest in the girl suddenly vanished. No, he wouldn't bother with her. She had no idea how lucky she was.

Besides, what was he doing slumming like this? His next victim ought to be classier.

Chiffon, he thought. He'd almost forgotten about Chiffon. *But maybe I've just been saving her for a special occasion.*

He could wait. It didn't have to be tonight. He drove away, gloating over his show of self-restraint, despite his enormous cravings. He considered that one of his best personal qualities.

He was, after all, a very civilized man.

Chapter Ten

The three young women in the interview room didn't look at all like Riley had expected. For a few moments she just watched them through the one-way window. They were tastefully dressed, almost like well-paid secretaries. She'd been told their names were Mitzi, Koreen, and Tantra. Of course Riley was sure that those weren't their real names.

Riley also doubted that they dressed so acceptably when they were on the job. Working for about 250 dollars per hour, they'd surely invested in elaborate wardrobes to cater to all sorts of clients' fantasies. They had been colleagues of Nancy "Nanette" Holbrook at Ishtar Escorts. The clothes Nancy Holbrook had been wearing when she was killed had been markedly less proper. But, Riley figured, when not actually on the job, the women wanted to look respectable.

Although prostitutes had played a role in some of the cases Riley had investigated in the past, this was the first time she'd been called on to work so directly with any of them. These women were potential victims themselves. They might even be potential suspects, although virtually all murders of this type were carried out by men. Riley felt sure that these women weren't the kind of monsters she hunted in her job.

It was late Sunday afternoon. Last night Riley and Bill had settled into their separate and comfortable hotel rooms not far from the FBI building. Riley had phoned April, who was in a Washington, DC, hotel with the history field trip. April had been giggly and happy, and had warned her mother that she didn't really have time for phone calls. "I'll text you tomorrow," April had said, shouting over the teenage clamor in the background.

Riley felt that too much of today had already been wasted. It had taken most of the day to round up the prostitutes and bring them in. Riley had told Special Agent in Charge Elgin Morley that she wanted to talk to the women without any men present. Perhaps they'd be more open with another woman. Now she thought she'd observe and listen to them unseen for a few minutes before actually questioning them. Through the speaker, she could hear their conversation.

Their styles and personalities were distinctive. Short, blonde, buxom Mitzi displayed a certain small-town, girl-next-door image.

"So has Kip popped the question?" Mitzi asked Koreen.

"Not yet," Koreen said with a conspiratorial smile. She was a slender brunette with something of the grace of a ballerina. "I've got a feeling he's bought a ring, though."

"Does he still want to have four kids?" Mitzi asked.

Koreen let out a high, lilting laugh. "I've talked him down to three. But between you and me, he's only going to get two."

Mitzi joined in Koreen's laughter.

Tantra gave Koreen a nudge. She was a tall African-American with a tawny complexion. She seemed to have adopted the glamorous poise of a supermodel.

"Better make sure he doesn't find out what you do for a living, girl," Tantra said.

All three women laughed heartily. Riley was taken by surprise. These three prostitutes were talking about having families, just like any ordinary women in a beauty parlor. Was that kind of normality really in the cards for any of them? She couldn't imagine that such a thing was possible.

Riley decided that she'd kept the women waiting long enough. When she walked into the interview room, she could feel the relaxed atmosphere suddenly pop like a bubble. Now the women were visibly on edge.

"I'm Agent Riley Paige," she said. "I'd like to ask you all a few questions."

All three women let out groans of dismay.

"Oh, God, not more questions!" Mitzi said. "We've talked to the cops already."

"I'd like to ask a few questions of my own, if you don't mind," Riley said.

Mitzi shook her head. "This is starting to feel like harassment," she said.

"What we do is perfectly legal," Koreen said.

"I don't care about what you do," Riley said. "I'm an FBI investigator, not a judge."

Koreen murmured under her breath, "Like hell."

Mitzi looked at her wristwatch. "Can we make this quick?" she said. "I've got three classes today."

"How many credits are you taking this semester?" Koreen asked.

"Twenty," Mitzi said.

Koreen gasped. "That's a pretty big load."

"Yeah, well, I want to get my degree as soon as I can."

Riley was taken aback again.

Mitzi is going to college, she thought.

She had heard that sometimes women pursuing an education chose prostitution as a way of paying tuition. With the money she was making, she might not have to go too deeply in debt. Still, it struck Riley as strangely unsettling.

"I'll try to keep this short," Riley said. "I just want to know more about Nanette."

Koreen's expression suddenly turned pensive. "Poor Nanette," she said.

But Mitzi seemed unperturbed. "What happened to Nanette's got nothing to do with us," she said.

"I'm afraid it does," Riley said. "We have good reason to believe that her murderer is a serial killer. And I can tell you from years of experience, serial killers are relentless. He'll kill again. And one of you might be his next victim."

Mitzi frowned disdainfully.

"Not a chance," she said. "We're not like Nanette."

Now Riley was shocked. Could these women possibly be naive enough to think that what they did for a living was safe?

"But you work for the same business, doing the same kind of work," Riley said.

Mitzi was starting to get defensive.

"Hey, I thought you weren't here to judge," she said. "You can look down your nose at us if you like. But what we do is as respectable as this kind of thing can be. And as safe. We can turn down any clients we don't like. We keep the sex safe, and we get regular check-ups, so we don't have diseases. If a guy gets too kinky or violent, we can walk away. But it usually doesn't come to that."

Riley wondered about that word "usually." Surely their business sometimes took them into pretty dark territory. And how "safe" could hired sex possibly be? How long could they continue without falling prey to AIDS?

"As far as Nanette goes," Mitzi continued, "she was on her way down. She'd lost all her class. She was meeting clients outside of the service, shooting smack, losing her health and her looks. She wouldn't have lasted at Ishtar's a lot longer. She'd have been fired for sure."

As Riley took notes, she eyed the women, trying to understand them better. Little by little, she sensed something behind their placid expressions. She was pretty sure it was denial. They refused to accept that theirs was a losing way of life, and that they'd all fall

51

into the same decline as Nanette sooner or later. Their dreams of family, education, and success were ultimately doomed. And deep down, they knew it.

Riley noticed that Tantra had gotten quiet and was looking off into space. She had something to say, but hadn't yet said it.

Riley said, "We believe that Nanette was killed about a week ago, probably on Saturday. Do you know who her client was that night?"

Koreen shrugged. "I've got no idea."

"Me, neither," Mitzi said. "Actually, that's none of our business, you'd have to ask Ishtar about that."

Riley knew that the local agents were already looking for the escort service owner and would bring her in for questioning.

"What about other places of work?" Riley asked.

"We're contracted to Ishtar," Mitzi said firmly. "We're not allowed to follow our line of work through any other agency or on our own."

The other two women were looking downward, avoiding Riley's eyes. She asked the question more directly.

"Did Nanette ever do extra work anywhere else? Did she ever go out on her own without having a date made through Ishtar?"

The room was silent. Finally, in a barely audible voice, Tantra said, "She told me she'd just started working at Hank's Derby."

"What?" Mitzi said, sounding surprised.

"She didn't want me to tell anybody," Tantra told the other women.

"Jesus," Mitzi said. "So she was turning into a lot lizard. She was in worse shape than I'd thought."

Riley's mind was buzzing with questions.

"What's a 'lot lizard'?" she asked.

"It's the lowest class kind of whore," Koreen said. "They work truck stops, like Hank's Derby. It's really a rock bottom life."

"She was just so strung out," Tantra said. "She wasn't getting the clients she used to at Ishtar's. She told me she wasn't making enough to feed her habit. She said she was just doing it on the side. I told her how dangerous it was. I mean, hookers just disappear from truck stops without a trace, it happens all the time. But she wouldn't listen."

A cloud of gloom had settled over the women. Riley didn't guess that they had a lot more information to give. They'd given her one important lead already.

"That will be all," Riley told them.

But as they got ready to leave, the women started chatting again as though nothing unusual was going on.

They really don't understand, Riley thought. *Or they don't want to understand.*

"Listen," she said, "this killer is dangerous. And there are many other men like him. You're making yourself into targets. If you think you're safe doing what you do, you're just lying to yourselves."

"And just how much safer is *your* job, Agent Paige?" Mitzi asked.

This retort left Riley speechless.

Is she really comparing what she does with what I do? she wondered.

As she followed the women out of the interview room, Riley's heart sank. She felt as hopeless for them as she would if they had been common streetwalkers. In a way, this seemed worse. Their superficial veneer of respectability concealed a life of degradation even from themselves. But there was nothing she could say or do to make them face the truth.

Riley felt sure that this killer wasn't finished murdering prostitutes. Was his next victim here right now, or would she be someone Riley hadn't yet met and warned?

*

Riley was in the field office hallway looking for Bill when her cell phone buzzed. She saw that the call was from Quentin Rosner, head of the dive team that was searching Nimbo Lake.

Her heart quickened. Surely he and his divers had found the second body by now.

"Hello, Mr. Rosner," she answered eagerly.

The voice on the line said, "I called Special Agent in Charge Morley. He told me I should report to you directly."

"Good," Riley said. "What have you got for me? Have you found the other body in the lake?"

She heard a faint, wordless grumble, followed by, "Agent Paige, you're not going to like hearing this."

"Well?"

"There's no body in that lake. It's a big area but we've looked everywhere."

Riley had trouble believing her ears. Had her hunch wrong?

No, she still felt sure that Nancy Holbrook's killer had previously dumped a different body in that lake. It helped explain why he hadn't gone down to the water to make sure that his latest victim had disappeared into the lake's depths.

As she puzzled over what to say, she saw Bill walking down the hall.

"I'm headed out to interview Ishtar Haynes," he said. "At her place of business. Want to come along?"

Riley nodded yes, but first she had to sort things out with Rosner.

"How was the visibility?" Riley asked.

"I won't lie to you, it really sucks down there," Rosner said. "Flooding a canyon stirs up a lot of sod and rotting vegetation and it can take several years for the water to clear up. Anything dumped here when the lake was new could actually be buried under debris."

"The body I'm looking for could have been put there several years ago."

"Then that's a problem. But we know what we're doing, Agent Paige. We're a well-trained unit. And we're really sure there's no body to be found in this lake."

Riley thought for a moment. She deeply wished that Morley had called in actual FBI divers. The Underwater Search and Evidence Response Team was amazing and those divers would have considered every possible angle without any prompting. Instead Morley had called in help from a local dive training school. He'd said that there was no legitimate reason for the FBI to be involved in this case anyhow. He wasn't going have an FBI team fly in here from LA.

She realized that in spite of what Riley had reported to him, Morley was still thinking of this as a single murder that they were investigating as a favor to a fellow agent. She would just have to work with the team they had. But what might these guys have missed?

She asked, "Have you looked at maps of the canyon before it was flooded?"

Rosner was silent for a moment.

"No, but what good would that do?" he said.

Riley stifled a groan of impatience.

How much training does this guy actually have? she wondered. *Do I really have to tell him how to do his job?*

She said, "How can you be sure that you checked every nook and cranny without knowing more about the terrain?"

Another silence fell.

"You should be able to call it up on your laptop," Riley added.

"We'll get on it," Rosner finally said, sounding gloomy.

"You do that," Riley told him.

She ended the call and stood in the hall wondering what to believe. Was there no second body after all? If there wasn't, then this probably wasn't even a serial case. She felt a flood of mixed feelings. She hated making mistakes. Even so, the possibility that Nancy Holbrook's murder hadn't been the work of a serial killer might be good news.

But Riley's gut still told her that there *was* another body in the lake. That this was a familiar type of monster who would strike again.

Chapter Eleven

When she and Bill walked into the Ishtar Escorts office, Riley thought that it actually looked very much like a high-class travel agency. A bulletin board was devoted to posters about things to do in Phoenix, suggesting visits to museums, art galleries, parks, and botanical gardens. A table carried brochures with details about a variety of places. The detail that would be missing from an actual travel agency was the second bulletin board, with images of the escorts. She recognized the ones that she had spoken with earlier. In these photos, they were all nicely dressed as if for an elegant event, with just an occasional flash of cleavage here and there.

The woman at the reception desk didn't seem at all nervous about a visit from FBI agents. The receptionist explained that many clients were visitors who weren't well informed on cultural and recreational activities.

"We help them out. We'll even book tickets for theatrical and sporting events. We want our visitors to have a good time here."

She punched a button and spoke into her phone, "The agents are here to see you." The receptionist guided them into the madam's office.

Ishtar Haynes stood up to greet them and gestured for them to be seated. Riley found the woman's appearance even more startling than that of the escorts she had talked to earlier. Ishtar Haynes was wearing an expensive pantsuit and had perfectly coiffed hair. A pair of reading glasses was perched on her sharp, long nose. She looked like any legitimate female CEO.

"Let me see if I understand your purpose for making an appointment with me," she said, taking her own seat behind an expansive desk. "You want me to give you the name of Nanette's client on the night she was killed."

She directed her question to Bill, who nodded. Riley let him carry the interview as she took the opportunity to look around the plush office.

"That's right," Bill said. Ishtar Haynes smiled. Riley saw a world of coldness in that professional smile. This wasn't the stern face of a competent businesswoman, it was the frozen face of a person who had experienced no real feelings for many years.

"Agent Jeffreys, what kind of business do you think I run?" she said. "Not that I have any reason to think that Nanette and a client were doing anything especially illicit on the night in question. If

56

they got, shall we say, *affectionate*, that was entirely up to them. But my clients trust me to keep things strictly confidential."

"But you keep records of your clients," Bill said.

Ishtar Haynes shrugged. "Well, yes," she said. "We insist on photo IDs, which we scan and keep in a database. But I'm certainly not going to give you access to that kind of information without a warrant."

That was pretty much what Riley expected her to say. She was sure that Bill had expected it too. On a late Sunday afternoon, obtaining a warrant could be a time-consuming process if it was possible to get at all. She wondered how her partner would handle it.

Bill drummed his fingers on the table. He said, "You know, we could just put the word out that you were glad to talk with us. And three of your girls came in to talk to us earlier. How much would your clients trust you if they knew that?"

Haynes spoke with icy cheerfulness. "Yes, I've heard it all before. This is where you tell me that law enforcement can make it hard for me to do business. Sorry, that little threat means nothing to me. I run an honest and perfectly legal firm that does a respectable service."

As Riley studied the woman's face, her coldness and ruthlessness showed through more and more. Then the woman's features formed a humorless smile.

Haynes leaned across the table toward Bill. "You could do me a favor, though," she said. "And maybe I can do you a favor as well. I'm sure you'll be shocked to know that there are a couple of bad apples among the local police. They treat me like a common criminal. They're a real nuisance."

She took out a note pad and wrote something down.

"I'll jot down a couple of names. And if you'll look into this little problem of mine, well ..."

She pushed the paper across the table toward Bill.

This tactic took Riley completely by surprise. She could see that Bill was startled as well. The cops in question were undoubtedly hitting Haynes up for bribes or special favors. Getting them off the streets would be good for both her and local law enforcement. It was a brazen move, but a smart one.

"I'll definitely look into it," Bill said, pocketing the piece of paper.

Haynes's smile broadened. It looked quite sinister.

"Well, then," she said, "we can do business."

She turned to her computer and started going through her database. When she found what she was looking for, she said, "I've got a name for you. And I don't mind giving him up. Maybe you've heard of him—Calvin Rabbe. His grandfather made a killing with a chain of restaurants. Calvin inherited the family fortune, never did an honest day's work in his life. I was already thinking about banning him from our service. The girls were complaining about his … proclivities."

"So he was Nanette's client the night she was killed?" Bill asked.

Haynes pushed up her reading glasses to study her record more closely.

"Well, yes and no," she said. "He'd paid for her companionship on Saturday night, but then complained that she never showed up. I had to refund his money. So whatever happened to the girl had nothing to do with her work at my company."

Haynes closed her laptop and put it back in her bag.

"I assume that's all you need from me," she said. "Now if you don't mind, I need to get back to work. And oh, Agent Jeffreys—I take it you've flown in from Quantico for a few days."

Bill nodded. Still smiling, Haynes handed him a business card.

"Well, once you've cracked the case, give us a call," she said. "We'll show you some southwestern hospitality."

As she and Bill left the premises, Riley found herself unsettled by the woman's confident attitude.

She needs to be stopped, she thought.

To Riley, Haynes seemed as vicious and dangerous as many of the killers that she had killed or put away. In a way she seemed even worse—a coldhearted exploiter of women who spread evil far and wide.

As for Mitzi, Koreen, and Tantra, what was their future? If they survived, they might eventually become as stone cold as their employer. But even that was truly a big "if." They were much more likely to sink into desperation like Nancy Holbrook, even to meet the same fate.

"It sounds like Calvin Rabbe is a viable suspect," Riley said as they walked toward their car. "He was likely covering his tracks by complaining that the girl didn't show up."

"Maybe," Bill said. "A spoiled rich perv comes pretty close to fitting our profile. Did you get anything from the women you talked to?"

"It seems that Nancy Holbrook was hustling at a truck stop called Hank's Derby. She might have been doing it around the time she was killed."

"We've got to cover our bases," Bill said. "Let's check out that truck stop too."

Riley agreed. "You go after Rabbe," she said. "I'll go to Hank's Derby."

As she started to walk away, Bill called out, "You be careful."

It sounded like good advice. From what the girls had said, Riley suspected that she was about to encounter evils that even she had never faced before.

Chapter Twelve

Riley spotted two women holding out their thumbs hitchhiker-style as a massive big rig rolled toward them. They were dressed almost identically, braless with T-shirts ripped away at their midriffs and ultra-short denim skirts. They were obviously hookers, and it was easy to see that they sold themselves as a single package.

With a mighty hiss of brakes, the truck ground to a halt. The driver leaned out his window and beckoned to the girls. They scampered around to the passenger door and climbed inside. Then the truck rumbled back into motion and continued on its way. Riley found it unsettling to consider whatever this impromptu threesome was about to do next. But now was no time to get distracted. Her job was to find out whether Nancy Holbrook had met her killer here.

Dusk had fallen by the time Riley had reached Hank's Derby. Even from the highway, she'd been able to see that this was a much seedier place than most modern truck stops. The neon lettering on a huge derby-shaped sign flickered unsteadily in the waning light. Both the restaurant and the adjoining bar looked like their best days were far in the past.

Riley parked, got out of the car, and walked toward the main building. A few provocatively dressed women were hanging around outside the place. It seemed that prostitution was as much a thriving business here as gas and food. Riley already knew that some of the country's ugliest human trafficking happened at truck stops. Far too often, runaway children were the prey.

Before driving out here, she'd done a little online research on recent years. In Arizona, the situation had been especially bad, and the FBI had worked with local authorities to clean up prostitution rings all over the state. They had focused on places such as this, especially to get underage girls out of the trade.

But somehow, dens of human trafficking like Hank's Derby managed to survive. Riley wasn't surprised. She'd learned long ago that the world's evils had a way of growing back even after you thought you'd gotten rid of them, like weeds.

Walking past a row of dumpsters, Riley recalled a case when a teenage girl's body was found in a truck stop dumpster. A serial killer had been haunting the stops across the country and picking up girl hitchhikers. Some of them were simply never seen again.

Riley hadn't worked that case, and the killer had long ago been put away. Still, it chilled her to look at the dumpsters. Might even these contain the remains of discarded humans? The thought was a distraction, and Riley knew better than to stop and search inside the big metal boxes. She needed to stay focused.

Alongside the well-lighted main building was a little clapboard bar called the Yucca Lounge. She knew she had to go in there and ask some questions, but the prospect worried her. She'd struggled with alcohol during her recent bout of PTSD and had stopped drinking altogether. She'd been managing just fine, but going in a bar meant walking straight into temptation.

She assured herself that she was strong and professional enough to resist, then walked into the building. The Yucca Lounge was a dimly lit little dive with country music playing on the jukebox. It wasn't very crowded at the moment—just a few truckers and even fewer scantily dressed women.

Riley hadn't yet decided how best to proceed. She had a printed-out photo of Nancy Holbrook that she wanted to show around. But flipping open her badge and flashing the picture to everybody would cause too much of a stir and possibly backfire.

She noticed a hulking, bearded man sitting next to the door. He was obviously the bouncer. She approached him quietly and showed him her badge.

"I'm Agent Riley Paige with the FBI," she said. When his eyes widened, she added, "Don't worry, I'm not here to make trouble."

She took the picture out of her bag and showed it to him.

"Do you recognize this woman?" she asked. "I think she may have been here last Saturday."

"I haven't worked here that long," the man grumbled.

Riley took a twenty-dollar bill out of her purse.

"I'd like you to check this out for me. That's less likely to spook the patrons. Just go around quietly asking all the folks here if they've seen this woman. If anybody has, tell them to talk to me."

The man took the money and headed on over to the bar. Riley sat down and watched from the shadows as he made his way through the place, showing everybody the picture. She saw a lot of people shaking their heads no.

Finally he showed the picture to a woman sitting at the bar who nodded. The bouncer pointed to Riley, and the woman signaled her to come over and sit beside her. The woman was dressed like any of the working girls, but she seemed tired, and she looked about Riley's age—much too old for this line of work.

Riley sat down next to her. A row of empty shot glasses and a glass half full of beer were on the bar in front of the woman. The smell of whiskey made Riley's throat burn with the expectation of alcoholic pleasure, but the bartender never had a chance to ask her what she wanted.

The woman called out to the bartender in a sandpapery voice, "Cabot, I'm buying for this FBI girl. Bring her what I'm having. And bring me another round while you're at it."

The order was out before Riley could decline the offer. Cabot brought two full shot glasses and a beer for Riley.

"I'm Justine," the woman said. She downed the contents of her shot glass at a gulp, then chased it down with a swallow of beer. "We're drinking Fireball Cinnamon Whiskey. Have you tried it? If you haven't, you haven't lived. Burns going down, but tastes just like Christmas. Hope that's OK with you."

Riley's stomach turned a little at the thought of candy-flavored whiskey. It wasn't going to be so hard to resist temptation after all.

"I'm on duty," Riley said.

"Suit yourself," Justine said. "I'll find a nice home for it," she added, patting her own stomach.

She handed the photo back to Riley.

"I seen her around here. Name's Nanette, ain't it?"

"That's right," Riley said.

"How's she doing?"

Riley hesitated for a second. Justine interrupted before she could speak.

"Nanette's dead, ain't she?"

Riley was startled. Justine's expression was steady and calm.

"How did you know?" Riley asked.

Justine emitted a gravelly chuckle. "Oh, it's always an easy guess. Everybody dies sooner or later. For us working girls around this place, it's usually sooner. Sometimes a whole lot sooner. And it's never pretty."

Justine swallowed more beer.

"I figure my number's long overdue to come up," she said. "Just biding my time."

The woman sounded resigned but not bitter. Riley felt a pang of sympathy. She didn't know which was worse—living a lie like the escorts she had talked to that afternoon or facing grim facts like Justine. She couldn't imagine how this woman had gotten to such a terrible point. How had her existence become so miserable that she didn't even try to get out of this kind of life?

"What can you tell me about Nanette?" Riley asked.

"I only seen her a couple of times," Justine said. "She was new around here. I could tell right off she wasn't going to last."

Riley said, "We think she was killed last Saturday. Did you see her that night?"

Justine thought for a moment.

"I think the last I saw her was Friday," she said. "I don't think I saw her Saturday. She might've been here then too, and I could've missed her. I might have been otherwise occupied, if you know what I mean. I keep a pretty busy schedule for an old lady."

Justine slumped a little. Riley could see that she was letting some of her sadness and weariness show through.

In a slightly choked voice, Justine said, "This is no place for the likes of you. Now I think you'd better get the hell out of here and find the bastard that did her in."

"I'll do that, Justine," Riley said. "Thanks."

Riley got off the barstool. It sure didn't sound like she'd find that particular bastard here. But before she left she wanted to get a better look around. The main building would hold a store and shower rooms for the truckers. And outside, there was the big parking lot occupied by dozens of resting trucks. What might she find out there? Whatever it was, she felt sure that it was going to be as ugly as hell.

Chapter Thirteen

Her stomach knotted with dread, Riley headed for the last part of Hank's Derby that she needed to investigate. After leaving the bar, she had shown Nanette's picture around the truck stop store, but no one there had been helpful. Now she had to see what might be happening among the parked trucks, and she wasn't looking forward to it.

When she walked out of the main building into the warm night air, she didn't see any hookers around. Maybe they'd been tipped off that an FBI agent was around.

Across a wide stretch of pavement, rows of silent trucks occupied a big parking lot. Most of the parking lot lights weren't working and those few that were created giant shadows. She walked slowly toward the mammoth vehicles.

Everything was very quiet, and at first she thought maybe no one was out here after all. But as Riley made her way between two trucks, a door to one of them swung open. A burly man with enormous tattooed biceps climbed out and stood in her path.

"Well, who have we got here?" he said, leering at her. "You don't look like one of our regular girls. Much too proper. Poor little thing, you must've lost your way. Maybe you'd like me to give you a ride home."

"I don't think so," Riley said, trying to move past him.

He grabbed her by the arm, swung her around, and pushed her backward against the truck. He leaned forward, straddling her with his arms. She couldn't get away. She could feel anger rising, feeding on her deep-seated fury that men like this viewed women as prey.

"Why not, baby?" he said. "I guess you're new around here and don't know how we do things. You just get in the truck with me. I'll make sure you get home safe and sound. Honest."

Without a word, Riley rapidly lifted her knee, aiming at his groin. But he deftly parried the blow with his own leg. He was strong, and he weighed at least twice as much as she did.

"Oh, so you're gonna put up a fight, are you?" he snarled. "I like that."

He grabbed her arms and held her fast. His breath reeked of beer as his face craned toward her.

Riley's anger mutated into rage. The face she saw in front of her was no longer a drunken trucker. She felt that she was looking into the eyes of a deeply evil man who had held both Riley and her daughter captive. A man who had killed other women and tormented a good friend until she killed herself. A man she recognized all too well ...

Peterson.

Riley snarled, giving him a head-butt and then whipping out her Glock and pointing it directly at his face.

The man in front of her staggered backward in shock and fear.

"Hey! Hey!" he cried. "No need for that!"

The image of Peterson's face faded back into that of a frightened bully.

Not a killer, Riley told herself. *You've already killed Peterson.*

Her hand was shaking. She had come very close to firing her gun—very close to killing a man in cold blood. Slowly she lowered the gun. Now she knew that it was just the trucker standing before her, but her anger hadn't dissipated. She landed a tardy blow to his crotch, using the sharp toe of her shoe instead of her knee. He buckled over, groaning and gasping.

Her weapon was still in her hand, and she smashed the butt of it against the back of his head. He fell flat on his face. She put her gun back in its holster and knelt down beside him. She grabbed him by the hair, yanking his head back. His face was bloody.

Short of breath, she managed to speak in a mock-kindly tone.

"I'm Agent Riley Paige, FBI. And you're right, I am kind of new around here, so maybe you could help me with a little something."

Still holding him by the hair, she pulled out the photo and held it in front of his face.

"Did you ever see this woman? She'd go by the name of Nanette."

He grunted, "Huh-uh."

She jerked on his hair, pulling some it out by the roots. "Are you sure?"

"I'm sure."

"OK. Thanks."

She let go of him. He clambered unsteadily to his feet and staggered away toward the truck stop, cursing under his breath.

Riley heard a voice from the passenger window of the next parked truck.

"Hey, hard-ass FBI lady."

Riley looked up and saw a young girl's face peering down at her. She gave Riley a thumbs-up.

"Very dime," she said.

It sounded like the kind of slang Riley might hear her own daughter use.

"I take it that's a good thing," she said.

"Yeah. It means ten on a scale of one to ten. Maybe you could give me a self-defense lesson."

Riley rubbed her forehead, which hurt quite a bit.

"To start with, go with head-butts only as a last resort," she said. Then she took a better look at the girl.

"What's your name?" she asked.

"They call me Trinda."

The girl looked shockingly young.

"How old are you?" Riley asked.

"None of your business, old lady."

The girl who called herself Trinda was wearing thick makeup, like a little girl trying to look like a grown-up. But she looked like she might be April's age.

"You're just about fifteen, aren't you?" Riley said.

Trinda said nothing, but Riley could see by her expression that she'd guessed right. Riley climbed up onto the foothold and peered into the cab of the truck. There was a mattress in the back of the cab with a pair of manacles on it.

"Jesus," Riley said. "What are you doing here?"

"What do you think I'm doing? I'm doing what all the other girls here are doing. And you'd better bone out of here fast. My john's just having a beer and he'll be back soon. He's big and mean, even for you."

"Do you have any idea what he might do to you?"

Trinda shrugged. "He says he's gonna pay me a hundred. He can do whatever he wants."

Riley felt positively sick to her stomach.

"Come with me," she said. "I'll get you out of here. I'll get you cleaned up and take you to some decent place to live."

Trinda sneered. "There aren't any decent places to live. I've tried them all. Look, what do you think I should be doing instead? Flipping burgers for eight dollars an hour? On a good night here I can pull in three hundred dollars turning tricks. And it's easy money—at least most of the time."

Then with a shrug, she added, "And when it's not so easy— well, I'm tough. I can take it."

Riley was almost trembling with rage and frustration.

"You shouldn't be flipping burgers, and you shouldn't be working for eight dollars an hour or three hundred dollars a night, and you shouldn't be here. You should be in school."

"And going home after school to a nice house with a loving mom and dad, right? Believe me, it's not an option. Look, if you're going to get all moral like this, leave me the fuck alone, OK? Go do your job, whatever it is. I'm sure you've got more important stuff to do than hassle working girls."

Riley pulled the truck door open.

"I want you to come with me," she said.

The girl yanked the door shut again.

"Not a chance. Do that again and I'll yell for help. You'll have truck drivers all over your ass. They'll fucking kill you—after they do everything else they like."

Riley had no idea of what to do. With her Glock and her considerable fighting skills, she figured she could handle a bunch of drunken truckers. But what good would it do to make that kind of scene? Trinda would undoubtedly slip away in the mayhem.

Still, she realized that there was something she could do. She walked away alongside the truck.

"Good riddance, lady!" Trinda called out.

While Riley jotted down the number of the license plate, Trinda yelled out again.

"Hey, if you really want to help a kid in trouble, check over there."

Riley looked and saw that Trinda was pointing along the line of trucks.

"Check out the truck at the end of the row," she said. "You'll find a girl named Jilly. She *really* needs help. She's never done nothing like this before. She's got no business being around here."

Trinda rolled up the window and disappeared from view. Riley walked across the blacktop toward the last truck.

"Jilly?" she called out.

A small, frightened voice called out, "What do you want?"

Riley climbed onto the foothold and looked through the open window into the cab. Crouched on the mattress in back was a skinny, dark-skinned girl who didn't look older than thirteen. She wasn't dressed like a hooker. She was wearing sneakers, shorts, and a T-shirt just like any girl her age. Riley was stunned.

"Are you Jilly?" Riley asked.

The girl nodded.

"What are you doing here?" Riley said.

67

"Waiting for Rex," the girl said in little more than a whisper.

"Who's Rex?"

The girl said nothing. She looked absolutely terrified.

"Who's Rex?" Riley said again.

"I don't know," Jilly said. "But the guy at the cash register said he'd be looking for a good time. He told me to just come out here and wait for him."

Riley opened the door and climbed inside the cab. "I'm getting you out of here," she said, offering her hand to Jilly.

"Who are you?" Jilly said.

Riley showed her badge. "My name is Riley. I'm an FBI agent. You'll be safe with me. I promise."

The girl looked straight into Riley's eyes. She came forward and Riley put an arm around her shoulders. The girl was trembling.

Before they could climb out of the truck, Riley heard a voice from below.

"Hey! Who the hell's in my truck!"

Riley looked down and saw a beefy middle-aged man.

"Are you Rex?" she said.

"Yeah, what's it to you?"

Riley knew she should reach for her badge, but she couldn't bring herself to let go of the girl. The man saw Jilly.

"Hey, what are you doing with this poor little thing?" he said to Riley.

"What are *you* doing with her?"

Rex's mouth dropped open with disbelief.

"Good God, I ain't doing nothing with her! She's just a kid. Who the hell *are* you? What kind of perverted shit are you up to?"

At that, Riley turned partly away from the child and pulled out her badge.

"Agent Riley Paige, FBI," she said.

Rex smiled, looking genuinely relieved. "Glad to hear it. We've got to get this girl home."

"I'm not going home," Jilly said. "My dad will beat me up if I go back."

Rex looked at Riley. "Maybe you could drive her to Child Protective Services."

Riley took Jilly's hand. They climbed down from the cab. She still didn't know what to make of Rex.

"I'll do that," Riley said. "But Jilly said some guy told her to come here. He said that you'd be looking for a 'good time.'"

68

Rex shrugged. "Sure, I like a little whorin' around as much of the next man. But only with grown women, for Chrissake, not with little girls. You get this runaway out of here."

Riley led Jilly toward her car, feeling more puzzled than ever. Rex seemed like a good-hearted guy. Still, he liked his "whorin' around." Didn't he understand that every working girl around here had once been a little girl just like Jilly? The whole thing didn't make sense to her.

Riley got Jilly into her car, then sat down in the driver's seat and called the local police. She gave them the license number she'd written down and described the truck.

"I'm at Hank's Derby truck stop," she said. "The driver's got a teenage girl. She goes by the name of Trinda. Get here fast before he can take her anywhere. And bust him but good for child trafficking. Throw the goddamn book at him."

When the policewoman on the phone agreed to send someone out, Riley said, "There's something else I need to know. I've got a juvenile with me, a fourteen-year-old who says she can't go home. I need the address for Child Protective Services. Or someone who will be open right now."

The policewoman gave Riley the address of an emergency shelter in downtown Phoenix. "I'll call and tell them you're coming," she said.

Riley turned to Jilly, who was looking up at her with a worried expression.

"Fasten your seat belt," Riley said. "I'm going to take you to someone who can help you out."

Jilly fumbled with the seat belt with hands that were still trembling, and Riley had to help her latch it. Then she started to drive.

"Where are we going?" Jilly asked, in a little more than a whisper.

"There are people who can give you a place to stay. They can even find you a new home if you need one," Riley said.

Jilly seemed to be thinking that over. "I can't go home anymore," she finally commented.

Riley asked, "You said your dad would beat you. What about your mom?"

"She's not there," Jilly said. "She went away years ago. My older brother left, too."

"So it was just you and your dad?"

"Yeah," Jilly replied. "And he drinks a lot now."

Riley concentrated on driving the car, following the automated instructions to the shelter. Beside her, Jilly sank down on the seat and seemed to be asleep. Riley wondered what was going to happen to this child now. Would she just run away again? Would she wind up like Justine someday? Or would she even live that long?

She had to ring the bell at the emergency shelter doorway, but after a few minutes a voice on the speaker asked what she wanted. Riley identified herself, and a tired but sympathetic-looking woman came to the door and let them in.

Jilly was still holding onto Riley's hand, so she followed them down a hallway to an office. She thought the place looked clean enough, and the woman seemed genuinely interested in the child. Jilly let go of Riley's hand and sat down in the chair by the desk. Riley gave the woman her card, and said she'd check in tomorrow. When she left, Jilly was cooperatively answering questions while the woman typed on her computer.

When Riley got back into her car, she realized that she hadn't found out anything about Nancy Holbrook's death. She might have to go back to Hank's Derby to further investigate. It all depended on how Bill had fared with his suspect, Calvin Rabbe. She'd check in with him as soon as she got a chance.

Meanwhile, nausea over all she'd seen threatened to overwhelm her.

I hope Bill's got something, she thought. *I want this case to be over with.*

70

Chapter Fourteen

Bill felt a rush of anticipation as he neared the gated entrance of Calvin Rabbe's sprawling Spanish-colonial home. The man who lived behind this fence was very likely to be the killer who had taken a woman's life and thrown her body into a lake. Bill was determined to find out for sure.

He had done a little research on Calvin Rabbe before driving out here. Ishtar Haynes had been right—the spoiled bastard hadn't done a day's honest work in his life. He'd spent his childhood and teen years getting expelled from boarding schools, then had gotten kicked out of all the best Ivy League universities without getting a degree.

Now he was living with his divorced mother in that mansion.

It figures, Bill thought.

Rabbe's dependence on the family matriarch added to Bill's suspicions. The man was sounding more and more like a spoiled rich momma's boy who might have a lot of unresolved resentment. Bill was starting to look forward to putting this guy away.

But as he drove past the entrance, he could see that getting to meet Rabbe might be complicated. Even getting admitted to the grounds would involve a bit of protocol. Security cameras flanked the gates to the property. You had to ring a buzzer and announce yourself. Bill wasn't sure how to proceed.

What would happen if he tried to ring himself in, announcing that he was an FBI agent? And who would he wind up talking to once he was admitted? Dusk had fallen, and the house was well lit. It was possible that a number of people were inside. Bill couldn't even be sure that Calvin Rabbe was one of them.

At the next corner, Bill turned his car around to drive past the front gates again.

In the well-lighted driveway, he saw a fancy little sports convertible wending its way through the grounds toward the gate. The top was down, and Bill could see the driver. The man was young with sandy blond hair, and he was wearing a polo shirt. He perfectly matched pictures Bill had seen of Calvin Rabbe. He had the look of a movie star approaching middle age, but still trying to project a carefree, youthful image.

Bill suddenly felt lucky. Now he wouldn't have to fake his way into the mansion. Rabbe was on his way out, very possibly headed for a night on the town. If Bill could just stay on his trail, the man might give himself away. The gate opened, and the little car went off down the street. Bill followed him, keeping an unsuspicious distance behind.

The night deepened as Bill followed the sports car through the expensive neighborhood. He found himself wondering what Riley was doing right now. Had it really been a good idea to let her go to that truck stop alone? Hank's Derby sounded like a vile and dangerous place for a woman.

Bill didn't really know why he was worried. Riley was far and away the toughest and most capable woman he had ever known. He'd seen her take down some truly dangerous characters. It was hard to imagine what kind of man could actually be a threat to her.

He decided that his unease was because this case was getting to him. He thought that it was getting to Riley too. Bill doubted that either of them would feel a lot of satisfaction once they took down this killer. Whoever had murdered Nancy Holbrook was just the tip of an iceberg, a symptom of a much larger evil. God only knew how many other women were being exploited, victimized, and killed. They were here to stop one man, but the whole ugly scene would just go on and on.

Soon Bill noticed that Calvin Rabbe was making his way into an especially unpleasant neighborhood. The streets were lined with seedy bars, motels, and strip joints. Rabbe parked his car in front of a place called the Lariat Strip Club.

The marquee sign showed a semi-animated neon lariat dropping around a nude woman's silhouette and tightening around her waist. Below the sign was a smaller one that announced "LIVE NUDES." So soon after viewing Nancy Holbrook's naked corpse, the sign struck Bill as chillingly ironic. Had the killer come here to hunt for another living target?

He parked just a couple of spaces behind Rabbe and watched him get out of the car. In the midst of the local riffraff of druggies and hookers, Rabbe really stood out in his preppy shirt, khaki shorts, and expensive sneakers. But Bill quickly realized that Rabbe wasn't headed toward the club's front entrance. Instead he continued around the corner of the building and disappeared from sight.

Bill jumped out of his car and broke into a trot. When he reached the edge of the building, he saw Rabbe walking away from him toward the alley behind the strip club. Bill waited until his prey disappeared around back, then followed. Once in the alley, Bill was able to hide alongside a dumpster and watch what Rabbe was up to.

Rabbe knocked on the back door of the strip club. The door opened, and Rabbe walked on inside. The door slammed shut behind him.

Bill felt more alert by the second. If Rabbe was making a drug deal, this might give Bill a perfect excuse to bring him in. But he had to be patient. He had to be sure.

After about five minutes, Rabbe stepped out into the alley again. He took a small package out of his front pocket and unfolded it. He brushed his finger through the contents, then rubbed it inside his mouth around his gums. He was sampling the product.

Bingo! Bill thought.

Bill stepped into the open, taking out his badge.

"FBI," he said. "You're under arrest."

Rabbe hastily refolded the package and stuck it in his pants pocket. For a moment, he looked at Bill with a slightly stunned deer-in-the-headlights expression. Then he smiled broadly, threw back his head, and laughed.

"FBI? Oh, this is a joke. This has got to be a joke."

"No joke," Bill said. "Hands behind your back."

Bill had come prepared with a pair of handcuffs. As he took them off his belt, he wondered if he was going to need to draw his weapon.

Shaking his head with apparent disbelief, Rabbe put his hands behind his back.

"No, really," Rabbe said. "This is a joke. I know it's a joke. Who put you up to this?"

Bill slapped the handcuffs on him. As he started reading his rights, Rabbe interrupted.

"I know my rights, believe me. I'm used to this kind of thing from the local cops, but the FBI? Seriously, I don't believe it. What are you even arresting me for?"

The corner of the paper package was poking out of Rabbe's pants pocket. Bill pulled it out and waved it in front of his face.

"This will do," he said.

"Oh, give me a break. You've got to be kidding."

Bill resumed reading him his rights.

"I said I know my rights," Rabbe said, interrupting again.

"Humor me," Bill said. He finished the recitation of rights and escorted Rabbe back to his car.

He had a good feeling that this really was the killer. He hoped Riley would get back to the FBI field office in time to help him make absolutely sure.

Chapter Fifteen

Riley got a text message from Bill just as she drove away from the emergency shelter where she'd left Jilly. All it said was that he had apprehended Calvin Rabbe. She hurried back to the Phoenix FBI building to check out the suspect.

She met Bill outside the interview room.

"What happened?" she asked breathlessly. "What did you get him for? We didn't even have a warrant."

"Cocaine possession," Bill said. "I got lucky. Real lucky. I'm glad you're here. I was just getting ready to talk to him. Come on in and help me out."

Riley followed Bill into the interview room. Calvin Rabbe was sitting there in handcuffs, sneering like some snotty overage schoolboy who had been sent to the principal's office.

"Will somebody tell me what this is all about?" Rabbe said. "I'm not an idiot. I know it's not coke. It's got to be something else."

Riley and Bill sat down at the table across from him. Riley stared at him quietly, trying to decide how to handle him. It wouldn't do to accuse him right away of killing Nancy Holbrook. He'd lawyer up in no time and wiggle right out from under them. A less direct approach seemed more promising.

Riley said, "We understand that you're an occasional client of Ishtar Escorts."

"Who told you that?" Rabbe said. "That's not true."

"We got your name from Ishtar herself," Bill put in.

Rabbe looked surprised, but hardly shocked, nor even especially annoyed.

"Well, that old whore," he said. "What's the world coming to? If you can't trust whores, who can you trust?"

Riley leaned across the table toward him.

"So you like whores, Calvin?" she said.

Rabbe shrugged. "As women these days go, whores are better than most. That's not saying a lot."

"So you've got a problem with women?" Riley said.

"Don't get me started," Rabbe growled, looking away from her.

I've hit his sore spot, Riley realized. She was starting to feel that the interview was on the right track.

"Tell us a little about Nanette," Riley said.

"Who's Nanette?"

"Oh, come on," Riley said. "You know perfectly well who I'm talking about. One of Ishtar's girls. You met with Nanette last Saturday night."

Rabbe let out a snort of derision. "I did no such thing," he said. "Sure, I had an appointment with her. But she stood me up. It really ruined my night. She was going to come with me to a charity event my mom was holding. It was written up in the news. Maybe you've heard of it, the Judith Rabbe Foundation."

He said the words with palpable disgust. Riley was becoming intrigued.

"No, I can't say I have heard of it," Riley said.

Rabbe rolled his eyes.

"Oh, my mom's got this thing about educating girls in all those countries with unpronounceable names. Trying to fix a problem that's not a problem at all. They've got the right idea about women in those places. Not like the fucked-up culture we've got here."

Riley could see Rabbe's character coming into clearer focus.

A misogynist pig, she thought. *Exactly the kind of guy we're looking for.*

Bill asked the next question. "So how does your mother feel about your bringing escorts to her fancy get-togethers?"

It struck Riley as an excellent question. She remembered the less-than-respectable outfit that Nancy Holbrook had been wearing when her body was found. She also pictured how it would have gone over at the kind of upscale charity event that Rabbe's mother had surely given.

A broad, satisfied smirk formed across Rabbe's face.

"She doesn't like it, you can be sure of that," he said. "And it serves her right. But Nanette left me high and dry that night. No time to schedule another girl. I got stuck there alone in a house full of shrill harpies going on and on about oppression and patriarchal hegemony and all that sort of thing. Jesus."

His expression changed. Something seemed to be dawning on him.

"Wait a minute," he said. "Is this about Nanette's heroin habit? Is that why you hauled me in? Because I didn't have anything to do with that."

It was a lie, and Riley instantly knew it.

"But you didn't *mind* that she was strung out on smack, did you?" she said.

Rabbe chuckled a little.

"I like them docile, if you know what I mean," he said. "More like nature meant them to be. You ought to read a little evolutionary psychology, baby. Women aren't wired for the kind of work you do, the kind of life you live. Nature designed you to stay in the cave while the men went out to hunt. You're supposed to have babies and take good care of them."

He looked her steadily in the eye.

"You're just making yourself miserable, you know," Rabbe told her. "Fighting your own DNA coding, I mean. And I pity your boyfriend or husband—unless you're a lesbian, which I guess would make sense."

She knew that he was trying to get her goat. But it wasn't going to work. It was going to take a lot more than pseudoscientific antifeminism to get her to flare up at him, especially after the ugliness she'd just witnessed at Hank's Derby.

Then he told her, "I can see right through you. I know your type through and through. And I'll bet anything—every cent I've got in the world—that you're a lousy lay."

It was Riley's turn to smirk.

"This from a guy who can't get laid unless he pays for it," she said.

The comment seemed to have no impact upon him at all.

"Oh, I can get laid," he said. "I can get all the pussy I want, anytime I want. It's an art and a science, and I'm a master at it. I could have you if I wanted you. I could make you beg for it if I put my mind to it."

Riley almost laughed at the idea of Rabbe trying to ply his pickup technique on her. Still, she detected that he was more than half telling the truth. He was cunning and amorally deceptive, and he knew exactly what he was doing. She sensed that he could drop this vulgar, woman-hating manner altogether and adopt a much more charming and attractive persona. He could present himself as thoughtful, gallant, and sensitive to a woman's feelings. He could get his way with many women before they had a chance to see their mistake.

But they always live to regret it, she thought.

Or maybe some of them *didn't* live to regret it.

And this creep had no regrets. Not for anything he did. Not even for anything he said. She could feel her innate disgust for this type of man stirring in her gut.

"So why go to whores?" Bill asked.

Rabbe looked at Bill. "Believe me, buddy, whores are the way to go. Or maybe you know that already. They're honest. You don't have to get into bargaining and bartering about 'consent.' These days it's all 'may I' this and 'may I' that. A man can go to jail just for having sex with his own wife."

"Nonconsensual sex," Bill said.

"In marriage, there's no such thing."

He made a point of saying it directly to Riley. But she had no trouble keeping her cool. She sensed that now was a good time to get to the point.

"Did you have anything to do with Nanette's death?" she asked.

Riley looked for even a flicker of reaction. Rabbe's face showed no change of expression at all.

"She's dead?" he replied blandly.

"She was killed on Saturday night," Riley said.

Bill added, "The night you had an appointment with her."

Rabbe actually looked bored now.

"Well, I'm all broken up about it," he said, pretending to stifle a yawn. "So that's what this is all about. You think I did it. Well, I've got an alibi. I was at home at my mom's charity event. You can even find photos of me there on the Internet."

He leaned back in his chair.

"OK, fun times over," he said. "I want my phone call. I want my lawyer."

She didn't know whether it was the artificial yawn or the comment about fun times, but Riley wasn't listening anymore. She lunged across the table and grabbed Rabbe by the front of his expensive shirt.

"Right!" she shouted. "No more fun times."

His scream when she threw him to the floor was deeply satisfying. She flung herself toward him and he scrambled backward across the floor, moving remarkably fast for a man in handcuffs.

Two younger agents rushed into the room, grabbing Riley's arms from both sides, but she was still moving forward toward Rabbe. She started to knock them away, but she didn't fight Bill off when he put his arms around her from behind, pinning her own arms down.

"Enough," Bill said. "You'll get suspended again," he said sternly.

"Again?" one of the younger agents said.

"All right," Riley said. "All right." Her fury was subsiding. She relaxed her body and Bill released his hold.

By then Rabbe was yelling for his lawyer and threatening lawsuits. Riley looked down at him and he grew quiet.

He was a rare suspect, she realized—the kind she didn't know how to read. She turned to Bill.

"Let's have a word outside," she said coolly.

She and Bill stepped outside the interview room.

"I think we should let him go," she said.

Bill looked shocked and surprised.

"You don't think he's our guy?" Bill asked.

"I don't know."

"Then shouldn't we question him some more?"

Riley let out a discouraged sigh. "We can check out his alibi. But right now, all we've got him on is a half-assed drug charge. Just possession of a small quantity. And with the kind of lawyer he can afford, we won't even be able to make that stick. He'll be out of here in no time. If we let him go now, at least we can assign some agents to keep track of him. Maybe we can trip him up."

Bill shook his head.

"I don't like this," he said. "But I'll go in and do it. Maybe that will keep him from bringing charges against you."

Riley watched through the one-way window as Bill took off Rabbe's handcuffs and told him he could go. Rabbe looked straight into the window. He obviously knew that Riley was watching him. He gave her a smirk but then lowered his eyes and hurried out of the room.

Riley wasn't used to feeling so full of self-doubt. And now she remembered how the diving team chief had said there was no second body in the lake. She hadn't had a chance to tell Bill about that yet, but it had shaken her confidence.

As she waited for Bill to finish escorting Rabbe out of the building, her head filled up with questions. Could she really be sure that the divers were wrong? Was it possible that this wasn't a serial case after all?

She was used to following her gut, but now her gut was giving her mixed signals. Maybe all the trauma of the last few months— being held captive herself and having to rescue April from captivity—had blunted her instincts. Maybe she wasn't up for this kind of work anymore.

Still, there was one thing she wanted to do, even if this was the last job she ever took as a field agent. She wanted to catch Nancy Holbrook's killer. But was she right to suspect Rabbe?

Or did she just want him to be guilty?

Chapter Sixteen

As the woman strolled down the posh hotel hallway with the man who called himself T.R., she wondered what kind of fun was in store for her today. The situation made her a little giddy and she gave herself a stern reminder …

Your name is "Chiffon." Don't forget it.

It wasn't that she usually had trouble remembering the name of her hooker alter-ego. She really liked the name Chiffon, and she'd used it with dozens of johns without slipping once. But T.R. was different. He disarmed her somehow.

Maybe it was because he'd shown a trace of vulnerability the only other time they'd been together. Things hadn't gone well for the poor guy. Of course, she'd dutifully taken the blame and cheerfully offered to make it up to him.

A little while ago in the middle of the day, she'd spotted him sitting in his parked car a block away from the Kinetic Custom Gym. He'd picked her up near the gym once before, although he'd insisted they meet somewhere else to play. She thought it was because he was too classy for a place like that. This time, she'd approached him and suggested they give things another try.

Right now, she was feeling a bit overwhelmed. She was used to holding her trysts in her sordid little cubicle behind the gym or sometimes in a cheap motel. But today he'd asked where she'd like to go if she could choose any place she wanted. She'd thought it was a little game. More or less as a joke, she'd suggested this expensive, out-of-the-way hotel. She'd never been here but knew it was a vacation spot for well-to-do tourists.

The next thing she knew, he was making a reservation on his cell phone. Then she was in his car and on her way here. T.R. was certainly full of surprises. She wondered what else he had in store for her tonight. She couldn't wait to tell Mitzi all about it. She was sure that her friend who also worked at the gym had never been to a place like this.

He had left her in the car and gone into the hotel alone to check in, carrying a suitcase and wearing a hairpiece and expensive-looking glasses that changed his appearance. She'd been surprised at how different those small changes made him look.

In a short time, he had come back to the car to escort her through a side door and to their room. When he opened the room door, she saw that it was beautiful and spacious. Peeking into the bathroom, she saw that it was quite elegant. A sliding door led from the room out onto a patio where pots of flowers were in bloom.

"How beautiful it all is," she exclaimed, heading toward the patio.

But he gently blocked her way. "Sorry," he said with a smile. Then he drew heavy drapes across the sliding door.

Of course, she realized. *How silly of me.* He obviously didn't want to be seen with her, and it was best for her to stay completely out of sight.

She wasn't bothered. How could she be? It was part of the job.

She sat down on the edge of the bed and looked around the room, eager to figure out what this john would want her to do next. This place was expensive, and he'd promised her a lot of money—money that she wouldn't have to divide with Jaybird, the manager of the gym. She was delighted with the opportunity, but one thing was bothering her. She realized that T.R. might be expecting to spend a lot of time with her here. That could be a problem for her.

The john didn't appear to be in a rush, and he seemed to be prepared for a leisurely afternoon. He pulled a bottle of chilled white wine out of the mini-fridge and poured two glasses. Handing one to her, he sat down in a plush armchair with his own. He nodded and gestured as if making a toast, then sipped his wine and seemed to relax into the chair.

She sipped her own wine for a few moments. Then she got up nerve enough to tell him, "I'm sorry, but I can't stay long."

"Why not?"

She fell silent. She didn't know what to say. She'd never told a john the truth about herself. She hadn't even told Mitzi everything. Jaybird was the only person who knew.

The man smiled a gentle, sympathetic smile.

"You've got a secret, haven't you, Chiffon?" he said.

She said nothing.

He chuckled a little. "I understand. I really do. I've got some secrets of my own." Then, after a pause, he added. "And I've got a bit of a confession to make. I feel a real a kinship with you. I feel like we understand each other in a special way."

She was becoming quite moved. She'd never known a john to show this kind of openness. A lot of them didn't even bother talking.

"Tell me about it." He patted the suitcase. "I've got little surprise for you. I'll give it to you if you tell me."

The woman took a long, slow breath.

"My name isn't Chiffon," she said.

"Well, mine isn't T.R.," he said, chuckling again. "Tell me something both of us don't already know. Tell me your real name."

She felt as if she were on the edge of a precipice. But yes, she really did want to tell him. It would be exciting to tell him. It would be a new kind of adventure.

"My name is Gretchen," she said.

"And?" the man asked.

"And—I'm married. I've got children."

The man looked quite delighted now.

"Two children?" he guessed.

"No, three."

He held her gaze for a moment. Yes, it felt good to be doing this. She wasn't sure just why, but it felt absolutely right.

"I'm supposed to be at home right now," she said. "I'm supposed to be doing whatever it is that stay-at-home mothers do. That's what my husband thinks I'm doing. But it's no kind of a life. There are too many hours in a day. I can't keep myself busy."

"And you get bored," he said.

She giggled, feeling relieved to be able to admit it aloud.

"Oh, yes! More bored than you can imagine! But I do need to be home when the kids get back from school."

The man fingered the top of his suitcase. "And you don't need the money?"

"No. Well, the money's nice. My husband keeps a pretty tight hold on the purse strings. I like having cash of my own."

The man rose from the chair and walked over to the bed, carrying the suitcase. He sat beside Chiffon. He opened the suitcase just a little, holding it so that she couldn't see its contents.

"Close your eyes," he said.

She did so.

She felt his hands at the back of her neck. He was putting something around her throat.

"Now you can look," he said.

She opened her eyes and jumped up to see herself in a nearby mirror, then squealed with surprise. She was wearing a thin silver necklace with an infinity sign. A little stone sparkled in the center of it. A real diamond, she was sure.

It must have been quite expensive. For a moment, she didn't know what to say. Should she accept it? She didn't know when or where she'd be able to wear it. She certainly couldn't let her husband know about it.

Still, it was a sweet gesture. It would be rude to reject it.

"Thank you," she said. Then she added, "I want to show you just how much this means to me."

The man said nothing. She looked into his eyes. They seemed to be full of affection.

"Aren't you going to tell me *your* name now?" she asked.

The man nodded. "In a few minutes. Go get ready."

She found it fascinating, the way he gave orders like this. Somehow, his orders didn't seem terse or controlling. His voice and his face were much too pleasant.

She giggled with delight and headed for the bathroom.

Wait until Mitzi sees this, she thought. *Won't she just die!*

And she felt sure that T.R. still had other surprises in store. It was a thrill to try to imagine what might happen next.

Chapter Seventeen

The man almost laughed aloud when the little whore came out of the bathroom wearing nothing but the necklace he had just given her. The view of her naked body didn't arouse him. He knew it would take something more to give him any satisfaction.

He was still fully dressed, sitting in the big upholstered chair across from the bed. He smiled at her, as if in appreciation.

"Get in bed," he told her.

Without a word, she climbed between the luxurious satin sheets.

She pulled the covers around her, looking like a shy little girl.

No, he thought. *She looks just like a hooker pretending to be a shy little girl.*

He smiled broadly, and detected the relief on her face. She was trying hard to please him. As he got up and walked toward the bed, she moved the sheet downward to reveal her ample breasts.

She smiled up at him, and he was struck by how indifferent her efforts left him. Her little antics were not serving any purpose. Her trusting smile was actually turning him off.

"Put your hands behind you," he said.

She rolled over on her side, facing away from him, and did as he had ordered.

"That's good," he said. "Just stay like that."

He had placed his suitcase on a table near the bed and now he drew what he needed out of it. Sitting on the bed behind the hooker, he deftly tied a rope around her wrists.

"Oh, my," she exclaimed. But she made no complaint. He was sure he wasn't the first john who had enjoyed tying her up. And after his show of generosity, he deserved to do whatever he liked with her. And he would do exactly what he liked.

"Now sit up," he said. "I'll help you."

"All right," she said. "What do you want to do next?" She was giggling again, perhaps a little nervously, he thought.

"Don't turn around," he said.

On his knees behind her on the bed, he stroked her hair.

"That's nice," she murmured.

Then he slipped the plastic bag over her head. She wasn't giggling now. Stunned, she sat still for a moment. Then she began to struggle. He held the bag there forcefully. She thrashed her legs and kicked off the satin sheets. She tried to reach him with her tied arms. With his hands he held the bag in place and kept her from moving away from him.

After a few moments he whispered, "I'll tell you my name now."

But he knew she couldn't hear him anymore, so he released her.

Then he sat on the edge of the bed, looking at the naked and pathetic little pile of a woman lying there. It had all happened much faster than he'd intended. He'd meant to dally with her for hours, until after dark. But he'd had to act faster after she told him that she didn't have much time.

Not that he was disappointed. To the contrary, having to improvise and change his tactics added to his enjoyment. And he'd felt a wonderful sense of connection with her before he had done it. This killing had given him more pleasure than either of the others.

Now the pleasure continued, a silent afterglow of satisfaction. He decided to just sit there and savor that lovely feeling. The other times, he'd felt rather rushed to get rid of the bodies. But there was absolutely no reason to hurry this time. He could just wait here until dark.

And what was he going to do until then? Well, he could watch television. But no, that didn't feel right at all. Chiffon—Gretchen—deserved more respect than that, a little pampering and attentiveness even in death. The last time he'd been with her, he'd found her a bit off-putting, and he hadn't been sure that he liked her. But now things were different.

He gently stroked her hair and remembered what she'd said …

"There are too many hours in a day. I can't keep myself busy."

He admired the sentiment. Really, he did. Most people he knew lived Thoreau's proverbial "lives of quiet desperation," day in and day out. Not knowing what to do with themselves, they never did much of anything at all.

Not Gretchen. She had been a worthy victim. There had been good sport in killing her.

Time passed at a relaxed, meditative pace. He raptly watched the shadows shift over Gretchen's body as night settled in. He was surprised at how soon it seemed dark enough to finish things. The rest of what he had to do was simple drudgery in comparison to the act itself. Even so, it had to be done.

He pulled a black body bag out of his suitcase. He'd used simple garbage bags in the past, but now he thought better of it. A body bag seemed a much more secure receptacle. He laid it across the bed, then arranged the body inside, still naked except for the silver necklace.

Then he zipped the bag up. He stepped out onto the patio to make sure nobody was around. His car was parked only a few feet away.

He went back inside, threw the remarkably lightweight burden over his shoulder, and carried it out to his car. He opened the truck and put it inside.

He went back into the room and looked around for anything Gretchen had left there. Her handbag and the clothes she'd been wearing were in a neat pile on the bathroom floor. Inside the handbag, he found her cell phone, a little cash, some keys, and some Kleenex. He picked up the phone and stared at it for a moment. He was sure she'd had no time to make a call, but when anybody started looking for her they'd try to locate that phone. He put it on the floor and smashed it with his heel. Her wallet held her driver's license, some photos of kids, and a little cash. He tossed it back into the handbag, then he put all her stuff into a garbage bag to sling into some random dumpster far away from anything that could be connected to him.

Then he walked around the room making sure that nothing was left behind, just like any hotel guest getting ready to leave. He hung a "DO NOT DISTURB" sign on the hallway door. He wasn't going to check out right now. He'd come back tomorrow morning and do that, so that it would look like he'd spent the night here alone. Of course, he'd checked in with a credit card with a phony name.

Finally he exited through the patio, got into his car, and drove. As he drove into the deepening night, he took stock of his current situation. Things were at a dangerous point now. Because of his sloppiness with Nanette's body, law enforcement at every level was now arrayed against him. He was at very great risk.

To her credit, Chiffon—Gretchen—embraced that kind of risk, positively lived for it. But his approach to life was different. As a connoisseur and an epicure, he wasn't out to live life on the edge. He didn't want to be famous. He'd be just as happy if nobody ever found out about these murders. All he wanted was to enjoy the moment of a woman's death. It was a private matter between himself and his victims.

Is that too much to ask of life? he wondered.

There was no question in his mind that he deserved those pleasures.

Such thoughts passed through his head during the two-hour drive to the lake. He'd chosen a different lake this time, of course—one that was farther away from Phoenix, where no one would think to look. This one, too, was an artificial, freshwater lake created by flooding a deep canyon. He liked to come to lakes like these recreationally, and he knew this one well.

With his headlights off, he drove along a gravel road until he found the spot he was looking for. He made no mistake this time. It was a ledge near the road that hung over the water, and he knew that it dropped straight down into considerable depths.

He parked, got out of the car, and looked around the scene. The moon shone but faintly through a thick bank of clouds. The weather was certainly in his favor.

He got the body bag out of the trunk. He zipped it open and arranged a number of heavy rocks around the body. He zipped the bag up again and rolled it off the ledge. It made a louder splash than he expected.

Suddenly a light appeared. It seemed to be from a boat a few hundred feet from the shore. He guessed that someone was nighttime fishing out there. But why had they turned on the light? Had they heard the splash?

He doubted it. They were probably changing bait or something. In any case, even with the light, he was sure they couldn't make out his form from such a distance. He went back to his car, got in, and started to drive, keeping his headlights off until he was a fair distance off.

It's been a marvelous night, he thought.

He felt a bit melancholy that the whole thing was over. But he promised himself that he'd do it again soon.

Chapter Eighteen

After Riley and Bill spent another tedious day at headquarters, she felt the exhaustion creeping in. The pessimism. It was getting late, and it was about time to wrap things up. They had been in Phoenix since Saturday under the flimsy pretext that Nancy "Nanette" Holbrook's murder *might* be the work of a serial killer. But with every passing hour, that seemed less likely. And if Nancy's death had been a one-off, it was time for the FBI to turn things back over to the local police—and for Bill and Riley to head back to Quantico.

Of course, if Calvin Rabbe's alibi didn't hold up, she and Bill would have some reason to stay on the case. Riley hoped that that would get sorted out soon, one way or the other.

Riley felt tired and apprehensive when she walked into the computer lab with its daunting array of screens and equipment. At the center of the vast array of computers sat the head of the digital tech department, a young woman who simply called herself Igraine. She was definitely an odd character—hardly the sort of technician Riley was used to back at Quantico. Special Agent in Charge Elgin Morley had told Riley that Igraine was a self-described technopagan.

Igraine had rainbow-dyed crew-cut hair, and her face and ears were pierced with a wildly colored array of plastic-head diaper pins. Her clothes, by contrast, were gothic black. Her workstation was decked and littered with amulets and little circles of colorful stones and crystals.

"What have you got for me, Igraine?" Riley asked, sitting next to her.

"I've got nothing," Igraine said. "Oh, lots of murders of prostitutes, naturally. We had a series of strangulations back in the nineties. But none of those MOs really fit."

Riley didn't know how she felt about this news. The fact was, the seemingly endless number of unsolved murders and disappearances of prostitutes nagged at her.

Riley asked, "Have you checked water-related deaths for the past few years?"

"Sure, for two whole decades. One dead prostitute was found in a creek, but her killer was caught and convicted. A serial killer murdered one of his victims in a bathtub, but none of his victims were prostitutes, and he's on death row now. Other bodies are found in lakes around Phoenix from time to time. Accidental drownings, boating and swimming accidents, that kind of thing, and the victims are mostly guys at that. As for using the lakes for corpse disposal, I've turned up zilch."

"Is there anything else you can do?" Riley asked

Igraine leaned back in her chair and let out a groan of impatience.

"You mean, to magically turn a single murder into a serial? Not without calling upon the forces of darkness. Frankly, I don't think the FBI ought to be dabbling in that stuff. Leave the black arts to the CIA. Believe me, I've tried every cyber-spell I can think of. Anything more, and I'll make the Uber-Spirit very angry."

Riley knew that, in her own special language, Igraine was telling the truth.

"That's OK, Igraine. You can call it a night."

Riley left the lab just in time to meet Bill in the hallway.

"What have you got?" Bill asked her.

"Not a thing. And you?"

"Well, we've checked out Rabbe's alibi. He was definitely at his house, at his mother's charity event. He's clean."

Riley sighed. Although she'd more or less expected this, it gave her no satisfaction. As far as she was concerned, Rabbe needed to be put away for good.

"Well, that's all we can do tonight," Bill said. "Let's get out of here."

*

About an hour and a half later, Riley and Bill were sitting together in a booth in their hotel's bar. She had just ordered her second bourbon on the rocks. It had been a long time since she'd had a single drink, but she figured tonight would be okay. Even so, she knew she'd better take it easy. This would be her last drink for the night.

Anyway, Riley could see that Bill needed someone to drink and talk with. At the moment, he was putting his whiskey away at a markedly faster rate than Riley. For a few minutes now, he'd been rambling on about the breakup of his marriage.

"It's hard to let it go," he continued wearily. "I mean, twelve years of marriage, two kids and all. It's just like a huge piece of my life is getting cut away. And it's leaving a big empty space."

He paused for a moment and took another sip.

Then he said, "I mean, yeah, I can see her point of view. Being married to an FBI agent is tough. But I thought she knew what she was getting into. I was already an agent when we got married. But little by little, all kinds of resentment started to kick in. And after the boys were born, she wanted me to get out of the agency altogether. But what else was I going to do?"

Riley simply nodded. She understood all too well. After all, she'd recently done her own share of trying to turn her back on this kind of work. But whether she liked it or not, she seemed to be in it for the long haul. Teaching hadn't been enough for her, and sitting around in an office trying to ignore all the evils in the world was simply out of the question.

Still, she said nothing, just let Bill keep on talking.

"You know, I think maybe at the start, she thought being married to an agent would be romantic and exciting. But when I got wounded five years ago, she really freaked out. Things never got back to normal."

Riley found herself trying to see things from Maggie's point of view.

"Well, at least she worried about you," she said. "Ryan barely seemed to notice that I had a job at all. He just couldn't get used to the fact that I wasn't the perfect little social hostess." Then she thought for a moment and added, "Maybe Maggie's ending it because she loves you."

Bill gave her a long, curious look.

"That's the stupidest thing I've ever heard," he said.

Riley started laughing.

"Isn't it, though?" she said.

Suddenly they were both laughing together. It felt good, talking and laughing with Bill like this. For years, he'd been her best friend in the world. But the last couple of cases had taken a toll on their friendship. She'd almost forgotten how close and comfortable she could feel around him.

Of course, she also knew that the bourbon was helping her relax.

Steady, she told herself. *Don't get* too *comfortable.*

Again she remembered that awful drunken night when she'd called Bill and said they should have an affair. The wounds from that incident were just starting to heal. She didn't want to open them again.

"But enough of my self-pity," Bill said. "What's going on with that girl you rescued?"

"You mean Jilly? Well, maybe 'rescued' is too strong a word. She's got a long way to go and needs a lot of help. I've called Child Protective Services a few times to check in on her. She's OK, and they're hoping to be able to take her away from her father. He really is an abusive man."

"What'll happen to her then?" Bill said.

"She'll wind up with a foster family, I guess. Unless …"

Riley fell silent. A far-fetched possibility started to occur to her. Bill was able to read her expression right away.

"Oh my God," he said. "You're not thinking about adopting her, are you?"

Riley didn't reply. He'd nailed it perfectly, of course. But she was pretty sure that the drinks were starting to kick in. She was definitely feeling a little tipsy now—and more than a little wistful about Jilly.

Bill was smiling at her sympathetically.

"Riley, this can't be a good idea," he said. "God only knows what kind of traumas that poor girl has gone through. She doesn't even know what it's like to be nurtured and cared for. She's going to need years of professional help. You don't have the resources."

"I know," she said, feeling a catch in her throat.

Bill really was right, after all. So why did this urge come over her? Maybe it had something to do with how she'd been thinking about her sister lately. She remembered how Wendy had sent her a letter some years ago, just to reach out and connect. But Riley hadn't replied. Looking back, she didn't know why. But she regretted it. And now she had no idea where Wendy was or what had become of her.

Riley couldn't shake the feeling that she had abandoned Wendy. Now she didn't want to abandon anybody else.

But now was no time to talk about all that. She just sat there, enjoying Bill's quiet warmth and sympathy. Then a strange fantasy started to shape in her mind.

Bill and I would be the perfect parents for a girl like that, she thought.

For just a moment, it seemed so real—she and Bill living as a couple, doing their best to give Jilly a better life.

"What are you thinking?" Bill said.

Riley laughed awkwardly. She wondered if she should tell him. Then her phone buzzed. It was a text message from April.

Having a great time! Capitol building today. White House tomorrow! How are U?

Riley smiled. It was a perfectly timed reminder. She already had a daughter, and a brave and bright one at that. Now was no time for Riley to tear up her own life and change everything.

She typed back:

Just fine. U keep on having fun.

April replied, *Will do!*

Bill said, "A message from April, I take it?"

Riley chuckled a little. "How did you guess?"

"Oh, maybe it was just that proud and loving mother look."

Bill's kind words sounded somewhat melancholy. His smile looked a little sadder now. Riley guessed that he was thinking about his own boys, and the ongoing custody battle he and Maggie were fighting over them. She suddenly felt lucky not to be going through all that with April.

At the same time, it seemed best to change the subject.

"You know, we've got to file a report with Morley," she said.

"Yeah, I know," Bill said tiredly. "I guess we've been putting it off."

"What are we going to tell him?"

Bill drummed his fingers on the table.

"There's nothing to say, except that we're coming up blank," he said. "We've got no reason at all to think we're after a serial killer. That means we've got no reason to be here at all. Garrett Holbrook's going to be disappointed, though. He was really hoping that we could crack his sister's murder."

"Do you think so?" Riley said.

Bill looked surprised by the question.

"Sure. How else would he feel?"

Riley simply shrugged. The words had been out before she'd thought about what she was saying. She couldn't explain what she meant. It was just that Garrett Holbrook still struck her as a bit of a mystery. She felt sure that there was something he wasn't telling them. But now they'd probably never find out what it was.

Riley said, "Well, I guess we can file our report tomorrow morning. Then we'll be out of here. Do you think the FBI will fly us back the way we came, in a company jet?"

Bill laughed.

"Nothing that ceremonious," he said. "My guess is we'll be flying back coach."

"You're probably right."

She saw that Bill had finished his drink. She was only halfway through hers, but she figured she'd had enough. She was feeling a little giddy now. She pushed the drink away. It felt good to consciously decide to quit for the night.

She and Bill paid the bar bill. Then Bill escorted her back to her hotel room. They paused a bit awkwardly outside her door. They maintained a distance of a couple of feet between them. Riley was sure that Bill was thinking just what she was thinking. If they so much as hugged, things might get out of control. And neither of them really wanted that. At least not tonight.

"You're a good woman, Riley Paige," Bill said.

Riley felt tears well up in her eyes.

"And you're a good man," she said. "And a good friend."

Bill turned and walked away down the hallway. She went on into her room and sat down on the bed. She couldn't help feeling disappointed in their trip. At the very least, she wished they could have gotten Nancy Holbrook's killer.

Besides, her gut had told her that they were dealing with a serial killer. She wasn't used to her gut being wrong.

Or am I really wrong this time? she wondered.

Chapter Nineteen

Rookie cop Robin Mastin scaled down the underwater cliff side, her flashlight barely breaking through the surrounding darkness. She was getting close to the base of the cliff, some fifty feet down, and the visibility was barely three feet ahead.

She and her class had spent two days combing the depths of Nimbo Lake for a woman's body. This was supposed to be their third day of searching, but their diving chief, Quentin Rosner, was sure there was no body to be found. When they had met here very early this morning, he had announced that they were going to give it up.

Robin had begged for the chance to make one more try. She had reminded Rosner that they were doing this search on orders from Special Agent Riley Paige from Quantico. Rosner had finally agreed to one more hour, but she knew that the hour was up now.

Riley Paige! The very name filled Robin with awe and admiration. The woman was a legend, and Robin wanted to be like her. And if Riley Paige thought there was a body down here, Robin felt sure that there really was one. If Robin could find it, she'd make her name even before she got her technologist certification. Then maybe she could get herself stationed somewhere with an active underwater CSI team.

That hope was why she had enrolled in diving school in the first place, even though her friends had laughed at her. They'd kept reminding her that Arizona wasn't the likeliest place to find diving jobs. But Robin had big plans. She'd already become a master diver, and when she had the CSI certification, she'd move anywhere she had to go for an exciting career.

Now she swam down the last few feet, hugging the cliff all the way, examining every square inch of its surface. As she touched the bottom, she felt an unwelcome tug on the yellow rope that reached back to the surface. It was Rosner, telling her it was time to leave.

She felt crushed with disappointment. She was sure that the search somehow had been handled wrong, sure that they had missed something.

At Paige's insistence, Rosner and the class had pored over maps of what the lake had looked like before it became a lake. If there was a body, Rosner was absolutely sure that it lay somewhere on the lake floor.

They'd searched every square foot without uncovering anything, just pieces of junk and a few animal bones. One of her classmates had found a rotting carcass of a dog. Nobody had any idea how it had gotten there. Dogs could swim, after all.

Rosner had laughed at Robin when she'd said that she wanted to search the side of this particular cliff.

Robin remembered what Rosner had said.

"You think she landed on a vertical surface? Gravity doesn't work like that."

She couldn't think of an argument against it. Even so, here she was, trying to prove him wrong. It was going to be humiliating to come to the surface one last time to admit her failure. But even now, she wasn't going to be rushed. She scaled the cliff as carefully as she'd descended, feeling and looking as closely as she could.

About twenty feet from the surface, a peculiar sensation caused her to stop. She became very still. Had she felt something real or was it just her imagination?

But there it was. She had felt a slight current in the water. But where could it be coming from?

She reached up and felt the edge of a ledge. It seemed that the cliff side was broken by jutting rocks. The current was coming from somewhere around those rocks.

She rose further to look above the ledge. The visibility was terrible, no more than a foot. But now she understood the source of the current. She had found a tiny entrance to a cave, which might well stretch back for miles under the rock. It might even drain separately into the river that had been dammed to form this lake.

A theory was rapidly forming in her mind. Possibly—just possibly—a body dropped from straight above might have hit this ledge and gotten sucked back into the cave, at least a short distance.

The entrance was so small that she had to squeeze to get inside. But she was only in to her waist when her fingers found something that wiggled under a layer of silt. She brushed it vigorously and saw that it was black plastic.

Her heart was pounding now. She remembered that the previous body had been found in a black plastic garbage bag. Those bags degraded very slowly, especially in cool temperatures. She struggled to keep her breathing under control. It would be dangerous to be overcome with excitement at this depth, in this tight space.

She fumbled around and found the bag's opening. Just inside, she could see it clearly—a rounded white bone surface where sutures joined together.

It was the top of a skull.

Chapter Twenty

Riley was sleeping later than usual when her phone rang. She hadn't awakened early because she and Bill were supposed to be going home today. She looked at the clock. They still had several hours to get to the airport.

But the call wasn't from Bill. It was from Morley.

"We have a new body," he said.

Riley was wide awake now.

"Another prostitute?" she asked.

"Looks like it."

"In the lake?"

"It's in a different one, Lake Gaffney. But it was dumped there in a black bag. It's a similar MO. I want you and Jeffreys to get out there. I'm getting a helicopter ready for you, but it will take over an hour to reach this one."

"How long has the body been in the water?"

"Just since last night."

Riley told Morley they would be right there. She phoned Bill. He said he was packing, but then she told him the news.

"Sounds like you were right all along," he replied. "This could be a serial case."

Riley didn't reply. Being right about something like this gave her no pleasure at all. But it did mean they had work to do. It did mean that there was a monster out there for them to track down and stop.

"I'll bring you some coffee," Bill said.

"And a bagel," she said. Bill agreed and hung up.

As Riley pulled on her clothes, she was grateful that whoever had found this body had made the connection.

"Lake Gaffney," she said aloud. She remembered seeing that one on the map. It was another artificial lake in the hills near Phoenix. She wondered whether the divers back at Lake Nimbo were having any luck with their search there.

*

Riley knelt down beside the dead woman in the unzipped body bag. The victim was naked and her wrists were bound with ordinary clothesline rope. She only wore a thin silver necklace set with a single diamond.

97

"Another real stone?" Bill asked.

"I'm sure it is," Riley replied.

"It must be the same guy."

She looked up at Garrett Holbrook, the agent who had called in help from Quantico when his half-sister had been found murdered. Today he had joined Bill and Riley for the helicopter flight to Lake Gaffney, where the new body had been found.

"I'm glad you insisted on getting the BAU involved in this case," she told the Phoenix agent.

Riley was still having trouble deciding what to make of him. As usual, he had said very little during the flight out here. And so far, his participation in the case had been pretty peripheral.

Holbrook just nodded grimly. "Glad you agreed to come," he said. Then he turned back to the newly found body.

"This one's in a body bag," he said. "Nancy's body was in a plastic garbage bag."

Riley always noted some vague emotion in his voice whenever he said his half-sister's name—Nancy. Riley still couldn't put her finger on exactly what that emotion was. She believed that something beyond his half-sister's death was troubling this man.

"The body bag shows both planning and premeditation," Riley said. "Could be that your sister's killing was spontaneous, maybe almost accidental. But this time he really intended to do it."

She looked over at District Ranger Nick Fessler, who was crouched on the other side of the body.

"How did you find her?" Riley asked.

A vigorous-looking yet taciturn man, Fessler looked dismayed by the question.

"I must have told the police a hundred times already," he said.

"Tell me again," Riley said. She'd already heard about it from the cops, but she wanted to hear it from Fessler's own mouth.

"I was out on the lake last night doing some night fishing. I heard a splash from right over there, near the little cliff. I figured it was some asshole dumping garbage or something. I steered on over there, figuring I could clean up a bit. But there wasn't anything floating. That seemed odd. So this morning I put on my diving gear and went down for a look."

He fell silent. Riley didn't need to hear the rest. Fessler had found the body bag and had gotten his staff to help him bring it up. Then he'd called the police.

Unfortunately, someone on his staff had indiscreetly emailed a friend about the discovery, and word of it went viral almost immediately. The media quickly descended upon Lake Gaffney. Right now the cops had taped off the area and were doing everything they could to keep reporters and television crews as far away as possible.

"She's given birth," Garrett Holbrook said to Bill and Riley, pointing to stretch marks on the victim's belly. "And she looks older than Nancy."

Riley could see that he was right. She added, "Both had been bound at the wrists. This time he didn't bother remove the rope."

Bill carefully took the necklace from the woman's neck and put it into an evidence bag.

"The earlier body wore a ring with a diamond," he said. "This woman's wearing a necklace—a pretty expensive one, also with a diamond. All of this sure looks like a recurring pattern."

Riley agreed. Right now a photo of the necklace was all over the Internet. Fortunately, no pictures showing the whole body had been posted.

She called out to the county medical examiner, who was standing nearby with his team.

"You can take her away now."

The examiner and his team obediently zipped up the bag and started to take it to their vehicle.

Riley stepped away from her colleagues and looked around where they stood. Beyond the hills and patches of dull green surrounding the lake, everything was just dry land and scrubby grass and brush. Saguaro cactus stood here and there like sentinels. Things looked much more alive out on the lake. It was a beautiful sunny day, and the water seemed crystal clear and blue. She could see that the marina across the lake was quite busy. Doubtless people in the village over there were going about their ordinary recreations.

Some boaters out on the water kept trying to veer close to get a look at what was going on here. Lake security busily waved them away.

It was a handsome lake, but from what the diving team leader had told her the other day, she knew that this appearance was deceptive. The depths of lakes like these were dark with sod and soot.

Just like this case, Riley thought.

Fessler had brought the body ashore where they stood now. It had apparently been dropped into the water from a nearby low cliff. But around most of this lake, the hills tapered gradually to the water's edge. The killer must have known the area well to find one of the few places where he could drop a body directly down and expect it to sink into the water. The killer had clearly been to both lakes before. He was familiar with the territory. He was likely to be a recreational boater, much like those out there now.

Riley's cell phone buzzed. She saw that the call was from Quentin Rosner, the head of the diving team. She'd been putting a lot of pressure on him to keep on searching, despite his insistence that there was no second body in Nimbo Lake. Now she didn't know what kind of news to hope for from him.

"What have you got for me, Mr. Rosner?" she said.

"Agent Paige," he began.

Then he hesitated.

"We've found a body," he said.

Riley's heart quickened.

"Tell me about it," she said.

"One of my divers found a skull in an underwater grotto. There's a whole skeleton there, inside a black plastic bag. It looks like a woman. She must have been killed some years ago, long enough for the flesh to completely decompose. But the skeleton is pretty solid. We might be able to identify her from dental records."

Riley asked, "Was there any jewelry on the body?"

"I don't know, but I'll check," Rosner replied.

Just then Riley heard Agent Holbrook call out for her and Bill.

"Good work, Rosner," she said. "I've got to go."

Agent Holbrook was looking at his smart phone as Riley and Bill walked toward him.

"I just got some news from the division," Holbrook said. "They forwarded this to me."

Holbrook showed Bill and Riley an image on his smartphone. It was a selfie of a smiling woman holding a necklace. It looked like she was standing in a bathroom. Riley immediately recognized the woman as the victim whose body had just been found. And the necklace looked exactly like the one Bill had just removed from her naked corpse.

"Where did this come from?" Riley asked Holbrook.

"A woman who calls herself Snowflake called the police tip hotline," Holbrook said. "She said that her friend Chiffon sent her this picture with a text message yesterday afternoon. Chiffon's text said that a 'gentleman' had just given it to her, and that they'd had a 'moment,' and that she'd call Snowflake with more details soon."

"Let me guess," Riley said. "Chiffon never got back in touch with Snowflake."

Holbrook nodded. "That's right. And Snowflake got worried. And this morning, Snowflake saw the necklace all over the Internet. She felt sure that Chiffon must be the victim."

Riley was processing this information.

Snowflake and Chiffon, she thought. *They sound like prostitute names. And Nancy Holbrook was an escort who called herself Nanette.*

"Did Snowflake say anything else?" Bill put in.

"Yeah, she said that she and Chiffon both worked at a place in Phoenix called the Kinetic Custom Gym. She said we should talk to a guy there called Jaybird."

Riley started walking toward the FBI helicopter.

"Let's go."

Chapter Twenty One

Riley thought that the Kinetic Custom Gym definitely looked like a front for a brothel. The place was seedy and rundown, even more so than the rest of this rough-looking neighborhood. A "CLOSED" sign hung in the door, but she was sure the place was actually open for a different kind of business.

The car she and Bill arrived in was the only vehicle in the parking lot. When they got out and walked toward the building, they could see some exercise machines through the front windows. The only person is sight was a man seated inside at the front desk. He was poring over a copy of *Scientific American.* Riley guessed that this was Jaybird—the man the tipster named Snowflake had said they should talk to. And Riley was sure that he was a pimp.

Whether he was the killer they sought was another question.

Bill was about to pull out his badge to display it through the window.

"Not yet," Riley said.

She wanted to get just a little sense of the man before he found out who they were. She smiled pleasantly and rapped on the window. The man looked up from his magazine. She waved as though she and Bill were just a pair of customers wanting to check the place out.

The man pointed at the CLOSED sign and started reading again. Riley rapped on the window again, still smiling. The man looked back up at her, realizing that she and Bill weren't going away.

He got up and walked toward the door. He was blond and about thirty—a short, muscular man who swaggered as he walked, with his fists clenched at his side. Riley could read a lot in his stride. She sensed that he'd experienced a lot of violence in his life, and that he could dish it out when he needed to—or wanted to.

Could this be our guy? she wondered. It started to seem more likely.

The man unlocked the door and poked his head outside.

"Closed," he said. "Can't you read the sign?"

Smiling as charmingly as ever, Riley pointed to the hours listed on the glass door.

She said, "Yeah, but according to this, you should be open. We just want to look around."

"I don't think so," the man said.

It was time to drop the pretense. Riley flashed her badge.

"I'm Agent Paige, and this is my partner, Agent Jeffreys."

The man's face broke into an impish smile. If he was the least bit fazed, he didn't show it.

"FBI, huh?" he said. "Why didn't you say so in the first place? Come on in."

Bill and Riley stepped inside.

Riley glanced around, taking note of the decrepit machinery—treadmills, a rowing machine, two weight machines. The smell was stale and stagnant. She also noted the overall space of this front area and realized there must be plenty of room in back to conduct illicit services.

"Are you the man people call Jaybird?" Bill asked.

"That's me," the man said. "But I guess you need my real name for, like, official purposes. I'm Jerome Kehoe."

He was pointedly not offering Bill and Riley a seat, not making any effort to make them comfortable. Even so, he maintained an outward show of hospitality.

"You know, you're just the people I want to talk to right now. I mean, you're in law enforcement. That means you're interested in questions of free will, right? Because I sure as hell am."

Jaybird picked up the magazine and waved it at them.

"This article says that scientists have all but *proved* that our whole reality is just a computer simulation," he said, his words pouring out very rapidly. "I mean look around you, look at everything you see, smell, taste, touch. It's all just VR in some big-assed giant mainframe."

Riley could see that he was giving them quite a tap dance with this nonsensical fast talk. But she detected that his interest was more than half genuine. He was intelligent, even philosophical.

She was also sure that he was emotionally volatile—extremely so. She guessed that his hyperactivity was periodically interrupted by emotional crashes, marked by terrible rages. Even murderous rages, she felt sure.

Above all else, he was good at conning people, keeping them off balance, manipulating them. If she and Bill didn't stay on their toes, they might well leave this place with nothing but a year-long membership to a nonexistent gym.

He continued, "I mean, *think* about the ontological implications of that shit, for the kind of work *you* guys do. Because, like, if I commit a crime, but it's preprogrammed in some kind of omnipotent God machine, am I really guilty? Am I responsible for my own goddamn behavior? Are you? Is anybody? Because that's an interesting question, huh?"

Riley knew better than to get drawn into any discussion. It was time to get to the point.

"We'd like to know where you were and what you were doing last night," she said.

"Like, what time?" Jaybird said.

"Between sunset and dawn," Bill put in.

Jaybird grunted a little impatiently. "That covers a lot of hours. And my nights can get kind of busy, if you know what I mean. And I don't sleep. I never sleep. I'm always out and around. So it's a tough question. Now I'm not a constitutional scholar, but I'm pretty sure you're not here to arrest me, but even so, I'm pretty sure I don't *have* to answer any questions. Correct me if I'm wrong. Am I wrong?"

Riley abruptly held up her cell phone to show him the selfie of Chiffon.

"This is one of your girls, isn't it?" Riley asked.

Riley could tell by his expression that she'd finally succeeded in catching him off balance. He knew better than to try to lie.

"Yeah," he said. "Chiffon's her name. She works here."

"In what capacity?" Bill asked.

Jaybird shrugged.

"She gives massages," he said. "I've got girls here who do that. There's nothing wrong with it."

"Nobody said there was," Bill said with an ironic edge. "Did my partner say there was something wrong with it? Did I say there was something wrong with it? Who said there was anything wrong with it?"

Riley enjoyed watching Bill take a go at the guy, playing him at his own game. She sensed that Jaybird was starting to get a little intimidated. Jaybird might be tough, but Bill was larger and equally imposing.

I'll just let Bill run with this for a while, she thought.

"Naw, nobody said that," Jaybird said. "Chiffon's not here, though."

"We know that," Bill said. "She's dead."

Jaybird said nothing. Riley didn't know what to make of his reaction—or lack of it. Maybe Bill could read him better.

At that moment, her cell phone buzzed. She stepped away from Bill and Jaybird to take the call. It was Elgin Morley calling from headquarters. Riley could hear Bill and Jaybird talking during the phone call.

"Agent Paige, we've had a bit of luck," Morley said. "We ran a search on dental records for the skull that was found this morning, and we got a match right away. The victim's name was Marsha Kramer. Her family reported her missing three years ago. She was in college when she disappeared."

"Could you text me a photo of her?" Riley asked.

"I'll do that right away," Morley said.

As Riley waited, she heard Bill and Jaybird continuing their little verbal tug-of-war. Bill was trying to get him to say more about Chiffon, without much success. Riley needed to get back into the conversation.

The photo of Marsha Kramer came through.

Riley thanked Morley and ended the call. She walked over to Bill and Jaybird, displaying the photo.

"How about this girl?" Riley asked. "Do you know her?"

Jaybird didn't say anything, but she could see a flash of recognition in his eyes.

Bill said, "Jaybird—Mr. Kehoe—let's stop playing games here. We don't have a warrant, but we won't have trouble getting one. Things will go better for you if you just cooperate."

"Yeah, I remember her," Jaybird said. "It's been a long time, though. Years, maybe. I don't remember her real good. Honest, I don't. Maybe my wife could help."

Jaybird turned and walked toward a door leading into the back part of the building. Riley trotted right after him, determined not to let him out of her sight. Jaybird made no effort to stop her. She heard Bill's footsteps right behind her.

On their way into the back of the building, they passed an open door. Riley stopped and looked inside. The room was a sauna, with cedar paneling and wooden risers. But it wasn't in use now, and it probably hadn't been for years.

Instead, the room now seemed to be a rest area for the women who worked here. Six of them were in there now, scantily clothed, of a mix of races. None of them was attractive, and all of them looked tired, ill, and listless.

Riley shuddered deeply. An image flashed in her mind, Peterson's dark cage, and his propane flame. She wasn't sure why it came to mind just now. She shook off the memory. There was work to do.

"These are my massage girls," Jaybird said. "And if you've got time, you can get a free massage." Pointedly to Riley, he added, "You too. But I guess you're on duty. Well, maybe some other time."

Riley knew that this wasn't a bluff—at least not exactly. If she or Bill asked, any of these women was prepared give them at least a crude rudiment of a massage. Still, she was pretty sure that none of the women was certified or even trained.

Jaybird led them back into a corridor of curtained cubicles, where clients surely got their services. Privacy was obviously not a priority in a low-rent operation like this.

The corridor ended at the back entrance. A woman in her twenties was sitting at a desk watching a small television and chewing gum. She was dressed just like the other women, and her expression was similarly vacant. Riley felt pretty sure that clients used this back entrance instead of the front, and that this woman was a receptionist of sorts.

"This is my wife, Chrissy," Jaybird told Riley and Bill. "Chrissy, I've got a couple of FBI agents here."

Chrissy looked worried.

"Don't worry, they come in peace," Jaybird said with a chuckle. "They've just got some questions."

Riley wondered whether Jaybird and Chrissy were really married. Neither wore a wedding ring. Whatever their actual relationship was, Riley was pretty sure it wasn't the least bit exclusive.

"They've got bad news about Chiffon, though," Jaybird told her. "They say she's dead."

Chrissy gasped. Riley sensed that she must have known the victim well.

"Who killed her?" Chrissy asked.

The words struck Riley as revealing—not "How did she die?" but "Who killed her?"

Before Riley could reply, Jaybird chortled and said, "Well, if you listen to these two, you might think it was me. They say it was last night. But you know it wasn't me, don't you, Chrissy?'

Chrissy smiled weakly.

"It sure wasn't Jaybird," she said. "I know what he was doing last night."

"Yeah, Chrissy knows," Jaybird said with a coarse laugh. "She can tell you some details, let me tell you. Not all of it would be appropriate for the lady, though," he added, indicating Riley again.

"I had a bad feeling about her," Chrissy said. "She'd sometimes go a long time without coming in to work, but this time felt different somehow. Does her husband know?"

The question took Riley slightly aback. She could see that Bill had the same reaction.

"She was married?" Bill asked.

"Yeah, her husband does something that's got to do with computers," Chrissy said. "She has—had—three children."

Chrissy shrugged and added, "She didn't have to work here. I mean, she didn't need the money. She was just bored."

Riley took note of the glances Chrissy kept exchanging with Jaybird. She was taking care not to say anything he didn't want her to say. He was giving her all kinds of scowls, nods, and squints as nonverbal cues. Still, at this point, Jaybird didn't seem worried about what Riley and Bill knew about the business. It certainly wasn't much of a secret. And after all, they weren't here to bust him.

He might have other worries, though, Riley thought.

She couldn't yet decide whether he was the killer.

Riley said, "Chiffon wasn't her real name, though, was it, Chrissy?"

Chrissy shook her head. "It was Gretchen something. Oh, yeah. Gretchen Lovick."

Riley showed her the picture of the woman who had just been identified, Marsha Kramer.

"Did you know this girl?" she asked Chrissy.

Chrissy knitted her eyebrows as she tried to remember.

"Oh, yeah," she said. "It was a long time ago. She called herself Ginger. I never knew her real name. I figured she'd died. I mean, maybe she didn't have long to live. She—"

Jaybird cut her off with a grunt. But Riley bent close to her and said gently, "She was what, Chrissy?"

"She was awful sick," Chrissy said.

Riley could see that Chrissy was frightened of Jaybird now. She'd better not push the issue. Besides, Chrissy's meaning was obvious. Marsha "Ginger" Kramer had been HIV positive, possibly with fully developed AIDS.

Then Bill asked Chrissy, "Do you know a girl named Snowflake?"

"Yeah, she used to work here, she—"

But Jaybird cleared his throat and she stopped in mid-sentence.

"Snowflake doesn't work here anymore," Jaybird said.

Again, Riley saw no need to push the issue. It was all pretty clear to her. Snowflake had fled this horrible place because of Jaybird's brutality. It was only because she was free of Jaybird that she'd dared to call in her tip.

"Hey, wait a minute," Jaybird said. "Wait just a minute. I know who you should check out."

"Who is it?" Riley asked.

"Now hold on, not so fast," Jaybird said. "I'll tell you only if you agree to not hassle me. I'm just doing an honest business."

Riley's stomach turned at making any kind of deal with this man.

"OK," she said, "but only if your tip is good."

"It's a guy named Clay Hovis. Yeah, I remember how Ginger was scared of him. All our girls were scared of him. Chiffon especially. In fact, I finally barred him from the place because he'd been too rough on Chiffon. Isn't that right, Chrissy?"

Chrissy nodded mutely.

Jaybird said, "Yeah, it's definitely Clay. He's really bad news. Give me something so I can write down his name and address."

Chrissy handed Jaybird a pad and pencil, and Jaybird jotted something down. While Bill asked him for a few details about Hovis, Riley turned to look at Chrissy.

Riley's heart sank. Still silent, Chrissy was staring at her with an imploring expression. After all the unspoken signals Chrissy and Jaybird had passed back and forth, it struck Riley likely that Jaybird would beat her badly as soon as she and Bill left. The poor woman desperately wanted someone to rescue her from this horrible life. But Riley knew that any rescue would be temporary. This woman would have to get to a point where she was willing to rescue herself. And all the others too.

As the men talked, Riley leaned over and whispered to Chrissy, "You can leave with me right now if you want to."

Chrissy just looked at her blankly.

"I can get you someplace to stay. There are people who can help you."

Chrissy shook her head no. Riley felt a little sick now.

She's too scared to even think about leaving, Riley realized.

She handed Chrissy her card and whispered, "Call me if you change your mind."

Chrissy took the card, but she looked away.

Now Riley knew why the sick, tired, despairing women in the sauna reminded her of Peterson's cage. Her own torment had lasted only a few days. Chrissy and the rest of women here were living under a life sentence.

In a way, it didn't much matter whether Jaybird was the killer they sought, or Hovis, or some other man.

They're all monsters, Riley thought.

And there was no way to stop them all.

Riley turned away from Chrissy and stepped menacingly toward Jaybird.

"Your tip had better be good," Riley said. "Just give me an excuse. Give me any reason at all. I'll put you down like a dog."

Jaybird stared at her with dark angry eyes.

"Come on," Bill said to Riley. "Let's go check out Clay Hovis."

Chapter Twenty Two

It wasn't a long drive to Clay Hovis's apartment. It was in the same rough neighborhood as the Kinetic Custom Gym. Riley wasn't looking forward to interviewing the man. After a career of dealing with horror, she'd had no idea that she could still be so horrified. Right now this case seemed to be getting uglier by the hour.

"Are you OK?" Bill asked Riley as she drove.

Riley didn't answer. She simply didn't know what to say.

Then Bill asked her, "What do you think of Jaybird? Do you think he's our guy?"

Riley thought for a moment.

"No," she said. "He's just a businessman. Oh, he's a businessman who hates women. And he's OK with beating up and abusing women. That's all in his line of work. But murder is bad for business. He doesn't like murder."

She thought for another moment, then added, "And he's not impotent."

"And our killer is?" Bill said.

"Intermittently, at least," Riley said. "Although I'm sure he doesn't like to admit it, even to himself. And maybe not when he first started killing. But now performance is an issue for him. He gets his enjoyment out of the murders themselves, not sex or sexual violence."

She thought about it for another moment. "And Jaybird's not like that," she said. "His bluster and bravado is genuine, not a way of compensating for a lack of virility."

"So his tip about this Clay Hovis guy might be legit?" Bill said.

"Could be," Riley said.

It made more and more sense to her. Jaybird had sounded truly angry with Hovis. The man must have caused some real trouble for Jaybird to have banned him from the place. And Jaybird was undoubtedly worried what would happen if or when word of these murders got out. That would really hurt his business. If Hovis was the killer, Jaybird had plenty of reason to want to put him away.

"You'd better call headquarters," Riley told Bill as she turned a corner into an especially seedy part of the neighborhood. "We need info about Gretchen Lovick. We'll need to find out about her next of kin. Chrissy said her husband does some kind of work having to do with computers. It shouldn't be hard to track him down."

Bill got on the phone. As he talked with Morley, Riley realized that she and Bill just might have to inform Lovick that his wife was dead. That thought only made the sick feeling in her stomach worse. Since the body had not been identified until now, the woman's husband probably wouldn't know that she'd been murdered. Unless, of course, he had killed her himself, but that wasn't at all likely in a case that included three dead prostitutes over a span of years. The man they were going to see now was a much more likely suspect.

Riley pulled the car up in front of a big, ratty-looking apartment building where Clay Hovis lived. They got out of the car and walked up three flights of stairs. As they continued down the hall toward Hovis's apartment, a cacophony of blaring music and loud voices surrounded them. It was hard for Riley to imagine living here. How could anybody ever sleep or even think?

As they approached the door to Hovis's apartment, they heard a dog barking inside. Before they could even knock on the door, they heard more hostile snarling and the scratching of claws against the door. The animal sounded big and extremely dangerous.

After a moment of animal fury, they heard a man's voice call out from inside.

"Who is it?"

Riley realized that the apartment's occupant was looking out through a peephole. Riley stepped back so that she'd be fully in view. She took out her badge.

"Agents Paige and Jeffreys, FBI," she called out. "We'd like to ask you a few questions."

The dog started barking again.

"Do you have a warrant?" the man yelled through the door.

"No," Bill said loudly. "We just want to talk."

The animal noise continued.

"No," the man's voice said.

Riley called out, "Mr. Hovis—I believe we're talking to Mr. Hovis—things will go better for all of us if you cooperate."

Once again, the man answered, "No."

Riley looked at Bill, uncertain of what to do. Things would be different if they had a warrant for his arrest, or to search his premises. But as things stood, Clay Hovis was well within his rights not to answer the door, even to law enforcement. And he apparently knew it.

Bill yelled over the barking, "That's OK, Mr. Hovis. We understand. You don't have to talk to us if you don't want to."

Riley looked at Bill with surprise. Bill gave her a half-smile that assured her that he knew exactly what he was doing.

As the dog's fury grew, Riley quickly understood Bill's tactic. Although Hovis had the right not to talk to them, she and Bill had every right to stay right where they were. And as long as they stood in front of the door, the dog's uproar would get worse. Hovis couldn't calm the creature down, and the situation inside the apartment must be becoming intolerable.

Soon the door opened a little, stopped by a chain. Riley could now see the black face of a Doberman pinscher. Its nose pushed through the opening as far as it would go. It flashed enormous teeth at the strangers, and its eyes were angry. The creature barked furiously.

An African-American man also peered through the opening.

"What do you want?" he said over the sound of barking.

"Like I said, we just want to talk," Bill said.

The man cursed and unlocked the chain. He opened the door, holding the dog tightly by its collar.

"It's OK, Genghis," the man said to the dog. Then he said to Riley and Bill, "Come on in."

Riley and Bill cautiously stepped into the apartment. The dog was growling, but he was calmer now that his master had invited them in. The man attached a leash to the dog's collar, walked the surly creature over to an armchair, and sat down.

"Genghis, down," he said.

The dog obeyed, lying down beside the chair with a whimper. It stopped growling but watched them alertly. Then Hovis glared at Riley and Bill.

Bill began, "We understand that you're familiar with the Kinetic Custom Gym."

"Yeah," the man said.

Riley added, "What do you know about two of its female employees—Chiffon and Ginger? Ginger worked there a long time ago. But Chiffon's very recent."

"I've never heard of them," Hovis said.

The man's face and voice were so lacking in expression that Riley couldn't tell if he was lying or not.

"Both women are dead," Bill said. "Chiffon died last night. Ginger died about three years ago."

Hovis said nothing.

Riley said, "Can you tell us where you were and what you were doing last night, between dusk and dawn?"

"I was right here," Hovis said.

"Do you have any witnesses to back you up?" Bill asked.

"No."

Then he fell silent again. The air was still full of ambient noise from the nearby apartments, and the dog kept whining a little. Hovis was obviously not going to be forthcoming. Riley couldn't yet tell whether he was concealing something or was reticent by nature.

But as a team, both she and Bill knew from experience better than to try to rush a situation like this. It was best to let Hovis think that they were in no hurry.

Riley looked the man over carefully. He was black, tall, and rather gangly. His gaze was direct and very intense. She noticed that he was wearing a long-sleeved T-shirt and full-length jeans, despite the fact that the room's air conditioning was audibly sputtering and the room was uncomfortably warm.

After a moment, Riley said, "We talked to Jaybird. It sounds as if you and he had a bit of a falling out."

Hovis's registered an ever-so-slight smirk.

"You could say that."

Bill said, "Care to tell us what it was all about?"

"Business," Hovis said.

Riley said, "Jaybird told us you were getting too rough on his girls. He said that both Ginger and Chiffon were scared of you."

Riley thought the man looked vaguely offended.

"I never touched his girls," he snapped.

Riley looked around the apartment. It was shabby and cheap, and all the furniture looked old and used. Still, the place was remarkably neat. Clay Hovis was anything but a slob.

Nearby was a chess set on a '50s-style kitchen table. It looked like a game was in progress. Was a partner coming in to play chess with Hovis from time to time, or was he playing the game alone? Either way, Riley had a hunch that Hovis was an excellent player.

And judging from the books on a nearby bookshelf, Riley gleaned that Hovis was intelligent and self-educated. All this was consistent with the profile of their killer. But she wasn't ready to jump to any conclusions.

Riley returned the suspect's gaze. He kept unflinching eye contact with her. She was starting to read something in that face. She wasn't sure just what. She reminded herself again not to hurry, not to push. This man demanded patience.

Then Hovis asked, "How did the girls die?"

Riley saw something in his expression. Was it a flash of concern? No, Riley sensed that it went deeper than that.

Guilt, maybe, Riley thought.

"They were murdered," Bill said.

Riley kept studying his face, trying to gauge his reaction.

"You don't think Jaybird killed them?" Hovis said.

"We haven't ruled out anybody," Riley said. She wondered if he knew that she was lying about Jaybird.

Hovis didn't try to evade Riley's gaze. To the contrary, he kept his eyes locked directly on hers.

"What do you do for a living, Mr. Hovis?" she said.

"Freelance construction work," he said.

Riley detected in both his voice and his look that this was a lie. She also sensed that he didn't much care if she knew it. He might very well want her to know it. He actually seemed to want to tell her something. But it was something that he couldn't tell her openly.

He wants me to parse it out somehow, she thought.

"Mr. Hovis," she said quietly, "I'm going to say a few things. Statements, not questions. You don't have to say anything in response to them. You don't have to do anything at all. Just listen."

Just a hint of a smile formed on his lips. Yes, this was what he wanted.

She looked around the sparsely furnished apartment. She didn't see a single object of real value. So why did Hovis keep such a big, fierce guard dog? What was he guarding?

Riley looked Hovis over again. She noticed that his face and hands were oddly pasty for a black person. And again she observed those long sleeves and full-length pants. He was in his stocking feet. He wasn't wearing a belt, and his fly was unfastened. He'd put these clothes on in a hurry when she and Bill had gotten here. He wanted to cover up something.

In a flash, Riley realized …

Needle marks. All over his body.

"You're a drug user," she said.

He stared back at her. Nothing in his gaze contradicted her.

Then she said, "You're an addict—but you're an extremely high-functioning addict."

That hint of a smile showed through again.

"You don't work in construction," Riley said.

His head tilted forward slightly, almost a nod.

Things were starting to come together in Riley's mind, without Hovis saying a word. He was a drug dealer—but not a sociopathic drug dealer. He was compelled to sell drugs to maintain his habit.

Then she remembered the question he'd asked earlier

"How did the girls die?"

She thought back to the women at the Kinetic Custom Gym— how wan and tired and strung out they looked. Chrissy too. Hovis had been afraid that he'd been responsible for their deaths.

"You didn't kill them," Riley said.

Riley saw something new in Hovis's expression. It almost looked like gratitude. She knew that her own little chess game with Hovis was over. It had ended in a draw, which suited both of their purposes perfectly.

"We'll go now, Mr. Hovis," she said. "Thank you for your time."

Bill seemed only mildly surprised that Riley was cutting the interview short. She knew that he was used to her coming to unspoken conclusions like this.

As she and Bill made their way out of the building, Riley said, "He's not our man. But he'd been dealing heroin to Jaybird. Jaybird likes to keep his women dependent and helpless. Hovis didn't like it. He prefers to do business with users like himself, people who've got some control over their lives. So he cut off Jaybird's supply."

"I get it," Bill said. "So Jaybird was pissed off, and he gave us Hovis's name just to get back at him."

"Yeah—the backstabbing bastard. Hovis just wanted to eliminate himself as a suspect, so we could get on with our work. He was actually trying to help."

She thought for a moment, then added, "Our deal with Jaybird is off. His tip was bogus. As soon as I get a chance, I'm going to make sure he's put out of business."

Bill suggested, "If we just tip the local police they'll clean up the place."

"I know," Riley said. She thought for a moment, then said, "But I also want to give those women some kind of alternative. I want Chrissy to have a chance to get out of the business. She hates it but she's terrified of Jaybird. I'm sure there are shelters in town that work with prostitutes who want out."

"If we can get Jaybird put away, it will be easier for the women. But they're gonna need a lot of help."

Riley knew that most prostitutes had been victims of violence or neglect before they entered the trade. They'd had terrible lives and often didn't regard themselves as worth saving. Some of them had PTSD problems just as devastating as her own.

"I'm sure there are organizations in Phoenix that will help," she replied. "I'm going to get someone on it."

Bill's phone buzzed when they were getting into the car. He checked it and said, "It's a text from Morley. They've got a name and address for Gretchen Lovick's husband. They've called him, and he's at home, and they're getting ready to send agents to break the news to him."

Riley agonized silently for a moment. She knew what had to be done next.

"Text Morley that we'll go over and talk to him. Get his address, then give me directions and I'll drive us there."

As she drove, Riley found herself haunted by the memory of Hovis's silent gaze. She'd encountered a strange and disturbing variety of people lately. Some of them were simply exploiters and abusers, like Ishtar Haynes, Calvin Rabbe, and the man who called himself Jaybird. Others were simply victims, like Justine, Trinda, Jilly, and Chrissy.

But others were harder to pigeonhole. There had been Rex the truck driver—a man who liked his whores but was horrified when they turned out to be children. And now there was Hovis, a man who meant no harm to anyone, but nevertheless destroyed lives with the drugs he sold.

It was weird moral territory, and Riley wasn't comfortable in it.

But now she had to put such thoughts out of her mind. They were going to have to pay a visit to Gretchen Lovick's husband and tell him the terrible news. Since the body hadn't previously been identified, he might not even know that there had been a murder. As far as she was concerned, this sort of thing was the worst part of her job. And this time would be worse than usual.

How were Riley and Bill going to begin explaining the whole sickening thing to the murdered woman's husband?

Chapter Twenty Three

Riley couldn't imagine how she was going to explain Gretchen Lovick's unnatural death to her family. The neighborhood where she had lived was made up of pristine rows of modern ranch houses with small but immaculate lawns and manicured shrubbery. Occasional tall, skinny palm trees stuck up along the street like giant feather dusters.

She said to Bill, "I thought this was a desert. But look at all the grass. And there are palms of all kinds all over Phoenix."

"People are willing to spend for whatever they think is important," Bill replied. "Looks like the folks around here can all afford some extras. I bet there's a pool in back of every one of these places."

Riley pulled up at the address they'd been given. The house and yard were scrupulously neat and well cared for.

Why? Riley wondered.

Why did a woman who lived here choose such a deviant path? How could she even go to a seedy place like the Kinetic Custom Gym? How could she tolerate a pimp like Jaybird?

As they walked up to the front door, she had to wonder if she and Bill were bringing this awful news to the wrong man. But Cyrus Lovick was expecting them and he opened the door as soon as she pressed the bell. He was wearing a polo shirt and casual slacks that could be golfing attire, but he looked somewhat rumpled and anxious.

"Are you from the FBI?" he asked. "They said someone was coming."

Riley and Bill showed their badges and introduced themselves. They stepped into the air-conditioned interior.

"What has happened?" Lovick cried.

"I'm sorry to have to tell you this," Riley said, "but your wife, Gretchen, has been found dead."

"We're sorry for your loss," Bill added.

"Oh, God," Lovick said. He sat down abruptly in an armchair. For a moment he looked around the room, as if expecting to see something that wasn't there. When he spoke again, his voice sounded numb. "I was afraid that something ... she ... yesterday when the kids came home, she wasn't here. Lexie—my oldest—she called me, worried. I came home from work right away. After a while I called the police and reported her missing. Then this afternoon the FBI called. I knew there must be something awful."

He looked back and forth from Riley to Bill, "But how did she …?"

Riley said as gently as she could put it, "I'm afraid she was murdered. Her body was found this morning in Lake Gaffney."

Lovick seemed stunned. After a few moments he asked, "Gretchen drowned?"

Riley glanced at Bill and he took over the explanations. Riley watched Lovick's expressions as he learned that his wife had been suffocated, and that her body had been stuffed into a weighted body bag. She thought that the bereaved husband's reactions looked real, but that he wasn't as shocked as she might have expected him to be.

After a while Lovick asked, "Do you know who did it? Do you know why?"

Bill explained that the FBI was at work on those questions. That's why he and Riley were here. The man's expressions grew more and more despondent.

Riley said, "Mr. Lovick, we have to ask. Can you account for your whereabouts for the rest of last night?"

Lovick didn't look as if he understood why she was asking the question.

"I was here. All night."

Bill asked, "Can anybody confirm your whereabouts?"

"My kids, I guess," Lovick said.

To Riley, it appeared that he didn't grasp that they were trying to eliminate him as a suspect. The truth was, they hadn't done that yet. They'd have to talk to his children. And even then, there might be some question as to whether he'd coached them with his alibi.

At the moment, though, he seemed like nothing other than a grief-stricken husband. And for the time being, Riley knew that she and Bill had to proceed on the assumption that he was exactly that.

Riley tried to think about how to ease him into the rest of what she and Bill needed to tell him.

"Where do you work, Mr. Lovick?" she asked.

"I'm a computer systems analyst. I've got my own business. I stayed home today."

He fell silent again. Then he managed to murmur a question.

"How could this happen?"

Those four words hit Riley like a punch in the gut. Things were about to get extremely difficult.

But before either she or Bill could speak, they heard the chattering of young voices just outside the front door. The door swung open, and in walked three children—a girl in her tweens, maybe twelve years old, and two younger brothers. One looked about ten years old, the other about eight. Judging from the time, Riley knew that they must be just getting home from school.

The kids' chatter stopped as soon as they saw their father sitting with two visitors. A smile vanished from the girl's face.

"Did Mom come back?" she asked.

Lovick couldn't bring himself to reply for a moment.

Finally he said, "Lexie, take your brothers out back. Go play by the pool."

With a deeply worried look, the girl herded her brothers away through the house.

Riley studied Lovick's face. He had the slender, small-jawed face of a guy who might have been a geek and a misfit in as a kid, but had since become thoroughly socialized and successful and doubtless well liked.

Speaking slowly and gently, Riley asked, "Mr. Lovick, were you aware that your wife was living a double life?"

Lovick looked puzzled. "What do you mean?"

Riley glanced at Bill uneasily.

Bill said, "It appears that your wife worked as a prostitute during the day. Out of a brothel called the Kinetic Custom Gym. Were you aware of this at all?"

Riley studied the change in Lovick's expression. She saw less shock in his face than she'd expected. Instead, it looked as if something was starting to make sense to him.

"I knew there was—something," he said. "I didn't know what it was."

As far as Riley was concerned, the whole thing was still completely baffling. But a possibility occurred to her.

She said, "Mr. Lovick, did your wife happen to suffer from some sort of dissociative disorder?

Lovick looked up at her and Riley went on, "I mean something like dissociative identity disorder? Did she ever exhibit multiple personalities?"

"No, not that," Lovick said. But he didn't sound surprised at the question.

Then he said, "She had ... extreme mood swings that scared me sometimes. Like, a couple of years ago, we took the kids to the Grand Canyon. I was driving us along the South Rim, and out of the blue she told me to stop. I did, and she jumped out of the car. She ran straight toward the canyon. I was scared to death, and the kids were too. It looked like she was going to throw herself off the cliff. But she stopped right at the edge, like stopping on a dime. She threw her arms open and looked out over the canyon and laughed."

"She was bipolar, wasn't she?" Riley said.

Lovick nodded. "Meds helped a little—when she was taking them. But she didn't like them. And when she went off them, her behavior got erratic, or worse. When she was depressed, she couldn't get out of bed for days at a time. When she was manic, she took crazy risks, drank too much, drove too fast, that kind of thing. Things had been worse lately. I didn't know how bad it really was. Obviously."

He shook his head.

"I just wanted her to be happy," he said. "I always wanted her to be happy. We met when we were in college, and she had all kinds of talent, could have been a great programmer if she'd wanted to. But she said she didn't want to. She said she wanted to be a stay-at-home mom, at least for now. There'd be time for a brilliant career later on, she said."

He stopped talking, but it wasn't hard for Riley to fill in the rest of his story. They'd started having children when they were both way too young. Gretchen found out that being a housekeeper and a mother wasn't all it was cracked up to be. Her husband had been building a business while she was stuck at home, bored literally out of her mind.

And this was how it had ended. With her murder.

Suddenly, Riley realized that her face was hot, her palms were sweating, and her hands were shaking. She knew what these symptoms meant.

She was angry. She was as angry as hell.

The emotion took her completely by surprise. Earlier that day, she had interviewed a drug dealer, a vile man whose only life's work was to deal in death and despair. Gretchen herself had surely partaken of his terrible merchandise.

But Riley hadn't been mad at Clay Hovis. Instead, she'd almost felt some strange kind of sympathy for him.

But now she was angry. She was angry with this man, Cyrus Lovick. Gretchen's husband.

Why? she wondered. Did she think he was guilty?

The answer to that question tore through her mind like the blade of a knife.

Yes.

But it didn't make sense. She knew that she was being crazy. She knew that she was being irrational. And she had to stick to the task at hand.

"Mr. Lovick," she said, "did you really have no idea what was going on? That your wife was living this other life?"

He looked shocked by her tone. She, too, felt shocked by her tone.

He said, "It's like I told you, I knew there was something."

"But how could you not know?" she said, her voice shaking now. "Didn't you ever just *ask* her?"

He stared at her.

"You have no idea how much I asked," he said.

He looked hurt and angry now. Riley didn't care. Her temper was rising by the moment. But why? She felt herself spinning out of control.

She sputtered at him, "You said you thought she wanted to be a housewife. But there must have come a time when you saw that it wasn't working out for her. Surely you knew she felt empty and lost and bored. Why didn't you do something? Why didn't you help her?"

She felt Bill's strong hand on her shoulder.

Bill said to Lovick, "I'd like to confer with my partner privately for a moment."

Lovick nodded, looking horrified by Riley's ranting. Bill hastily escorted Riley to the kitchen and shut the door behind them.

"What the hell do you think you're doing in there?" Bill snapped. "You're treating him like a suspect."

"He *is* a suspect, for all we know," Riley said.

Bill looked like he could hardly believe his ears.

"Riley, for Chrissake, *think* just a minute. Use your brain. Do you really think this man killed his own wife? And those two other women? One of them three years ago? Were those just warm-ups or decoys or what? This isn't some stupid TV cop show. It doesn't make sense and you know it."

Riley didn't know whether she knew it or not. She did know that she wasn't making sense—or at least she didn't *seem* to be making sense.

"We've got to talk to the kids," she insisted. "Check out his alibi."

"Like hell we will," Bill growled.

"It's procedure."

Bill seemed to be struggling to keep from shouting.

"To hell with procedure. Riley, are you seriously going to break the news to those kids that their mother was murdered, then grill them about what their daddy was doing when she was killed? Their whole world's just been wrecked. Do you want to make it worse? What's going on with you?"

"I'm trying to do my job."

"No. You're not. A couple of days ago you almost beat up a suspect. Are you going to beat up this guy too?"

Riley could hardly believe the insinuation.

"This is different," she said.

"Yeah," Bill said. "It's worse."

The words stopped Riley short. It was starting to dawn on her that Bill was exactly right.

"I'm getting us out of here," Bill said.

Riley followed him back into the living room. Bill managed to address Lovick in a steady, soothing voice.

"Mr. Lovick, we're terribly sorry for your loss. We don't have any more questions."

Lovick looked at him dumbly. Bill handed him a card.

"Here's the number for a victim assistance hotline. I don't think you should wait to call them."

Riley realized that Bill had come here prepared with this information. By contrast, she hadn't been prepared at all.

They left the house and walked to the car. Bill stopped Riley as she headed around to the driver side.

"You're not driving," he said. "Not in your state of mind."

She couldn't disagree, although Bill was awfully agitated himself. She walked around to the passenger side and got in.

"Where are we going next?" she asked.

"Back to HQ, I guess."

Bill started to drive in stony silence.

Riley mentally replayed her words and actions of the last few minutes. What had she been thinking? What had triggered her anger?

She began to understand now. She and her own daughter had been locked in cages, Jaybird's girls passed their days in a prison cell of an extinct sauna, girls like Trinda got tossed from the back of one truck cab to the next, and God only knew what kinds of torments Justine had endured at the hands of countless men.

But Gretchen Lovick had been tormented in her own respectable, upper-middle-class home. She'd lived in a hell that she hated so much that she took refuge in another kind of hell.

It seemed small wonder that the situation had pushed Riley's buttons. But since when did she let this kind of thing get the best of her?

I've got to get myself under control, she thought.

Her phone buzzed. She saw that the call was from Morley.

"What have you got for me, Agent Paige?" the field office chief said when she answered.

Riley didn't reply. She couldn't bring herself to say the word "nothing."

There was a note of barely subdued anger in Morley's voice. "We brought you and Jeffreys all the way from Quantico. We expected results."

Riley's anger started to rise again. She and Bill had just gotten here on Saturday, and they hadn't even known for sure that they were dealing with a serial killer until this morning. What kind of results did Morley expect just yet?

But Riley swallowed her anger.

"We'll get you results," Riley said. "We're on our way to headquarters."

"Damn straight you are," Morley said. "I'm holding a meeting here in twenty minutes. We're going to regroup. We've got to crack this thing before more women wind up dead."

"We'll be there, sir," Riley said.

She ended the call.

"Morley?" Bill said.

"Yeah. He's holding a meeting. We'll get back just in time."

"He's not happy, I take it," Bill said.

"No. He's not."

Bill kept driving, and a chilly silence settled between them. Riley couldn't blame Bill for being upset with her. She felt herself drowning in a sea of self-doubt. She didn't know what to make of this case. And it was starting to look like she didn't know what to make of herself.

Chapter Twenty Four

Riley could feel a sense of urgency in the FBI conference room when she and Bill got there. They sat down at one end of the big table and looked over the group of people shuffling chairs about and finding places to sit. Special Agent in Charge Elgin Morley obviously wanted to make sure not to leave anybody out of the loop.

Chief pathologist Dr. Rachel Fowler was here. So was Igraine, in all her colorful technopagan regalia. Riley even recognized the faces of the two agents who had stopped her from demolishing Calvin Rabbe. There were several others that she hadn't met, and Riley wondered what they all expected to find out here today.

She spotted Agent Garrett Holbrook placing his chair back from the table a bit and close to the door. She wondered if he was trying to be inconspicuous or was planning an early exit. Perhaps both, she thought.

At the far end of the room a gigantic map was projected, showing where the three bodies had been found. The sheer size of the visual struck Riley as overkill. After all, the map wasn't particularly informative. Still, it made the statement that Morley obviously wanted it to make—that they were deadly serious about bringing a murderer to justice.

Once everybody had settled down, Morley stood up to get things underway. He wasn't a large man, but he had an intense presence that commanded everyone's attention. Riley could see why he was in charge here.

"I'm glad you're all here," he said. "We now know for sure that we're dealing with a serial killer. It's going to be a tough case, and we don't have a moment to lose. Even now, our subject might be targeting his next victim—or maybe he's killed her already. We've got to stop him now, if not sooner."

Riley heard more than a trace of impatience in his voice. She'd noticed this about him before. If Morley had a fault, she figured, it was that he expected progress to made at some impossible rate. Still, she admired his drive to get results.

Morley gestured across the table toward Riley and Bill.

"I think most of you have already met Agents Paige and Jeffreys. They're here from Quantico to lend us their expertise. Let's hear what they've got to say about where things stand."

He sat down. Riley and Bill exchanged glances. She nodded slightly and Bill smiled almost imperceptibly. They were silently exchanging a familiar signal. Riley wanted him to talk first, so she could simply take in the faces and reactions of the people present.

Riley was pleased that they could still communicate wordlessly like this. It was how they'd worked together when they'd been at their best, each supporting the other. It felt good to Riley to be getting back into that rhythm.

Bill stood up. "Here's what we've got so far," he began. "Agent Morley is right. We're dealing with a serial killer, and he's picking up his pace …"

He launched into a summary of what had happened during the last few days, beginning with the discovery of Nancy Holbrook's body. Riley knew that he'd continue to report all that she and Bill had been doing since their arrival on Saturday. But she didn't need all this review. Instead, she focused her attention on the people sitting around her. From experience, she could spot any weak links in the team—agents who weren't up to the job, or whose judgment was likely to be off. She would also notice any who appeared to be holding back, perhaps not sharing information that they all needed to know.

She was pleasantly surprised to find herself in a small sea of enthusiasm, alertness, and apparent competence.

No obvious weak links here, she thought.

But something did catch her eye. Garrett Holbrook had gotten up from his chair and was heading toward the door. He looked rather agitated and shaken. She told herself that he was simply upset about having to review details of his own sister's death. Maybe he didn't think he could deal with it all over again.

That sort of made sense to Riley—but perhaps not really. Holbrook was an FBI agent, after all—a trained professional. He was used to dealing with horrifying crimes. Besides, it had been his idea to make this an FBI case in the first place.

Holbrook slipped out the door and was gone. What bothered Riley most was that she didn't yet know what to make of him. She hadn't been able to nail down what was bothering her about the brother of a murder victim.

Another presence hovered in Riley's mind—the killer himself. Where was he right at this moment? Was he laughing at their efforts to track him down?

No, she thought. *We don't matter to him that much.*

But he mattered to Riley intensely. In order to bring him down, she knew that she would have to find a way to delve into the dark recesses of his mind. She was already beginning to sense a man in full control of what he was doing, a secure man …

Her musings stopped when Bill said, "And now my partner, Agent Paige, will give us what we've got in the way of a profile."

Riley rose to her feet and spoke to the group.

"We can make a few assumptions. The killer was a male between twenty-one and forty-three years old when he committed his first murder, and he's probably still within that age range. He's got at least a high school education, and I'm pretty sure that he's spent some time in college. In fact, this one might be very well educated. He's got a job, probably one that pays well. There's a good chance that he's got a wife and kids, or at least that he's been married with children in the past. He's highly intelligent, and very sure of himself."

A hand shot up. One of the agents who had pulled Riley off of Rabbe had a question.

"How much of what you're saying is fact, and how much is hypothesis?" he asked.

Riley smiled. It was a perfectly good question.

"Facts are in short supply at this point," she said. "But I'm not just making this stuff up."

A ripple of laughter went through the room.

"These are more than educated guesses," she said. "The BAU has gathered important data on serial killers of prostitutes. I'm basing some of my assumptions on that data. For example, in each of these cases we've seen here, the killer transported the body away from the murder scene and disposed of it in water. These types of serial killers want to place time and distance between themselves and their victims. Unlike serials who are out for publicity, they don't want anyone to know that a murder has taken place. They don't get their pleasure from panicking the general public."

The agent who had asked the question looked thoughtful. He added, "Then this type gets all his kicks from the killing itself?"

"Right," Riley answered, "and if I may say so, some of what I'm saying comes from my own many years of field experience. And I think this killer is atypical in some ways. For example, I don't think he has a police record. That won't make him any easier to track down. His everyday behavior is probably quite normal. This is a sociopath who takes prostitutes because they easily available. He considers them disposable.

"He's intelligent, but not a practiced criminal. He would have gotten away clean with the first murder if he hadn't fumbled on the second one. The third was a case of bad luck, but also a sign that he didn't anticipate all of the possibilities. He may change his MO the next time … and there will be a next time."

Another hand went up. Riley didn't recognize the young woman.

"Your name, please?" she asked.

"Robin Mastin," she said. "I'm with the local police."

Riley knew the name at once. This was the student diver who had found Marsha "Ginger" Kramer's skeleton. Riley also knew that the young rookie had insisted on searching even after team leader Quentin Rosner had been ready to give up.

Riley said, "That was some pretty good work you did at Nimbo Lake."

Robin Mastin smiled and blushed. "Thank you, Agent Paige," she said.

Riley got the strong feeling that the young woman especially appreciated praise from a seasoned agent.

"Your question?" Riley said.

"The body I found was still wearing an expensive-looking bracelet. Is that significant?"

"As a matter of fact, it is," Riley said. "Nancy Holbrook's body was still wearing a diamond ring. Gretchen Lovick was wearing a necklace, also with a diamond. Not extremely high-end pieces, but well beyond what we might have expected to find on them."

Riley thought this was a good moment to give the eager rookie a chance to pitch in.

"What does that suggest to you, Officer Mastin?" she asked.

The young woman thought it over for a moment.

"Well, it seems likely that the killer gave those trinkets to the women as gifts. That must mean that he was on good terms with them when he killed them. They thought they could trust him."

"Very good," Riley said. Robin Mastin blushed some more and smiled proudly.

Riley continued, "This is important to keep in mind. Our killer doesn't snatch his victims off the street, or abduct them by force. He uses some kind of ruse. We can be pretty sure that he poses as a john—and a kindly, generous john at that. He's a deadly con man."

Riley paused for a moment, then said, "Here's an important detail. His first victim was HIV positive. The killer is very likely to be as well. If so, he probably knows it."

Pathologist Dr. Rachel Fowler looked up from her note-taking.

"That's interesting," Fowler said. "The last two victims didn't have HIV. But then, he didn't have sex with them, or at least not when he killed them. Marsha Kramer's remains were too decomposed to tell."

"According to her associates, Kramer had the virus," Riley said. "And I've got a hunch that our killer was sexually active three years ago and got it from her. Considering his probable social status, he's most likely taking drugs for it, either illicitly or by prescription."

Riley caught the eye of the pagan digital tech chief.

"Igraine, is there any way you can use that information to track him down?" Without irony, she added, "With the magic at your disposal?"

Igraine tugged on one of her safety pins thoughtfully.

"I wouldn't get optimistic, Agent Paige," she said. "We could try getting a report from pharmacies. But more than ten thousand people in the area are known to be HIV positive or have AIDS. Even if we leave out women, the elderly, or the very young, that still leaves too many people to sort through fast enough to be of any immediate help."

Riley was impressed by Igraine's display of ready knowledge.

"I understand, Igraine," she said. "We'll think of another approach for you and your team."

Now Riley noticed that Morley had gotten up and was heading for the door. He seemed to be responding to a phone message.

It must be something important, Riley thought as he stepped quietly outside.

Riley and Bill took a few more questions, then called the meeting to a close. Everybody left the room except for the two of them.

"Where's Holbrook?" Bill asked. "I thought he'd stay around afterwards."

"I saw him leave early on," Riley said.

"That's kind of odd," Bill said.

"He's kind of odd," Riley agreed.

Morley came back into the room, looking more hopeful than usual.

"We just got a tip," he told Riley and Bill. "It's from a woman named Ruthie Lapham, who runs the bar at the Desert King. It's another truck stop where prostitutes hang out. Ruthie's something of a mother hen to the hookers there, watches out for them as much as she can. She's worried about a girl named Clover, who has been AWOL for a few days."

Bill shook his head doubtfully.

"A missing prostitute isn't exactly a lead," he said.

Riley had to agree. "It's sad, but it happens every day."

Morley said, "Yeah, and with the media coverage of the murders, our tip lines have been flooded with useless calls. But this might be different. Ruthie says a suspicious guy has been cruising the girls there from time to time. He really stands out. The usual clientele are truck drivers, and this guy just doesn't fit in. He's always made the girls nervous and of course now they're jumpier than usual. But Ruthie says she thinks they could be right about this one."

Riley's interest was piqued. "So why did Ruthie call just now?" she asked.

"Because the guy just showed up there again," Morley said. "She thinks maybe we should check him out."

"He could be gone by the time we get there," Bill said. "Still, we'd better go. If nothing else, we can talk to the women, find out what they might know about him."

But Riley remembered how hard it had been to talk to most of the women at Hank's Derby.

"It won't do to just go charging in as FBI," she said. "We'd never nail the suspect that way. And believe me, the girls won't talk to us."

"You'll just have to get them to talk," Morley said.

A long silence followed, and in that silence, slowly, Riley came to a decision.

"There's only one way to do that," Riley said.

They looked at her.

"I'm going undercover."

"Exactly how do you intend to do that?" Morley asked.

"I'll join the hookers," Riley explained.

Bill looked stunned, while Morley stared at her, frowning.

Bill sputtered, "At the truck stop?"

Riley nodded.

"That's too dangerous," Bill protested. "You'll make yourself bait for a killer."

Riley was thinking the same thing. But she was also thinking of these other girls' lives, of the urgency of time. She could not sit idly by while another girl died.

"It's out of the question," Morley said. "I won't authorize it."

She stood.

"I'm not asking for authorization," she said. "I'm doing it."

Chapter Twenty Five

Bill pulled into the Desert King truck stop and parked the big car he'd checked out from the FBI. He chose a space far enough from the main building not to draw too much attention from anyone inside, but close enough to watch all the comings and goings. He had insisted that if Riley was going undercover as a prostitute, he was going to be at the truck stop too.

He had to admit that going undercover was actually a pretty good idea, even if it might be dangerous. If their killer really was stalking victims around here, she might be able to draw him out, maybe even stop him cold.

Riley hadn't shown up yet, though. She'd told Bill she had to stop and find some more appropriate clothes. He didn't know how long that might take, but she was planning to head straight into the bar when she got here. Bill would keep an eye on things outside and give her backup if she needed it. He noted that the convenience store and the Iguana Lounge were housed in a single building, so he should be able see whoever went in and out of either place.

He also hoped to talk to some of the women, find out whatever he could about the man who had alarmed them. They must deal with some weird characters on a regular basis, and he had to wonder what could be so different about this one.

Of course, he didn't expect any of them to talk openly to an FBI agent. He had decided to pose as a john.

"Here goes nothing," he murmured to himself aloud.

He got out of the car and stood leaning against it, hoping to look like a potential customer. He saw four scantily clad women standing just outside the convenience store. He waved in their direction and they all looked at him.

He smiled and nodded toward his car. They stared at him for a moment, then huddled a bit closer together, making no move in his direction.

I must be doing something wrong, he thought.

He saw another pair of women wending their way among the cars toward the building. This time he whistled to get their attention. They looked at him, and he waved. They kept walking toward the building a little faster than before.

Then he heard a woman's voice nearby.

"Fish not biting tonight, huh?"

Bill turned and saw a woman who was obviously a prostitute approaching him. She was well along in years, and her garishly heavy makeup didn't make her look any younger. Her hair was an impossible shade of red, and her physique was sagging.

She leaned against the car right next to Bill.

"Hope you don't mind if I smoke," she said. "I know, it's a nasty habit. I've got a lot of those."

She took out a cigarette, lit it, and took a long puff.

"I'm Opal, by the way."

"I'm Jerry," Bill said.

The woman let out a sandpapery little laugh.

OK, she doesn't believe that. Bill thought. He realized that a lot of people might use fake names in a place like this, but he suddenly felt nervous and unsure what to do next. He hadn't done any serious undercover work for years, and he'd never tried posing as a john before.

"I was wondering if we could maybe just talk," Bill said.

She laughed again. "You're new around here, aren't you?"

"You could say that," Bill said.

She nudged him with her elbow.

"Well, if you're looking for a good time, you picked an odd spot," she said.

"Really? I hear this is where the girls are."

She laughed again. "If you're a trucker, sure. But you're no trucker. You're not even pretending to be a trucker. As a general rule, the girls here don't go with nobody who doesn't roll into here in a big rig. It's a safety thing."

She snuggled up against him seductively.

"Me, I'm different," she said. "I don't get to be that picky. I'm what you might call a casualty of the law of supply and demand. My 'supply' has got kind of stale over the years, so I can't be too particular about 'demand.'"

Then, whispering in his ear, she added, "Besides, I've got nothing against cops."

Bill felt a jolt of surprise. He was sure that she could feel it too.

Opal said, "Nope, I've got no problem with cops at all. I've been in jail too many times for it to bother me. I can even do business there when I need to."

Bill was embarrassed, but he saw no point in trying to lie.

He took out his badge.

"Actually, I'm FBI."

Opal purred with amusement. "*Are* you now? Well, you should've gotten in touch with Truckers Against Trafficking. They might of put you on a rig and got you in here looking like a real trucker."

"I've heard of them," Bill said. "Good guys. But I'm really just here to back up my partner. And we're not out to bust hookers."

"Well fine, we can still do business. I can talk just as good as I can do the other stuff."

She held out her hand. It was obvious what she wanted. Bill reached for his wallet and handed her a hundred-dollar bill.

"My, my," Opal said appreciatively, depositing the bill in her cleavage. "This will get you a lot of talking! Well, I don't like to do *anything* professional out in the open. Let's get in your car, shall we? Make ourselves comfy."

Feeling thoroughly ill at ease, Bill walked around to the passenger door and let the woman in. Then he got in on the driver's side. Opal continued to puff away at her cigarette.

Bill said, "I hear that a girl disappeared here recently."

"You'll have to get more specific," Opal said. "Girls disappearing 'round here is kind of a regular thing."

"She called herself Clover."

Opal sighed sadly.

"Oh, yeah. Clover. She got all freaked on account of this guy who calls himself T.R. He offered her some kind of jewelry last week—diamond earrings, I think it was. Now, regular johns don't give gifts like that, especially not to the likes of us 'round the Desert King. She got scared, thought maybe he was gettin' obsessed with her, might do something awful to her."

"Do you think he did do anything to her?" Bill asked.

Opal shook her head. "Oh, no, she didn't give him a chance. She lit out of here—out of Phoenix, probably out of the state. She told me she wanted to go where he'd never find her. I told her she was overreacting, taking his attentions too personal, that he probably pulled that gift number on lots of girls. But Clover wouldn't listen. I've got no idea where she'd be by now."

Opal reached over and stroked Bill's thigh.

"By the way, your options are open for more than talk. Just sayin'."

Bill firmly moved her hand away.

Just then Riley came into view, walking toward the bar. She'd put on very snug short shorts and a blouse that was unbuttoned lower than he'd ever seen her wear. She was displaying a lot of curves and cleavage, and she'd done something different with her hair. He had to admit she looked hot. Strolling along on extremely high heels, she vanished into the bar without even a nod in his direction.

Now it was up to him to keep watch. Meanwhile, maybe he could find out more from Opal. He started thinking up questions to ask her.

*

The man was sitting in his parked car when he saw the woman walk into the bar.

Good God, he thought. *Does she really think she's going to pass for a whore?*

He smirked at the thought. She might as well have a sign that said LAW ENFORCEMENT hanging around her neck. He glanced around, but didn't see any obvious backup.

Still, he was intrigued. She was out looking for him, no doubt about it. But what had made her come here? How could she have gotten this lead? Was the law trying to cover all the hooker hangouts now? If they were, it would just mean they had no idea where to look.

Or was she here because that skittish little hooker had complained about him?

He decided that it didn't matter. He wasn't going to let the woman's presence ruin his evening. As far as he was concerned, she was just making things more interesting.

So far, he'd never picked up a victim in this place, and he was always a bit surprised by his occasional urge to come here. If hanging around streetwalkers meant slumming, prowling among lot lizards meant something even lower. It also meant taking certain precautions—for example, renting a cheap used car. His own expensive vehicle would draw the wrong kind of attention. A visit here wasn't exactly convenient.

But his other regular haunts were problematic at the moment. News of his murders had made even the streetwalkers skittish. And Jaybird's gym had just gotten raided and shut down. And he was through trusting the escort service. That bitch Ishtar Haynes had no respect for confidentiality.

Besides, he was oddly fascinated by the whores who haunted the Desert King. They were more desperate than the streetwalkers, less feisty and exuberant. And they were strangely elusive. For some reason, they seldom approached him. And since he made a point of never approaching a whore himself, that meant that he didn't make much direct contact with them.

Clover had been an exception, though. She'd been friendly at first, but he'd gotten careless and scared her off. He reminded himself never to offer jewelry to whores until they were fully under his control. That's what seemed to have driven Clover away—his extravagant generosity.

He remembered what she'd said as she ran away …

"I'm getting away from here for good. Don't try to find me. You won't be able to."

He laughed a little at the memory. As if Clover was even worth the trouble!

But the woman who'd just walked into the bar—might she present a unique challenge? He'd never tried his luck with a decoy. It had never occurred to him. At the very least, he was sure that she would get into his car.

And after that?

The sheer brazenness of the challenge was tantalizing. He wasn't going to rush right into it, though. He'd bide his time for a little while.

Chapter Twenty Six

As Riley made her way through the bar, she felt horribly exposed.

I might as well be naked, she thought.

On her way here, she had bought uncomfortably tight shorts, cheap shoes, and some makeup. She'd stopped at a gas station and changed in its restroom. She'd known better than to try to look like a youngster. She knew from her visit to Hank's Derby that lot lizards ran the gamut of age, weight, and looks.

Of course, the shorts revealed her muscular legs. She wondered whether hookers ever went to the gym—a real one, not like Jaybird's outfit.

Probably not, she guessed.

Tottering along on spike heels that severely restricted her movements made her feel especially vulnerable. If she had to run or fight, it would have to be barefooted. And to make matters worse, there was nowhere to carry her gun. She'd had to leave it in the car.

But then, looking vulnerable and available was exactly the idea. She reminded herself that hookers were always this defenseless. It deepened her sympathy for them. How vulnerable and defenseless they must feel.

She only hoped that her outfit was passable. She'd put it together in a great rush, and she had her doubts about it. She was worried that maybe she couldn't look sufficiently at home in her scant wardrobe. The lot lizards she'd observed had seemed completely comfortable showing off all their assets.

An obese woman with a goiter on her neck was working at the bar. Riley felt pretty sure she was Ruthie Lapham, the bar's owner. Before coming here, she'd called Ruthie to tell her she was on her way, and that she'd be calling herself Tina.

Riley headed straight to the bar. But before she could introduce herself as Tina, Ruthie looked at her dismay.

"Oh Good Lord," she said.

She called out to a brawny fellow who was sitting at a table reading a newspaper.

"Burt, take over for a few minutes, OK?"

Burt ambled over to behind the bar. Ruthie came around in front of the bar and took Riley gently by the arm.

"Come with me, girl," she said.

She led Riley to a dark empty booth, where they both sat down.

Ruthie said. "I thought you said you were going to be undercover."

Feeling deflated, Riley said, "I am."

"What did you do, go out just now and buy those duds in some big-box store?"

Ruthie sounded as if she was just making a snide joke. The truth was, Riley had done just that.

"I was in a hurry," she said.

"Oh Good Lord," Ruthie repeated. "You did everything short of leaving the tags on. These girls never buy anything new. It's always thrift shops and rummage sales, that kind of thing, cheap and used and tatty. You'll never pass for a working girl looking like that. Did any of the girls see you on your way in?"

Riley remembered getting looks from some women as she'd walked through the parking lot. She nodded.

"Well, you can be sure they're not happy to see you," Ruthie said. "They've probably put the word out that a sting is on."

"That's not why we're here," she said.

Ruthie shook her head in resignation. "But never mind, we'll make do somehow. Like I said over the phone, some of the girls told me they spotted that man again—T.R., he calls himself. He hasn't come in here yet, but he will before he goes home, he always does. Don't worry, I can see good enough from here—both the front door and the hall that goes into the store yonder. I won't miss him."

"Now what can you tell me about this guy you reported?" Riley asked.

"Well, he's not a trucker, that's for sure. He tries to pass himself off as one, goes around in a T-shirt and jeans, but nobody's ever seen his rig. And he hasn't got a trucker's build or look, or the right kind of talk neither. He comes around here time to time, talking up girls, but he never seems to score, or even try to real hard. It's like he's got something else in mind. And from what I've seen on the news lately, it could be something real bad. That's why I called."

"What does he look like?" Riley asked.

"Well, he's sort of medium size. He has a lot of blond hair and always wears a cap. Big glasses. Expensive-looking clothes."

Ruthie glanced across the room.

"There he is now," she said. "Right over there. Lurking in the hallway."

Riley knew better than to move too quickly. Besides, she had to alert Bill that she was about to make her move. She got out her cell phone and sent him a text.

Suspect in view. I'm going after him. Meet us outside the bar.

Her plan was simple. She'd proposition the man, then escort him out of the bar to where Bill would be waiting and ready. Together she and Bill would nail him for simple solicitation. With luck he'd give himself away while they had him in custody.

To her own shock and surprise, Riley suddenly felt deeply afraid. An image of darkness and fire flashed in the back of her mind. She'd been held and tormented by one monster, and now here she was, offering herself up to another one.

But she wasn't going to let that residual trauma get the best of her. Besides, this time she had backup. Her partner was right outside.

She got up and stepped out of the booth. She could see the man standing in the hallway but he was keeping his face in shadow. As she looked toward him, he actually turned away.

Riley headed across the room, determined to walk up to the man and make her best try at a come-on. She wanted to at least get a look at his face. She wanted a chance to evaluate him as a potential killer.

But she had only gone a few steps when a woman stepped directly in her path. In a blink of an eye, the woman was flanked on both sides by two more. They were clearly prostitutes, and they all looked as mad as hell.

"Well, ladies, looks like we've got a new girl," the woman in front said, a note of threat in her voice. "My name's Jewel, what's yours?"

"Tina," Riley said, trying to push past her.

The three women clustered together to block Riley's way forward. She started to cut around a table and take another route, but the women moved to block that way too.

Riley was stumped. She'd taken on lots of men in her time, many of them strong and tough. Under normal circumstances, she wouldn't find three men much of a threat. But women? She didn't want to beat these women up and couldn't think what to do. Besides, she was anxious not to blow her cover.

"Now don't be rude, girl," Jewel said, her face uncomfortably close to Riley's. "What's the matter? Is there something you're not telling us?"

One of the other women snapped, "Yeah, she doesn't want to tell us she's a cop."

Riley heard a man's voice to her right.

"A cop? Hell, Dusty's no cop. Stop bothering her, Jewel. The rest of you too."

Riley turned and saw a familiar face walking toward her. It took her a moment to recognize Rex, the trucker who'd helped her rescue Jilly back at Hank's Derby. He must have just come in, because she hadn't seen him sitting in the bar earlier. He done some fast thinking and made up a name to call her by.

The women gaped at him with surprise, but they obviously knew him.

Rex offered Riley his arm, and she took it.

"Where've you been, Dusty?" he said, escorting her away from the angry hookers. "I thought you'd never show up."

"I got held up," Riley said. In a whisper she said, "I'm on a case. I've got to go." She steered him toward the hallway and then let go of his arm.

"After a bad guy, huh?" Rex whispered back with a wink. "Go get 'im, girl."

Riley darted away from Rex and into the hall, but the man Ruthie had pointed out wasn't there now. She saw another door leading into the adjoining convenience store. He'd obviously gone through there. If she could catch up with him, maybe there was still a slim chance that she could proposition him.

But inside the well-lighted store, she just saw a handful of men who were obviously real truckers, not the one she was looking for. A couple of them ogled her with interest and one even stepped toward her. But Riley didn't have time for this. She slid her FBI badge out of her handbag and flashed it at them. He stopped in his tracks and the other one got very interested in the doughnuts on a nearby rack.

She headed straight to the front door and darted outside. Nobody was in sight, except for Bill, who had gotten her message and was waiting outside the door to the bar.

*

On the opposite side of the building, the man started up his rented hatchback. He berated himself for his close call just now. The truth was, he didn't know how he'd have handled her if she'd

138

approached him. And had she seen his face? He felt sure that she hadn't.

When she'd gotten up from the booth, he'd hurried down the hallway into the convenience store and joined several truckers who were just leaving. He'd seen the man standing outside the bar—the woman's partner, ready to back her up. He doubted that the partner could have noticed him among the other truckers. Then he'd cut around the front of the building to his car. He'd gotten away clean.

For a moment he felt an urge to drive by and see if she would get in the car with him. But he knew that she and her partner were both surely armed. It had already been a close call for him.

Stupid, he thought. *I was stupid.*

What had he been thinking? Since when had he gotten a thrill out of playing cat-and-mouse like this? It just wasn't his way.

No more cheap thrills, he reminded himself.

From now on he would stick to the part he really enjoyed—the shock, the gasping, the weakening struggle, the silence at the end. And he promised himself to treat himself to that pleasure again very soon.

Chapter Twenty Seven

Over breakfast the next morning, Riley and Bill barely spoke to each other for a while. Riley wasn't sure where the tension was coming from. Sure, they were still discouraged over last night's failed attempt at catching the killer. But there was more to it than that. She couldn't put her finger on it.

"We'll get him," Bill finally said, chewing on a piece of toast. "From what Opal told me about him, he's got his weaknesses."

Riley didn't reply. She remembered the aging prostitute who'd still been sitting in Bill's car after the killer got away. Bill had discussed the situation with her while Riley was in the bar. From what he'd said, Opal sounded like a shrewd observer who knew what she was talking about.

Still, Riley felt bitterly disappointed that the evening had been such a bust. Her own hasty disguise hadn't worked very well, and she'd let three whores slow her down enough to let the subject get away. And although Bill had glimpsed several groups of men leaving the convenience store, he'd hadn't been able to pick out the suspect among them. A lot of truckers fit the description they had gotten from Ruthie and several of the prostitutes.

It seemed that T.R. was white, a little heavy in build but average in height. His age was somewhere between thirty-five and fifty, and he often wore a baseball cap. Some of the women had mentioned thick blond hair brushed forward. Ruthie had found no useful picture of him on her security camera footage. And of course, they really had no reason to believe that the man was anything more than a nuisance to the hookers.

Having to wake Morley up last night to phone in the bad news had been especially embarrassing.

And this morning Bill was looking at her in an odd way. Riley didn't know what to make of it. She took another swallow of coffee and tried to clear her head.

Suddenly, Bill reached across the table and put his hand on hers. "I mean it, Riley," he said. "We'll get him."

He didn't let go of her hand. She knew that this was more than a reassuring gesture. Under different circumstances, she might have welcomed it. But she was in no mood for it right now. No mood at all.

She growled, "Bill, you'd better move your hand away if you want to keep it."

But Bill didn't move his hand. He only smiled.

"C'mon, Riley."

"C'mon what?" He squeezed her hand and looked directly into her eyes.

No doubt about it—he was making a pass at her. It wasn't as brazen as her own drunken phone call a few months back that had nearly wrecked their friendship. But it was a pass nonetheless.

But why right now? Riley wondered. Then she remembered the expression on Bill's face when she'd joined him after they lost the suspect—a look of interest she hadn't given any thought to at the time. But now this morning that look made an unpleasant kind of sense to her.

"This is all because of the part I was playing last night," she said. "Because of how I was dressed and how I behaved."

Bill blushed a little. She knew that she'd called it exactly right. She jerked her hand away.

"You thought I looked hot because I looked like a hooker," she said. "High heels and bare skin made you feel all warm and fuzzy?"

"So what if it did?" Bill said.

Riley could hardly believe her ears.

"So what if it did?" she echoed. "Bill, listen to yourself."

"Well, you know it's more than that," Bill said. "You know I'm attracted to you all the time. And don't pretend it's not mutual. There's something between us. Isn't it about time we stopped pretending that there's not?"

Riley felt the truth in those words, but she also felt a little sick with disgust. She thought back to Jaybird and Calvin Rabbe, two men who weren't capable of seeing women as human beings.

Was it possible that Bill had something in common with them? Did her longtime partner harbor the same tendency to think of women as sex objects? Were all men like that deep down—the straight ones, anyway?

"It's not mutual right now," she said firmly.

"You're overreacting."

Riley was about to launch into a heated tirade about how she wasn't overreacting at all. But her phone buzzed. Seeing that the call was from April, she answered it.

"Hi, dear. What's going on?" she said.

To her alarm, she heard her daughter sobbing.

"I saw him," April said.

"Saw who?"

"Peterson. He's alive. He looked right at me. He recognized me."

Riley's heart was pounding.

"What's wrong?" Bill asked. He had seen the change in Riley's expression.

Riley didn't answer. She needed to get away so she could talk to April alone. She left the hotel restaurant and walked toward her room.

"You know that's not possible, April," she said.

And of course, it wasn't possible. She remembered as if it were yesterday. April herself had struck Peterson down with a rifle stock, and then Riley had caved in his forehead with a sharp rock. Finally there had been his dead eyes gazing up at her as river water trickled over his face.

But even then, she couldn't believe it until April said …

"Mom. He's dead."

Peterson was dead, all right. It had only been because of Brent Meredith's sympathy and discretion that Riley hadn't gotten a stiff reprimand for the force she'd used. But she understood what April was going through all too well. Riley herself had experienced a flashback just last night at the Iguana Lounge, and she still had nightmares about being caged and threatened with flames.

April was still sobbing. Her gasping voice on the phone sounded terrified.

"We were getting off our tour bus just now," she cried. "There he was, right in the street. He looked straight at me. He grinned. I know he's going to kill me. I need your help."

Those last four words—"I need your help"—stung Riley's heart. It didn't matter that Peterson was dead. April *did* need her desperately. But here she was, all the way across the country.

"Have you called your dad?" Riley asked. "He's probably in DC now."

"No. I didn't think of him."

Riley sighed. She knew that after a lifetime of emotional distance April had scant reason to want to call her father.

"I need you, Mom. I need you right now."

Riley didn't know what to say. April seemed to have forgotten that Riley was in Phoenix. And that was the last thing April needed to hear right now.

"Let me talk to your teacher," Riley said.

A moment later, Riley heard a different voice on the line.

"This is Lorna Culver. Is this April's mother?"

"Yes, this is Riley Paige."

The woman's voice sounded terribly agitated.

"Ms. Paige, I don't know what to do. She's calmer than she was a minute ago, but she was completely hysterical. You've got to get here right away."

"I can't," Riley said. "I'm in Arizona."

"Well, I'll take her right back to the hotel," she said. "But I can't be responsible for her while she's in this state of mind."

Riley wanted to yell at the woman.

Can't be responsible? Isn't that your job?

But she kept her voice under control.

"Give me your cell phone number," she said.

During the conversation, Riley had gotten back to her room. She wrote down the number on a pad and told Ms. Culver her own number.

"I'll call April's father," she told the teacher, then ended the call.

She paced anxiously back and forth as she called Ryan's cell phone number. She was relieved when she got her ex-husband and not his answering service.

"Hi, Riley," he said, trying to sound cordial. "How are you? It's been a while."

It was all Riley could do to keep herself from bursting into tears.

"Ryan, it's April. She's in Washington, and she's having an attack of PTSD. It's from the whole awful thing with Peterson. She's—"

Ryan interrupted her.

"Wait a minute. Slow down. What's she doing in Washington?"

Riley sat down on the edge of the bed. She took a long, slow breath.

"She's on a class field trip," Riley explained, speaking slowly and carefully. "She's been there since Saturday. It's supposed to be a whole week."

She wanted to add, *And if you cared at all about your daughter, you'd know that already.* But she stopped herself.

She continued. "She thought she saw Peterson—the man who abducted her. She didn't, of course. He's dead. But this is serious, Ryan. I've been through my share of PTSD and believe me, it's terrifying. You've got to go help her."

"Why me? Why can't you go?"

"Because I'm in Phoenix, Ryan. Phoenix, *Arizona*. I'm working on a case. I just can't get there."

"Well, I'm in Philadelphia. I'm working a court case. I can't get there either."

Riley couldn't keep her voice from shaking with rage.

"You *can* get there, Ryan. You can fly there in an hour. Hell, you can drive there in less than three hours. I can't get there that soon. I can't get there at all."

Ryan replied in a patronizing tone that Riley had heard thousands of times.

"This is your responsibility, Riley. And it's your fault she's going through this. It's that damn job of yours. You're the one who put her in harm's way. You couldn't just stay at home and be a normal mother. You fly back to DC. Right now. This isn't my problem."

Riley fought down a stream of curses and still said nothing.

"Did you hear what I said, Riley?"

Riley knew that there was no way to get him to face facts. He'd always assumed his right to be distant. His work was always too important for him to get caught up in everyday problems. His job was to be successful. His job was to make rich clients even richer. He'd never accepted that Riley's job of catching monsters was at least as important.

"Riley?" Ryan said. "Did you hear me?"

She had to find another way to help April, and this was a waste of time. She hung up.

If I never have to talk to that bastard again, it'll be too soon, she thought.

To make things worse, he'd hit her where it hurt, the very core of her guilt and self-doubt. Might life have been better for all three of them—Riley, April, and Ryan—if she'd never become an agent? But what would she have become if she had stayed at home? One of those secret drunk housewives? How could that have been better for anybody?

Worst of all, how could she have failed to see this coming? She'd convinced herself that April was doing fine. But of course it was too good to last. From her own experience with PTSD, she should have known better. There was no way April could have recovered so quickly and easily. She couldn't possibly be fully free of the trauma of her captivity or the added trauma of helping her mother kill her captor.

An image flashed through Riley's mind.

It was her friend Marie Sayles, suspended in mid-air, hanging by her neck from a cord tied to a light fixture on her bedroom ceiling.

Riley's mouth went dry at the memory. Marie, too, had been held captive by Peterson. Her fear of her tormenter drove her to suicide. Riley had desperately tried to talk her out of her fear on the phone, assuring her that Peterson was dead. But it made no difference.

"You killed his body but you didn't kill his evil," Marie had said just minutes before she took her own life.

And Riley knew that April was experiencing exactly the same despair at that very moment. She might do anything to escape her terror. Her greatest danger was to herself.

Just then she heard a knock at the door. When she answered it, Bill was standing outside.

"Riley, are you OK?" he asked.

Riley was relieved to see him. She vaguely realized that she'd just been angry with him. But at this moment, she couldn't even remember what it was all about. It seemed like a long time ago.

"Come on in," she said. "It's April. She's having a PTSD attack."

Bill nodded sympathetically. Riley knew that he didn't need to be reminded of the trauma that April had endured.

"Bill, I don't know what to do," Riley said. "Ryan refuses to help. And here I am, thousands of miles away!"

"What about Mike Nevins?" Bill said.

The very mention of the name brought a wave of hope. Yes, who could be better to turn to right now than the forensic psychiatrist who had helped her through her own trauma?

"Of course," Riley said, grateful for Bill's suggestion. She'd been too distraught to think of the obvious answer. She dialed his direct number, then heard a comforting, familiar voice.

"Riley?"

Riley felt a swell of gratitude that Mike had answered his phone.

"Mike, I need your help. April's in Washington on a field trip, and PTSD has kicked in. She's sure that she saw Peterson. She thinks he wants to kill her."

"How bad is she?" Mike asked.

"I don't know. Her teacher doesn't seem to know what to do. Ryan is out of town. I don't know who else to turn to."

145

There was a short pause. Then Mike spoke in a steady, reassuring voice.

"Have you got the teacher's number?" he said.

"Yes."

"Give me the number, and your daughter's too. I'll get in touch with them. And I'll find out where April is and go pick her up. Meanwhile, I think you'd better get over here."

For a moment, Riley was at a complete loss for words. She managed to gasp out, "Thank you, Mike. Thank you." She gave him the numbers, then ended the call.

Bill was sitting in a chair. Riley was still pacing.

"I've got to fly back right now," she said.

"I understand," Bill said. "I'll explain things to Morley."

"No, I'll call him. I'll tell him myself."

Bill shook his head uneasily.

"Riley, I don't know …"

"It's my responsibility, Bill. This is *all* my responsibility. I'm calling him right now."

"All right," Bill said. "I'll get online and book you on the next flight I can get."

Riley opened her laptop for Bill to use. Then she dialed Special Agent in Charge Elgin Morley's number. When she heard his gruff voice answer, she knew that this wasn't going to be easy.

"Agent Morley, I've got to leave Phoenix," she said. "I'm flying straight back to Washington."

"You're what?"

Morley sounded understandably incredulous.

"My daughter's having a nervous breakdown. I don't have time to tell you the whole story. But it's serious. She needs me."

Morley's voice was sounding angry now.

"*We* need you," he said. "There's a killer out there, and he's going to kill again soon, if he hasn't done so already. I'm not giving you permission to leave. You need to stay right here and do your job."

Riley gathered up her nerve and said, "I'm not asking for your permission," she said. "I'm catching the next flight out."

"Agent Paige, you'd damn well better not get on that plane. It's bad enough that you and your partner botched things up last night."

"I'll come back as soon as I can," Riley said.

"No, you won't be coming back. Don't even bother. If you leave, I'm calling Meredith. I'll have you taken off the case. You might never work for the Bureau again."

Riley knew that she ought to be upset by this threat. But she couldn't bring herself to worry about it right now.

"I understand," she told Morley. She ended the call.

Bill was poring over information on the computer screen.

"I've booked a nonstop flight," he said. "But we've got to hurry. It leaves in an hour."

Chapter Twenty Eight

Watching the earth roll by below was torturous to Riley. The plane seemed to be moving at a mere crawl. The slowness was only an illusion, she knew. But she also knew that a lot could happen during the four and a half hours she was going to be airborne.

Terrible things, she thought. And again, she remembered Marie's hanging body.

But she drove the horrible image from her head. No, nothing like that was going to happen this time. Mike had called Riley back and told her that he'd found out where to pick up April and was on his way there. And before takeoff, Riley had managed to get through to her daughter, who still sounded terrified but promised her that she'd be all right.

Riley was anxious about other things as well. She kept remembering Morley's anger and what he had told her just a little while ago.

"I'll have you taken off the case. You might never work for the Bureau again."

Was it true? Was her career as an FBI agent over? At the moment, she wasn't entirely sure that she cared. This was the first time she had ever put being a mother over working a case.

Maybe, she thought, it was about time she did just that. Maybe this decision was long overdue. Still, she more than understood Morley's point of view. Her decision had been thoroughly unprofessional. She'd left an important job unfinished. It was just like Morley had said …

"There's a killer out there, and he's going to kill again soon, if he hasn't done so already."

As the plane lifted higher, that distorted sense of motion became even more bizarre. In her mind, she was still crawling toward her daughter. At the same time, she knew that she was hurtling away from another responsibility at unthinkable speed. She had no idea which feeling was worse.

*

When she arrived at Reagan National Airport that evening, Riley hastily rented a car and drove through heavy traffic to Mike Nevins's office. It took at least an hour to get there. When she found Mike Nevins sitting in a chair just outside of his office, she felt a stab of concern. Where was April?

But Mike's smile as he stood up to greet her was deeply reassuring.

"She's here, Riley," he said. "Don't worry."

He opened the office door, and he and Riley walked inside. She saw April sitting in a chair, talking intently with a young woman who looked concerned and sympathetic.

April leaped to her feet and threw herself into her mother's arms, sobbing.

"Oh, Mom, I'm so sorry," she cried.

Riley could barely hold her upright. The poor girl felt absolutely limp and exhausted from her ordeal.

"What are you talking about?" Riley said, stroking her hair. "It's not your fault. Nothing's your fault."

"I know he's dead. I don't know what happened to me."

"It's OK," Riley said.

When Riley finally released April, the young woman rose to shake her hand.

Mike explained, "Riley, this is Rose Shepard—a resident. Rose, this is April's mother, Riley."

"Your daughter is going to be just fine," Rose said.

"Thank you," Riley said.

"Rose and April are doing some great work together," Mike said. "Let's you and I go talk."

Mike gently took Riley by the arm and escorted her out of the office. They sat down together in two chairs in the hallway.

"April's in good hands with Rose," Mike said. "She's young and smart and empathetic. I'm a little too used to dealing with psychopaths to be of much help in a situation like this. I just don't have the right touch."

"How is she?" Riley asked.

Mike stroked his chin thoughtfully.

"This has been coming on for a while," he said. "She's been repressing things too long. It's good that it's starting to come out."

Riley flinched at that word, "starting." Mike obviously meant that April wasn't out of the woods yet.

"I should have seen this coming," Riley said.

"Beating yourself up about it won't help, Riley. April has to do her own healing at her own pace. It's not up to you. This is a necessary part of the process."

The dapper, bookish man leaned toward Riley with a concerned look.

"But how about you, Riley? How are you doing?"

Riley shrugged. "I'm fine."

"No, you're not. I can see it in your face. You need to talk to me."

Riley wanted to tell Mike that it was only the time change bothering her. Flying through time zones could stress out her body clock. But he was right, of course.

"Mike, I don't know what to do anymore. I left in the middle of a case. The Arizona chief is furious. Did I do the right thing?"

"Only you can decide that, Riley."

Riley sighed miserably. "Said like a true shrink," she said.

Mike chuckled a little. "Yeah, and you know it's true," he said.

Indeed, she did know it was true. And she knew that Mike wanted her to talk it out.

She said, "I keep finding myself up against the same problem over and over again. How can I be both an agent and a mother? Is it even possible? Am I wrong to even try? Ryan's mad at me too. Of course, he's always mad at me, but this time I almost wonder if he's right. He says I should have just stayed at home and been a mother. Is that true? Maybe April would be better off with him."

Mike scoffed a little. "You know better than that."

Riley said nothing. But of course Mike was right again. She did know better than to think that April belonged with her irresponsible, philandering, emotionally distant father. She was letting her self-pity get the best of her.

"The impossible hours are bad enough," she said. "It's worse that I'm always putting myself in danger, and that she might lose me one of these days. But I wound up putting her in danger too, and look at what it's done to her. I'm so afraid that something like that is going to happen again."

Mike knitted his brow, giving Riley's words his best professional attention.

"You seem to think that your situation is entirely unique to you," he said. "Sure, the stakes are more dire for you than for most parents. But it's a simple fact of raising a child—there's not always a single *right* thing to do. Most parents make peace with that fact sooner or later. But not you. You keep right on thinking that you should be able to do the impossible. Why is that, do you think?"

Riley's eyes stung with tears. It sometimes hurt that Mike understood her so well. But then, that was exactly why she often turned to him for counsel and friendship.

He said, "I know this isn't what you want to hear, but you've reached a crisis point. Now that you're pulling out of your own

PTSD, you're still riddled by self-doubt. I'm not sure you can get through this without some kind of emotional catharsis."

A single sob forced its way out of Riley. She fought to control herself.

"Mike, I don't know what to do next."

"It's OK not to know what to do," Mike said.

"Not at a time like now. I've got to make a decision."

Mike held her gaze for a long moment.

"I don't know if this will help," he said carefully. "But the situation with April is well under control. I've made arrangements with a colleague of mine in Fredericksburg. Her name is Lesley Sloat, and she's an excellent pediatric therapist. She's willing to work with April every day for as long as she needs to. You and April can meet her tomorrow morning."

Riley detected an unspoken hint in Mike's words. He seemed to be saying that Riley's immediate presence wouldn't be necessary for long. She could go back to work soon if she wanted to.

But did she want to? She felt terribly lost and confused.

The door to Mike's office opened. Rose and April stepped out into the hallway. Rose's arm was around April's shoulder.

"I think we did some good work today, don't you, April?" Rose said in a warm, pleasant voice.

April's smile was weak but genuine.

"I think so too," she said.

"Let's head on home then," Riley said.

Riley held her daughter's hand tightly as they left the building and walked toward the car.

"I'm so sorry about all this, Mom," April said.

"Please stop saying that," Riley said.

*

April went to bed soon after they got back to their home in Fredericksburg. She was exhausted after her ordeal, and Riley hoped she would sleep soundly. But Riley didn't feel ready to sleep. It was more than the time change. She was deeply troubled.

As soon as she was sure that April was asleep, she went to her own bedroom and stretched out on the bed. She called Bill on her cell phone.

"Riley!" Bill said when he answered. "How's April doing?"

"She'll be OK," Riley said.

Riley heard Bill sigh with relief. It felt good to hear his voice.

"What's going on with the case?" Riley asked.

"We're just completely stalled here. I wish you were still here."

A silence fell. Riley sensed that Bill was trying to find the right words for something she might not want to hear.

Finally he said, "Riley, Morley did what he said he was going to do. He called Brent Meredith in Quantico and gave him an earful about how pissed off he is with you. He got you taken off the case."

It was Riley's turn to fall silent. She had no idea what to say.

"Riley, I can fix this," Bill said. "I've already called Meredith. He understands what you're going through. He can pull rank on Morley. He can get you reinstated. But the final decision is up to you."

Riley's anxiety was so intense that she could barely breathe.

"I need some time to decide, Bill," she said.

Bill let out a slight groan of impatience.

"Time's something we don't have a lot of," he said. "Morley's already talking about bringing in a replacement from Quantico. I'm stalling him for now, but I can't do it for very long. And once a replacement gets here, it'll be a lot harder for you to come back."

"I understand," Riley said. "Thanks, Bill."

They ended the phone call. Riley just lay there on her bed, feeling stranded and helpless and depressed. It was a new and terrible feeling. During her life she'd known anger, terror, grief, and just about every other kind of negative emotion she could imagine. But somehow this was worse. She barely recognized herself right now—a wavering, quivering mass of indecision and despair. Where was this unfamiliar misery going to end?

She remembered something Mike Nevins had said.

"I'm not sure you can get through this without some kind of emotional catharsis."

As far as she was concerned, that didn't bode well for her at all. Things were going to get worse before they got better. She remembered how she'd almost cried when she'd talked to Mike earlier.

Maybe that's what I need right now, she thought. *A good cry.*

But no tears came.

Chapter Twenty Nine

The next evening, Riley was in the kitchen just starting to fix dinner for herself and April when she heard the front door open.

A familiar, Spanish-accented voice called out, "Where is she? Where is my sweet *muchacha*?"

Then Riley heard April yell happily, "Gabriela!"

Riley hurried to the living room where she found April and Gabriela hugging each other. Gabriela's suitcase was on the floor near the door.

"Gabriela!" Riley said. "I didn't expect you home until tomorrow."

"You didn't think I'd stay away after all that happened, did you?"

Riley understood. Yesterday she had called Gabriela, who was still visiting her family in Tennessee. Of course Riley had told her what had happened with April. Gabriela was family, and Riley wouldn't think of leaving her out of the loop. Riley shouldn't have been surprised that Gabriela had hurried back as soon as she possibly could.

"You go get unpacked, Gabriela," she said. "I'm fixing dinner."

Riley headed back into the kitchen. As much as she loved Gabriela's cooking, she liked to switch places with her to cook once in a while. And she was sure that Gabriela could use a break after her trip.

It had been a long, emotional day. Early in the afternoon, Riley had taken April to Dr. Lesley Sloat's office. First, Riley had talked alone for a while with Dr. Sloat, who had explained her therapeutic approach to her. Riley immediately took a liking to the short, stout, warm-hearted woman. She felt so grateful for the help with April's post-traumatic stress. She shuddered to think what her daughter must be going through.

Then Dr. Sloat had talked with April alone for an hour. April had seemed to feel much better after the session had ended.

On the way home, April had said, "Your friend Dr. Nevins really came through for us. Dr. Sloat is going to be great to talk to. She has a way of making me see things I couldn't figure out on my own."

Now, washing vegetables in the kitchen, Riley felt glad that Gabriela was back. She was a calming, comforting, and loving presence in their lives. Riley wondered what she would have done without her through their recent difficulties.

April came into the kitchen and started helping her mother.

"You know what this means, don't you, Mom?" April said. "Gabriela coming back, I mean."

"I don't think so," Riley said.

"It means you can fly right back to Phoenix and get back on the job."

Riley was startled by the suggestion.

"But I just got here yesterday," Riley said.

April laughed a little as she chopped up some celery.

"Look, it's not like I'm not glad you're here," she said. "But you've got a bad guy to catch. And I'm going to be fine. I can get to Dr. Sloat's office by bus. And if I get shaky, I've got her number, and she says I can call her any time. And with Gabriela here, well …"

Gabriela had just stepped into the kitchen doorway.

"Your *hija* is right," she said. "April and I can handle things here."

Riley felt a surge of panic. April and Gabriela were both right, of course. She no longer had any excuse not to return to Phoenix. But to her alarm, she still couldn't seem to make a decision.

What's the matter with me? she wondered.

Then she remembered something else Mike Nevins had said …

"You keep right on thinking that you should be able to do the impossible. Why is that, do you think?"

In a flash, Riley knew the answer to that question—or at least where and how to find an answer. She collapsed into a kitchen chair, her tears finally flowing hard.

Gabriela and April huddled close to her, trying to comfort her.

"Mom, what's wrong?" April asked.

"I know where I've got to go," Riley said through her tears. "I know who I've got to see."

Chapter Thirty

Rain was pouring down hard the next day as Riley wended her way up into the Appalachian Mountains. The dirt roads were deep with mud, and the driving was rocky and rough. The disagreeable weather mirrored her feelings. Her rare visits to her father were never pleasant.

Still, she knew in her gut that this visit was necessary. The drive was taking her into more than just a mountainous wilderness. It was taking her into the very heart of her self-doubt. It was a part of her soul that she needed to look into without flinching. Otherwise she might never shake off her indecision and uncertainty.

Besides, she found the rain oddly refreshing. It was certainly a change after the dryness of the hot Arizona air. And the surrounding forest was still lush and green. The first frost hadn't yet hit to turn the leaves.

The rain showed no sign of letting up as she pulled up to the little cabin. Her father had bought this place and some surrounding acreage when he retired from the Marines. Generally speaking, visitors weren't welcome here. He didn't even have a phone or a computer to communicate with the outside world, although he sometimes got news during his occasional visits to the nearby town.

She opened an umbrella and rushed toward the door. She knocked—not that she expected anyone to answer or to welcome her inside. That just wasn't her father's way. But she heard someone coughing inside the cabin.

She opened the door and stepped inside. The single room was warm and dry, heated by a wood-burning cook stove. Grizzled and stooped, her father was seated on a stool, skinning a dead squirrel. Several naked squirrel carcasses were piled up next to him.

"Hi, Daddy," she said.

He didn't look up from his work. She didn't expect him to. He had just made the initial cuts and was pulling the pelt off of the carcass. Ever since she'd hunted with him as a little girl, she'd admired how he did that. He made it seem as smooth and graceful as helping a lady out of her coat on a dinner date.

He coughed loudly for a moment. Riley found it a strange sound coming from him. She couldn't remember him having been sick for a single day in their life together.

When he got control of his coughing, he said, "You came back in a hurry."

Riley understood what he meant. The last time she'd come to see him was a couple of months back, in July. Before that, more than two years had gone by without her making any attempt to contact him. And of course, no attempt at contact ever came from him.

Riley sat down, making herself as comfortable as she could on an uncomfortable wicker chair. Her father coughed again. He looked paler than the last time she was here—maybe a little thinner too. His hair was just slightly longer than the marine-style buzz cut he'd always worn.

"Are you sick, Daddy?" she said.

He chuckled grimly. "You'd like that, wouldn't you? Nothing would make you happier than to see me helpless and sick and at death's door. No such luck, girl. Not this time."

Riley felt her jaw tighten and her whole body tense up. This visit was turning ugly even faster than the last one.

"So what kind of a case are you working on these days?" he asked.

"Pretty much the usual," Riley said, finding herself dropping into his cold, detached manner of speech. "A serial killer out in Arizona. Murders prostitutes."

"Arizona, huh?"

He slit the squirrel down its abdomen and started to pull out its entrails.

"Scrawny little bastard," he grumbled.

The smell of squirrel guts wafted across the room toward Riley. She remembered it well. It wasn't pleasant, but it wasn't as bad as a decomposing human corpse.

"You're a long way from Arizona," he said. "What are you doing here?"

Riley didn't reply. Her back stiffened.

"Don't tell me," he said in a snarling half-cough, half-chuckle. "Things got the best of you. You went AWOL. You're wondering whether you're cut out for your line of work. Yeah, I felt that way in 'Nam from time to time. I never ran away from it, though. Deserting's frowned on in the Marines. Guess the Bureau's a little more lenient. Spoils you."

Riley emotionally braced herself. It was time to open up to a man who had no concept of what openness might be.

"A lot's happened since the last time I was here," she said. "April got captured by the last killer I took down. She almost got killed."

"April?" he asked with a grunt.

"My daughter. Your granddaughter."

156

He coughed a bit more. "Oh, yeah. How did she cope with it? Did she turn into a shivering ball of helpless fear?"

Riley felt pleased at what she got to say in reply.

"No. She helped me kill him."

Her father tossed the skinned and gutted squirrel into the pile and started to work on another carcass.

"Good girl," he said. "You ought to bring her around one of these days. I'd like to meet her sometime."

Not in this lifetime, Riley thought.

Her father kept on talking.

"So now you feel all guilty. You think maybe you're in the wrong line of work. You want to be a good little mother raising a good little girl. Shit. You know what I've got to say to all that."

"There are monsters out there, Daddy," Riley said. "I took her into a world of monsters."

He started to laugh, but his laughter broke down in coughing.

"What a load of crap. You think you're up against a monster in Arizona? A man who kills prostitutes? You're not dealing with a monster. Hell, you're not even dealing with evil. You're dealing with what folks call *normal.* This killer of yours—when he's not killing, he's a good man, a pillar of the community, a good husband, a good father. The opposite of me—and the opposite of you."

Riley knew, from the profile she herself was putting together, that he wasn't altogether wrong. But that didn't answer anything.

"If he's so good, why does he keep killing women?" Riley asked.

Her father stopped cutting the squirrel in mid-knife stroke. The question seemed to interest him. He looked Riley straight in the eye.

"Why do you keep killing men?" he asked.

Riley felt as if she'd been plunged into a freezing lake. It was a good question. It was an important question. It was exactly the question she'd come here hoping to have answered.

"You're a hunter," her father said, still holding her gaze. "What folks call normal—it would kill you if you tried living it too long. Truth is, it kills everybody, all that goddamn *normalness.* It's not natural, it's against human nature. Makes folks crazy with boredom. Makes them kill for no reason at all. Now, you and me, we've got our reasons for killing. We're good animals that way. We know who we are. These killers you hunt down and kill—they just don't have the proper insight. They don't know themselves. They get all out of control."

He continued to hold her gaze.

157

"Reminds me of a saying. 'In a mad world, only the mad are sane.' Can't remember who said it. But it's true, and that's you and me all over. Mad people in a mad world full of people who've got no reason to be sane. We're the only folks who've got any idea what's really going on."

He lowered his eyes and stared at the floor, speaking almost in a whisper.

"You'll go back to work. You'll head back on the next plane you can catch. I know it. You don't have a choice. I never gave you a choice. I raised you right, to be a hunter. Wish I'd done as well by your sister, but it's too late to fix that."

Riley felt like she'd gotten an electric shock. She couldn't remember the last time he'd ever mentioned Wendy. It seemed uncanny, because Riley had been thinking of her a lot lately.

"Maybe I didn't treat her right," he said.

"You used to hit her," Riley said.

Her father grunted and nodded slowly. "That's what I mean. I only hit her with my hands. Bruised her up a little on the outside, that's all. Didn't hit her deep enough. I knew better by the time you were growing up. I never laid a hand on you. I hit you a lot deeper than that. You learned. You learned."

He coughed for a long time now. Riley could see that he was very sick. But there was no point in trying to talk to him about it.

When his coughing passed away, he said, "I'd ask you to stay for some squirrel stew. But you don't want to hang around with a mean old bastard like me. You're ready to get the hell out of here."

He was absolutely right, but Riley didn't say so.

Instead she said, "I don't hate you, Daddy."

"You're either lying or you're a fool," he said.

Riley bristled at this.

"What the hell's that supposed to mean?"

"It means just what I said. If you don't hate me, I didn't do my job right."

He coughed some more. He seemed very ill. Riley wanted to pity him. But she wasn't going to let herself do that. He'd really made her mad.

Sarcastically she said, "Well, while we're on the subject of the 'job' you did, maybe I should thank you. I learned a lot from your example. I learned everything there was to learn about how *not* to be a parent."

"Stupid," he said. "You're probably raising that girl of yours to *love* you. She'll grow up weak. You'll live to regret it."

158

"What do you know about regret?" Riley snapped.

"Not much. And I'm proud of it. You ought to be grateful, you whiny little bitch."

By now Riley had had enough. She'd put up with this kind of abuse all her life. She'd never fought back. All she'd ever done was walk away. The time for walking away was over.

She stood facing him, too close for either of their comfort.

"Do you have any mirrors here, Daddy? I'll bet you don't. You wouldn't like what you saw."

"And what might that be?"

"A coward. A sick, frightened little man who never had the guts to love. A man who bullied little children instead of men his own size."

His eyes twisted with fury. He raised his open hand and swung it hard at her face. She deftly deflected the blow with her wrist.

"Go ahead, try to hit me," she said back, defiant. "You can't anymore. I'm stronger than you now, Daddy. You can't touch me ever again."

With a roar of rage, he reared back, then launched a punch at her face. Riley reached up and caught his fist with her hand, holding it in her own viselike grip. She took a step toward him.

She snarled, "Try that again, and I swear to God, I'll kill you where you stand."

Now his mouth curled into a malicious grin. Riley felt an icy chill. He was loving this. Her hatred was what he lived for. It was all that he had left to call his own.

But she refused to become like him. She wasn't going to waste her hatred on him.

She loosed her grip on his fist and shoved it away. She looked him squarely in the eye.

She said again, "I don't hate you, Daddy. I refuse to hate you, no matter how hard you try."

He looked wounded now. He hadn't looked wounded when she'd said that before. What had changed?

He believes me this time, she thought.

After all, it was the most hurtful thing she could possibly say to him. She'd taken away his most treasured possession in the world.

Riley turned and walked away. Just as she opened the door to leave, she heard him yell one more thing.

"Never trust a man whose kids don't hate him."

Even for her father, it seemed to her like a cynical thing to say. But she wouldn't respond to it. She stepped outside and shut the door behind her. She didn't bother to open her umbrella. The rain felt good. She just stood there on the front stoop and let it pour all over her.

The visit had turned sour, just like she'd expected. Still, it had served its purpose. She remembered what Mike Nevins had said to her.

"I'm not sure you can get through this without some kind of emotional catharsis."

Her father had given her that catharsis. And now she even had rain to complete the cleansing.

No doubt about it, her father was sick. But if he wasn't going to reach out for help, or even admit he was sick, there wasn't anything for Riley or anybody else to do. She didn't have to see him ever again. And she sure as hell didn't plan to.

She felt like herself now. And for the first time since she'd started working on this case, she felt the palpable presence of the killer. And he wasn't the least bit like her.

He's lived a successful life, she realized.

Unlike her, the killer had done everything that he was supposed to do, and he'd never felt any contradiction about it. As far as he was concerned, killing whores was just a way to let off steam, like playing golf or bridge. There was nothing wrong with it. There was nothing wrong with him.

It was all falling into place now. He was a killer, nothing more. But Riley was a hunter. She knew what she was doing in life, he didn't. He was her unsuspecting prey. And she was going to take him down.

She got into her car and started to drive. As she made her way down the rain-drenched mountain, she remembered something else Mike Nevins had said to her …

"There's not always a single right *thing to do."*

She smiled. She was at peace with that now.

Chapter Thirty One

As the john opened the motel door for her, Socorro wondered why she was feeling nervous about him. T.R. had a lot of class.

But maybe that's what's weird, she thought as she walked into the room. What kind of classy john would pick up a streetwalker? Wasn't he more of the escort or call girl type?

When he had picked her up, she'd actually thought he would want her services right there in the car like some johns did. Instead he had driven her all the way outside of Phoenix, saying he wanted to find some peace and quiet. He'd brought her to this motel near a small town, renting a room in the back part of the building. From what she had seen there was nothing behind the place but desert.

She wasn't completely comfortable with the set-up. For one thing, she wouldn't be able to catch a bus home like she usually did in the city. She'd have to wait for him to drive her back into town.

She'd get home later than usual. But her daughter, Mari, was old enough to take care of her two younger brothers. Mari could fix them dinner, but she'd have very little to work with tonight. Socorro had planned to stop on the way home and pick up fast food burgers for all of them. And fries. And something sweet too, maybe milkshakes.

Most johns didn't seem to pick up on the fact that she was a mother. Of course, she worked hard not to act like one. Out on the streets, she always played the feisty stereotypical spitfire of a Latina *chola.* The men she went with wouldn't even recognize the mother she was at home.

Meanwhile, it was a decent motel, and T.R. was being very nice. He'd brought a bottle of scotch with him, and he was pouring two glasses. He handed one to her.

"Water or ice?" he asked. "Or anything to mix it with?"

"I'm good," Socorro said with a smile. It was rare enough for a john to treat her to a drink. She wasn't going to get picky about it. She took a sip. It tasted expensive.

"Take off your blouse," he said.

Socorro was happy to follow orders. She pulled off the blouse and leaned back on the bed. She had nothing on underneath, but she had no problem with going half-naked, or fully naked. She would do whatever the johns wanted as far as clothing was concerned, and most activities too.

"Anything else?" she asked.

"Not right now."

So she would wait until he told her to take off her short skirt, fishnet tights, and spiked heels. Or maybe he would want to do that for her. Socorro told herself that she was only feeling wary because he was smoother and slower than her usual clients. He wasn't in a hurry like so many of them were.

He sat down beside her on the bed and began to stroke her body. He ran his fingers across her breasts and then up her legs, feeling her beneath her skirt.

But something seemed off. He was breathing rather loudly—but it wasn't the kind of breathing she expected with arousal.

He's having trouble getting it up, she realized.

But she could take care of that. Sometimes the johns couldn't perform well, but Socorro could usually make them happy one way or another. She might have to really work at it, but T.R. was worth some effort.

After all, she was spooked about nothing. Those news stories had gotten her all worked up—all that stuff about some serial killer taking prostitutes. Not that there had been a lot of details. Socorro figured maybe it was just hype during a dull news week. But it was messing up life on the street. More cops were out there than usual, scaring both johns and working girls away.

But Socorro didn't have the luxury of staying off the street. She needed money, and she needed it today. She had kids to feed and rent to pay. And although none of regulars had showed up, she'd gotten lucky with T.R.

She'd seen him before in that big expensive car of his. She'd even tried to talk to him once, but he'd driven away when her stupid pimp barged in.

¡Pinche Pablo! she thought.

Anyway, T.R. had to be all right. It was not like he was hiding from the law or anything like that.

After a few moments of idle fondling, he got up from the bed.

"I've brought you a gift," he said.

Socorro was surprised. Who ever bought gifts for streetwalkers like her?

He took a little flat box out of his pocket and held it out to her.

Socorro gasped when she opened it. Inside was a lovely little necklace.

"This is for me?" she cried.

"Especially for you," he said. "I picked it out with you in mind. The diamond is real."

162

She smiled with delight. She knew he was lying, of course. He hadn't had *her* especially in mind. How was that even possible? He'd have given the necklace to any whore who'd gone with him. But she wasn't complaining.

"I don't know what to say," she said.

He smiled back at her. "How about *muchisimas gracias?*"

She laughed aloud. "*Muchisimas gracias*—and then some!"

He glanced around the room. "Put it on," he said. "I've got some toys out in the car. I'll be right back."

As soon as he went out the door, Socorro got up and put on the necklace, checking it out in the mirror. It was a slender silver chain with one nice simple stone. She thought she looked rather glamorous, naked to the waist except for the necklace.

She sighed. She deserved this and much more. She often thought that she should try for a better class of work, like an escort service. Then she could get away from *pinche* Pablo. Working with a madam instead of a pimp would be a welcome change.

Meanwhile, she wasn't going to get all sentimental about this expensive trinket. She was nothing to T.R., and he was nothing to her. She'd sell the necklace as soon as she got a chance. She could buy groceries, maybe even take a week off.

Or maybe not, she thought.

If she was going to move up in the world, shouldn't she keep it? A call girl or an escort needed her jewelry. Maybe this was a start in that direction.

But as she looked at herself in the mirror, something vague started to trouble her. It had something to do with a necklace and nakedness …

Then she remembered. It had been on TV—a necklace a lot like this one. A dead woman had been found in some lake outside of town, naked and wearing just such a necklace.

The woman had been one of the killer's victims.

Panic overwhelmed Socorro. She couldn't meet the same fate. She had a life to live. She had kids to feed and take care of. What would become of them if she never came home?

But maybe she was wrong. Maybe she was scared about nothing. Maybe everything was going to be all right.

She opened the front door slowly, just a little, hoping he wouldn't notice. It was dark outside, and the light above the door was out. The parking lot wasn't well lit. Even so, she could see him by the trunk light of his car, not more than fifteen feet away. His back was toward her and he was searching for something. In one hand he held a coil of rope.

Her heart was pounding now. Should she scream? Would anybody hear her? Nobody else was in sight. There weren't even many cars parked out back. The motel seemed to be mostly vacant.

There was only one thing to do. She kicked off her spiked heels, pushed the door wide open, and ran. She heard the man cursing as she rushed past him.

Socorro had no idea where to run, so she just went where her feet carried her. In moments, the parking lot pavement gave way to gravel and then to rocky dirt. Darkness closed in on all sides as she mindlessly ran on and on. Her feet hurt badly from the rough, stony sand and desert weeds. Her legs and her naked torso were whipped by low brambly plants. But her feet kept carrying her on and on.

Soon she had no idea how far she'd run. She was in shock from pain, bleeding, and fear. How much time had passed since she fled that motel room? Just a few minutes? An hour?

She felt like her heart would explode and her lungs would burst. She stumbled to a halt and fell to her knees, momentarily deafened by her own gasping and the pounding of her pulse.

But as her breathing slowed, she heard another sound. It was distant traffic. She looked around and saw headlights moving along some distance away.

¡Tonta! she thought.

In her panic, she had angled toward the desert instead of toward the highway. She turned around. The lights of the motel were far behind her. She saw no one between her and the motel. Hadn't he followed her?

She hurt all over and couldn't run another step. It was chilly now, and she was almost naked, and she was shivering from both the cold and fear.

But she had to keep moving. She limped painfully toward the highway.

As she neared the road, an approaching car slowed down. It was a big, fancy car—T.R.'s car, she was sure of it. The car pulled beside her and came to a stop.

The passenger door opened. She could see T.R. driving.

"What's the matter with you?" he called out. He was holding her blouse in one hand. "You forgot this. Get in, put it on. I'll drive you home."

But there was no way she was getting into the car with him. She ran past the car out onto the highway. Big headlights were bearing down on her. It looked like a truck. She hoped it was a truck.

Socorro ran toward the lights, waving her arms. For the first time since she'd started running, she screamed.

Chapter Thirty Two

At seven a.m. Riley walked into the office of Special Agent in Charge Elgin Morley. Bill was already there, and Morley was sitting behind his desk.

Bill smiled at her. Morley scowled.

Well, the feeling sure is mutual, Riley thought, taking a seat.

This whole situation seemed like a dream. Her life had taken a mad whirl after she visited her father yesterday. As soon as she'd gotten home, she'd called Brent Meredith in Quantico to tell him she wanted to get back to work. He'd said he'd work things out with Morley and get back to her the next day.

Instead, she'd been awakened by a phone call at 3:00 this morning. It had been Morley. He'd gruffly told her that she was needed in Phoenix right away. A BAU car had picked her up at home and driven her to Quantico, where an FBI jet was waiting to take her back to Phoenix.

And now here she was, feeling exhausted and disoriented. At the same time, she was glad to be back on the job. And she was grateful that Gabriela and April had everything under control at home. They'd more than understood that she needed to get back to work.

Morley's gaze was anything but friendly. Riley reminded herself that he'd had perfectly sound professional reasons to take her off the case. Still, she couldn't help but be pissed off about it.

Without so much as a word of greeting, Morley started right in his explanations.

"We've had a new development. Maybe even a break in the case. Bill already knows the details, but I'll fill you in too, Agent Paige."

He looked over notes that he'd written down.

"Late last night, a trucker couple picked up a woman near the town of Luning. She was half naked, cut up, and hysterical. They didn't know what was wrong with her, except that she seemed to be running away from somebody. They took her to the Luning cops, who noticed that she was wearing an expensive necklace. That led them to think it might have something to do with our case. So they brought her here, along with the trucker couple."

"Are they still here?" Riley asked. "I mean the couple and the woman?"

"They're all here," Morley said. "The couple, Hannah and Troy Coddington, are in the interview room right now. We've identified the woman as Socorro Barrera. She's in the clinic, still in shock and pretty much incoherent."

Riley mulled over the situation. She wanted to talk with the woman. But was that even possible? Perhaps, but she needed more information first.

"Bill and I will talk to the couple," she said.

"Let's go, then," Morley said.

The three of them left the office and headed toward the interview room. Riley and Bill went into the room, and Morley entered the adjacent room. Riley knew that he'd be watching and listening. That was fine with her.

Hannah and Troy Coddington were sitting at the table. They were both rugged, heavy-set, and clad in overalls. Riley wasn't sure which of them was the more heavily tattooed.

As Bill and Riley introduced themselves, Riley noticed that the Coddingtons looked worried.

"Should we get in touch with a lawyer?" Troy asked.

Hannah added, "We ain't got a regular lawyer, but maybe you can fix us up with one."

Riley was a bit surprised by the question.

"Why?" she asked.

Hannah said, "Well, me and Troy know it don't look good, us picking up a half-naked woman on the highway, and probably a hooker at that. But we ain't traffickers, we swear to God. We hate those bastards. We really do. We were just trying to help this poor girl."

Riley and Bill smiled at each other.

"We understand," Bill said. "We're not holding you as suspects. We're not holding you at all. But we'd appreciate any help you can give us."

"Could you tell us exactly what happened?" Riley asked.

Hannah began, "Well, it was getting close to midnight. We'd just dropped off a shipment in Luning and were planning to stay in a motel that night."

"The Nopal Inn," Troy said. "Right near Luning."

Hannah continued. "Troy was driving, and suddenly we saw her in the road up ahead. First she looked like a ghost in the glare of the headlights, but she wasn't no ghost. She was naked from the waist up, and she wasn't wearing shoes. I yelled for Troy to stop."

Troy shuddered at the memory.

"Scared me half to death," he said. "I braked and swerved, almost jackknifed the truck, could have killed us all. It's a miracle I didn't."

Hannah also shuddered and shook her head. She said, "She came running up to my side of the truck, yelling mostly in Mexican. We couldn't understand much of it, except somebody was after her and she wanted us to save her."

"We didn't stop to ask a lot of questions," Troy said. "Hannah got her up into the truck, and I drove us on out of there."

Hannah said, "I took her to the back of the cab, we've got a mattress there. Poor thing, she was cut up from head to foot, and what few clothes she had on was all tore up. I wrapped her up in a blanket. She was shivering and her teeth was chattering. She went into shock right then and there—and I'm talking *deep* shock. Never heard her say another word."

"We drove her straight to the police, and they brought us all here," Troy said.

Riley tried to visualize the scene. A lot of details were missing. Where had the woman come running from? Had she jumped out of a moving vehicle? She hoped that Socorro would soon be coherent enough to tell more of the story.

"Did you see any vehicles parked nearby?" Bill asked.

"There was a good-sized car pulled over on the shoulder," Troy said. "Black, I think. But I didn't get the make. Guess we should have thought to get the plate number, but everything happened so fast. The car sped away."

"That's all right," Riley said. "You did everything you could. In fact, I'm sure that you saved that poor woman's life. When she gets better, I'm sure she'll want to thank you personally."

Bill turned toward Riley. With a look, he was silently asking her if they had further questions. She shook her head no.

"You may go, Mr. and Mrs. Coddington." Bill pushed a pad of paper and a pencil across the table toward. "But before you go, please jot down your contact information. And give us a call if you remember more details. Anything at all."

After the exchange of information, Bill and Riley escorted the couple out of the interview room. As Troy and Hannah walked away down the hall, Morley stepped out of the adjoining room.

"I didn't tell you to let them go," he grumbled.

"They told us all they know," Riley snapped. "Let's go to the clinic. I want to talk with the woman."

"She's in no condition to talk," Morley said.

"Let me be the judge of that," Riley replied.

As they walked toward the clinic, Riley realized she'd better ease up on her hostility toward Morley. She was tired and jetlagged, and she was letting her crankiness get the best of her. He could still yank her off the case for insubordination. And after her previous suspension, that could spell real trouble for her.

Try to be civil, she told herself.

A single male physician was on duty in the clinic. Socorro Barrera, clad in a hospital gown, was sitting upright in a bed. She was holding a silver chain, running it through her fingers, nodding her head monotonously and muttering in Spanish.

"She's been like this for hours," the doctor said. "She was a little more coherent when she first got here. She kept asking about her *hijas*—her children. She gave us an address. We sent a social worker to look after her kids. They're there right now. The kids are OK. But she's been like this ever since."

The woman kept muttering and fingering the chain.

"That chain is evidence," the doctor said. "We tried to take it, but she won't let go of it."

Riley bent closer to her. Now she could make out what she was saying …

"Dios te salve, María. Llena eres de gracia: El Señor es contigo …"

Riley understood right away. In her state of shocked dissociation, Socorro had convinced herself that the necklace was a rosary. She was fingering it and repeating Hail Marys in Spanish.

Damn it, the doctor ought to have figured that out by now, she thought.

And now here the poor woman was, surrounded by men except for Riley.

Riley wanted to yell at the others to get out of the room. But she reminded herself to keep her cool.

"I'd like a few minutes alone with her, please," she said.

The men went out of the room, leaving Riley and Socorro Barrera alone.

"Socorro," Riley said in soft voice.

But the woman just kept fingering the chain.

"Santa María, Madre de Dios, ruega por nosotros pecadores …"

Riley at her closely. Her face wore the remnants of heavy, colorful makeup—a flamboyant Latina look. But the makeup was all a mess now from tears and sweat and dirt. Socorro was heavily bandaged all over, and she was bruised in many other places.

Did somebody beat her up? Riley wondered.

No, these didn't look like those kinds of wounds. They didn't come from a fist or a knife. She'd gotten them running, probably through some tough terrain. The truckers had said it was near a town called Luning. The town must have been out on the desert. The woman's feet were under the bed sheet. Riley guessed that they must have been cut up especially badly.

"Socorro, *me llamo* Riley. I know something terrible happened to you. I'm here to help you."

The woman kept murmuring her prayer and fingering the chain.

Riley touched Socorro on her fingers. Socorro stopped moving her fingers and stared into Riley's eyes. Riley shivered. In all her years as an agent, she'd seldom seen such a frightened look.

"*¿Hablas inglés?*" Riley asked. She doubted that her Spanish was good enough to conduct such a delicate interview.

To Riley's relief, Socorro nodded.

Riley fingered the chain herself.

"This is pretty," Riley said. "Where did you get it?"

The whole time Socorro had been fingering the chain, she hadn't looked at it. Now she did. Her eyes bulged with terror. She fumbled with the chain, taking it off and pushing it into Riley's hands.

"*Tómalo,*" she said. "Take it, please. I don't want it."

Riley held the chain up for her to see.

"But it's pretty," she said. "Where did you get it?"

Socorro cringed, backing away from Riley, shivering violently.

"He gave it to me," she said.

"Who gave it to you, Socorro?"

Socorro broke eye contact now, and her eyes began to glaze over again. She was about to slip back into her state of shock. Riley squeezed her hand gently.

"I want to help," Riley said. "But you've got to talk to me."

Riley's touch and kindly tone brought Socorro back. She looked at Riley again with the eyes of a frightened animal.

"I was out walking," she said, in much the same numb voice as when she'd been saying the prayer. "Down on Conover Avenue."

"Where the working girls go," Riley said.

Socorro nodded. "Yes, but I …"

Her voice trailed off. Riley patted her hand.

"It's OK, Socorro. I'm not here to judge. Nobody's going to arrest you. Everybody's on your side. All I want to do is help."

Socorro squinted, trying to remember.

"He had a nice car and he looked like he had money," she said. "His car was parked and I walked right over to him. I told him I'd like to go with him. Right there in the car if he wanted, I said. But he wanted to go someplace else. He drove way outside of town. To a little motel."

Riley remembered the motel that the Coddingtons had mentioned.

"The Nopal Inn?" she asked.

Socorro nodded.

"We went into the room," she said.

"Did you have sex there?" Riley asked.

Socorro shook her head. "No. I was ready to. But I don't think he could."

Riley had suspected that the killer had problems performing sexually. Again she held the necklace for Socorro to see.

"And he gave this to you," she said. "Was it in a box?"

"I think so."

"Was the name of a store on the box?"

Pain showed in Socorro's face as she tried to remember.

"I don't remember. But then he went out to the car, and I got worried, because I knew that another woman was murdered wearing a necklace. I looked and he was getting a rope out of the car."

"And then you ran," Riley said.

"*Sí.*"

The rest of her story was pretty easy to fill in. Riley's earlier guess had been correct. She'd gotten her physical wounds during her escape, running through rough vegetation and across rocky ground. She'd been extraordinarily lucky.

"What did he look like?" Riley asked.

Socorro just stared at her as if she didn't understand the question.

"Was he tall, short, medium height?" Riley asked.

Socorro seemed even more confused.

"Can you remember anything about his face?" Riley asked. "The color of his hair, maybe?"

Tears formed in Socorro's eyes. Trembling all over, she shook her head.

Riley sighed. She understood exactly what was going on. She'd seen this happen with witnesses before. The poor woman was repressing all memories of the man's appearance. It was simply too painful to remember. They'd have to work with her on retrieving that image, but she might never allow herself to remember.

Yet again, Riley flashed back to her own captivity with Peterson, and how she'd struggled with those memories.

Riley couldn't blame Socorro for blocking it out. Trying to force her to remember would only cause her pain and produce no results.

"I'm sorry," Socorro said. "I can't remember."

Riley stroked her hand.

"It's all right," Riley said. "I understand."

Tears began to pour down the woman's face. She started to sob.

"I thought he was OK. He seemed nice, classy. I thought T.R. was OK."

The initials hit Riley like a bullet.

"T.R.?" she said. "His name was T.R.?"

"*Sí,* it was what he called himself."

Riley was seized by self-reproach. She remembered what Ruthie had said about the man back at the Iguana Lounge …

"T.R., he calls himself."

T.R. was the name of the man who had frightened the women at the Desert King truck stop. In some part of her mind, Riley had been hoping that the suspect that she and Bill had failed to catch that night wasn't the real killer. But now there could be no mistake about it.

If only we'd caught him, Riley thought. *If only we hadn't let him get away.*

And now, after his bungled attack on Socorro, Riley knew exactly what to expect.

He was going to strike again soon—if he hadn't already.

Chapter Thirty Three

It was morning, and the man was driving along the familiar stretch of Conover Avenue. He didn't see any of the usual streetwalkers—nor did he expect to, not at this hour. The truth was, he didn't know what to expect, or what he hoped to do.

He was exhausted. And he hated to admit it even to himself, but he was scared.

The whole thing with Socorro late last night had been a disaster. For the first time, a woman he had targeted escaped his clutches. And where was she now?

After he'd pulled up beside her, she had run out into the highway and seemed about to be run down by a truck. He'd driven away fast, but then had turned off the highway and stopped to see what had happened. She'd watched a woman help Socorro into the truck.

Why couldn't the bitch have been killed? he thought.

He'd tried to follow the truck, but quickly got separated from it in traffic. So where had she gone next? Had the truckers taken her to the police? Had she told the police that a man had tried to kill her?

No, he wouldn't let himself believe that. A whore, turning to the police for help? Surely not.

All the same, he wasn't sure he was thinking things through rationally. He'd barely slept last night, despite taking a strong sedative. He'd kept awakening himself with his own curses of frustration.

And now here he was—hoping to do what? Did he seriously think that he'd find Socorro here this morning? No, but maybe he could get some clue as to where to find her. And he really needed to find her, before she talked. If she hadn't talked already. He needed to finish the job he'd failed to do last night.

It angered and upset him that killing her would be no pleasure. He'd never killed from necessity before. If only the others he had selected hadn't gotten into the news. If only he'd been able to keep them his own personal secret.

Damned publicity, he thought.

It was the last thing he'd wanted, but now he was stuck with it.

He saw a woman walking his way—a streetwalker, there was no mistaking her for anything else.

He rolled down his window and called out to her.

"Hey, I wonder if you could help me."

The woman turned and smiled and walked toward his car.

"Anything you'd like, pal," she said.

As she came toward him, he thought he recognized her face. Where had he seen her before. He thought it might have been at one of those truck stops, maybe. Hank's Derby. Or the Desert King.

She seemed to recognize him too, and her smile disappeared.

"I'm looking for a girl named Socorro," he said. "Could you help me find her?"

The hooker didn't reply. She wheeled around and walked away from him.

"I owe her money," he called out. "I didn't have enough on me last night, and I don't want to shortchange her. She gave me a great time."

The woman didn't seem to be listening. She'd gotten out her cell phone and appeared to be making a call.

Determined to ignore me, he thought. *What's the matter with that stupid whore?*

Just then he was startled by a loud tap-tap on his passenger window. A girl he'd never seen before was tapping on the glass.

He lowered the window.

"How about giving me a ride, mister?" the girl said.

She was a slender blonde, and she was wearing a backpack. He smiled at her. He was pleased that she'd approached him. It was the first thing that had gone right so far today.

"Do you know Socorro?" he asked.

The girl shrugged and grinned.

"Sure. We go way back, Socorro and me."

"Then get in," he said. He unlocked the passenger door, and the girl plopped herself inside.

"So tell me about Socorro," he said.

"Hey, give me a ride first," the girl said. "I don't care where. To the edge of town, maybe. Anywhere."

He wondered if she really knew Socorro at all. But maybe it didn't matter. She was a obviously a hooker, or she wouldn't be walking alone in this neighborhood. She'd serve his purposes nicely.

Yes, she was exactly what he needed right now. She'd get his mind off of Socorro. He'd have his fun with her. And she was so charmingly unsuspecting. She really had no idea.

As he pulled away from the curb, he heard somebody shouting behind him. He couldn't make out the words. He looked into the rearview mirror and saw the other older hooker chasing after his car, waving an arm and yelling.

The crazy bitch, he thought.

She'd deliberately ignored him, and now she was mad that he was driving off with someone else.

To hell with her, he thought.

She'd missed her chance. And she had no idea how lucky she was.

Chapter Thirty Four

Riley was still in the FBI clinic when an assistant informed her that she was being called to the conference room. Morley wanted to talk to both Bill and Riley.

Grill us is more like it, Riley thought with dread.

Meanwhile, she wasn't at all happy with how Socorro had been treated so far.

She snapped at the male doctor, "Call the social worker who's with Socorro's kids at home. Bring the kids here. They need their mother, and she needs them. When Socorro's better, get them all to a shelter where they'll all be safe."

The doctor gave Riley a condescending smile.

"Yes, *ma'am*," he said.

Jesus, Riley thought. *The last thing Socorro needs right now is this patriarchal pig.*

"And get a female nurse in here to take care of Socorro," she said. "Get *two* female nurses. And you—make yourself as scarce as possible."

The doctor repeated, "Yes, *ma'am*."

Riley's blood boiled. But now was no time to lose her temper. She headed straight for the conference room, where Morley and Bill were waiting.

"Did you get any information from the woman in the clinic?" Morley asked.

"The man at the Desert King was our guy for sure," Riley said. "He calls himself T.R."

"And you two lost him," Morley said, glaring at Riley.

Riley gulped hard.

Bill said, "Yes, sir. We did. It won't happen again."

"Did she give you anything else?" Morley asked Riley.

Riley shook her head.

"She's repressing any details. She couldn't give me a physical description at all."

Morley drummed his fingers on the table.

"Maybe we should have her hypnotized," he said.

Riley breathed slowly. She didn't like the idea at all. But given Morley's present mood, she had to state her objections coolly.

"Sir, with due respect, how often has hypnosis worked out for you in the past? In my experience, all it does is get a witness to confabulate. It's like any kind of recovered memory—extremely unreliable. Anyway, now is not the time. All we'd do is cause her further trauma without getting information."

Morley nodded reluctantly.

"So we've got precisely nothing," he said.

Neither Bill nor Riley replied. Riley's phone buzzed. She saw that the call was from Ruthie Lapham, the woman who ran the Iguana Lounge at the Desert King truck stop.

"I'd better take this," Riley said to Morley and Bill.

She retreated to the far side of the room to talk to Ruthie.

"Ruthie, what's going on?"

Ruthie sounded breathless and upset.

"Agent Paige, he's got a girl. T.R.'s taken a girl."

"What?" Riley asked. "Who? How do you know?"

Ruthie said nothing for a few seconds. She seemed to be trying to collect herself.

"Maybe you remember Jewel," Ruthie said. "She's the woman who stopped you in my bar."

A sour taste rose in Riley's mouth. She remembered how Jewel had blocked her way just when the suspect had been in sight. Flanked by two other women, Jewel had ruined everything.

"Yeah, I remember Jewel," Riley said.

"Well, Jewel was just now working on Conover Avenue. It's not usual for a working girl to go out on a morning, but Jewel needed cash, and the girls on Conover can get real territorial at night, so morning was the best she could do, and …"

"Please get to the point, Ruthie," Riley said.

She heard Ruthie take a deep breath.

"Jewel saw this girl on the street, not more than fourteen, wearing a backpack, probably a runaway looking for a ride. Jewel told the girl she was in a bad neighborhood, tried to talk her into going home, but she wouldn't. Jewel didn't get her name. That very same minute, T.R. rolls up in a big car, and yells out to Jewel something about a girl named Socorro."

The names piqued Riley's attention.

Ruthie continued, "Well, I'd told the girls 'round here that T.R. was dangerous, and to call me if they ever see him. So Jewel got on the phone to me right away. But while she and I were talking, she saw that poor girl climb into T.R.'s car. Jewel ran after them yelling, but T.R. drove away and didn't stop."

Riley's heart was beating faster now.

"Did Jewel get a license number?" Riley asked.

Ruthie let out an irritated sigh.

"Well, no, she did not. You might have noticed, Jewel's not too smart even for a hooker, which is really saying something. I asked her, and she said she didn't even think of it. She said it was a big car, though—a Buick or a Cadillac or a BMW, something like that."

Riley thought fast about what to do next.

"Can you get in touch with Jewel?" she asked.

"Sure, I can call her right now."

Riley was about to suggest that Ruthie tell Jewel to go to the police. But of course, a hooker wasn't going to do that.

Finally Riley said, "Tell Jewel to come out to your bar right away. Do you think she'll do that?"

"Sure, if I tell her to," Ruthie said.

"Good. Keep her there until I can send an agent out to talk to her. Surely she can remember something more."

"I'll get right on it," Ruthie said.

Riley ended the call and hurried right over to Bill and Morley.

"The suspect has been spotted. A hooker saw him cruising along Conover Avenue. He picked up a young girl with a backpack—probably just a teen runaway, not a streetwalker."

Morley's expression looked doubtful.

"That doesn't sound like his MO," he said.

Riley didn't say so, but she couldn't disagree. Abduction wasn't this man's style, nor was taking any woman who wasn't a prostitute. She'd never have predicted that he'd snatch up a teen runaway.

But Bill said, "I'm not surprised. He's getting sloppy, and he let things get out of control last night. He's liable to start doing things differently. He also might start making more mistakes."

This made good sense to Riley.

"Well, right now he's got a girl," she said, "so we've got no time to lose. The hooker's name is Jewel. She'll be at the Iguana Lounge at the Desert King truck stop. I need to get out there to talk to her."

Morley said, "We can send an agent to get her statement."

"I need to see her myself. You should put out an APB for the car."

"For what?" Morley scoffed. "Buick? Cadillac? BMW?"

"I don't know. For a big dark car leaving Conover Avenue."

"That's too vague to do any good."

"Something needs to do us some good," Riley snapped.

A knock on the conference room door interrupted the argument.

"Come in," Morley said.

A familiar shock of closely cropped rainbow-colored hair popped through the door. It was Igraine, the technopagan technician. She looked eager and excited.

"I've got a feeling maybe the Uber-Spirit is smiling," she said, coming into the room.

"What have you got, Igraine?" Morley asked.

"Well, Agent Paige, you said it was likely that our killer was HIV positive. And I said that it wouldn't be easy finding him among ten thousand local patients. But you also mentioned that he might be taking drugs illicitly. Actually, that seems pretty likely to me, doesn't it to you?"

Riley thought for a moment. Their profile, after all, was of a successful, educated man. Such a man might be very anxious to keep his condition a secret.

"It makes sense to me," Riley said.

Igraine said, "I did some searching and ran across a cop who has been investigating thefts of drugs from hospitals. Some of them are HIV medicines. The cop told me that we should get in touch a certain Dr. Gordon Poole. He's offered his services to help the police on cases like that. Does everything pro bono. He could have lots of information."

Morley nodded with approval.

"I know Gordon," he said. "A very well-respected man, an infectious disease specialist. He's offered us his expertise on several cases. Paige, Jeffreys, you should go talk to him right now. I'll let him know you're on your way."

"That could be helpful," Bill said.

"And," Morley said firmly to Riley, "I will send an agent to get this Jewel's statement."

Riley stifled a retort and went out the door.

Chapter Thirty Five

A little while later, Riley and Bill arrived at Dr. Gordon Poole's house.

This isn't where I'm needed, Riley thought.

Still, Bill had persuaded her to follow orders.

Poole had told Morley that he wouldn't be in his office today, and had suggested that Bill and Riley visit him at home.

It was a big, modern, single-story home spread across a wide green lawn. The front yard was adorned with hedges and leafy trees. Unlike the little patches of green she had seen in some Phoenix neighborhoods, the lawns here were expansive, their wealthy owners pointedly ignoring the desert beneath the city.

They were greeted at the door by a cheerful but rather tired-looking man of about forty. Dr. Gordon Poole had thinning hair and a boyish face with an open, kindly expression.

"Gosh, I hadn't expected you so soon!" he said. "Come on in!"

Riley was slightly amused. She couldn't remember the last time she'd heard a grown man say "gosh." The expression struck her as delightfully quaint.

Poole escorted them into a comfortable, carpeted living room and invited them to sit down.

"It's some hot weather we're having, isn't it?" Dr. Poole said. "Maybe the two of you would like some fresh-squeezed lemonade. I always keep some in the fridge, and I like to share it when I can. Please say yes!"

Riley was utterly charmed by his smile and the innocent twinkle in his eye.

"I'd love some," she said.

"I would too," Bill said.

"Excellent!" Dr. Poole said. He disappeared into the kitchen.

Bill sat down on the sofa, but Riley was drawn to a cluster of family photographs hanging on one wall. They all showed Dr. Poole sharing happy moments with children—his kids, Riley felt pretty sure. In one, Dr. Poole and a boy of about twelve were holding a huge fish they'd just caught. In another, Dr. Poole was beaming over a little girl dressed up as a honeybee.

Must be a Halloween costume, Riley thought. *Or maybe for a school play.*

Her musings were interrupted when Dr. Poole came back. He was carrying a tray with glasses and a pitcher of lemonade.

"I see you've discovered my kids," he said.

Riley heard a world of warmth and pride in his voice.

"I take it they're at school right now," Riley said.

A pang of sadness flashed across his face.

"I'm afraid they don't live with me," he said. "Their mother and I are divorced. Have been for four years now."

Riley felt embarrassed to have touched on such a sensitive subject.

"I'm sorry," she said.

"Oh, gosh, don't be!" he said, his boyish smile returning. "It was perfectly amicable. She's a lawyer, got a job in Connecticut she couldn't refuse. My roots here are deep, and I couldn't just pick up and leave."

The doctor looked a bit uncomfortable, standing there still holding the tray. Riley wondered if having strangers gawking at his family portraits was making him uneasy.

Then he turned and headed for a pair of doors that stood open on the other side of the room.

"Let's take our drinks out back, sit by the pool," he said. "It's a shame to waste a beautiful day like this."

Riley and Bill followed him out to a pleasant terrace beside a large pool surrounded by landscaped gardens. Dr. Poole set the tray down on a deck table and closed the doors behind them.

As he poured lemonade and handed each of them a glass, he continued his comments about his family.

"Still, it's tough having the kids on the other side of the country most of the time. But we still do a lot together. I never miss a chance to spend time with them."

"Well, I could see that your kids adore you, Dr. Poole," Riley said.

"And I adore them," he said. "But if you don't mind, I don't much like being called 'Dr. Poole.' Gordon or Gordy is the usual thing, even with people who don't know me really well." Then with a chuckle he added, "If you really must be formal, 'Dr. Gordy' will be OK."

Riley laughed. She liked this man more by the minute. She saw signs of weariness in his face and she could understand why. A man as kindly and dedicated as he seemed to be must put in very long hours. She could relate to that.

Riley found the setting to be quite idyllic. Still, she had trouble getting quite comfortable. All this luxury seemed so far away from the world she'd been immersed in during the last few days—a world of pimps, prostitutes, and killers. She felt vaguely guilty just being here.

"I can access everything we want to know right here," Dr. Poole said, opening up a laptop computer that was on the table.

Bill said, "We understand that you've been helping the police investigate drug thefts from hospitals. Chief Morley says you do that kind of thing pro bono. That's very generous of you."

Dr. Poole shrugged modestly.

"Well, it's the least I can do. Phoenix has been good to me, as you can see. I like to give something back whenever I can. And the theft of HIV drugs—well, that deeply troubles me, and I feel like it's a personal issue. And Elgin tells me that you think this serial killer might be HIV positive and stealing drugs for himself."

"That's right," Riley said. "Have you got any suspects in this spate of medicine thefts?"

Dr. Poole squinted at the computer screen.

"As a matter of fact, I'm narrowing it down to just a few," he said. "There's one in particular that …"

He paused for a moment.

"I'm not sure I should give you this information," he said.

"Why not?" Bill asked.

"Well, the person in question is a rising administrator in a Phoenix hospital. He might be the man you're looking for. But the evidence is still thin. And to be perfectly honest, I hope I'm wrong."

Dr. Poole shook his head worriedly.

"I'd hate to ruin an innocent man's reputation. Still, I'm sure that Elgin will know how to handle this."

He took a pad of paper out of his pocket and jotted something down.

"I'll tell you what. I'll write down his name right here, and you can pass it along to Elgin. I'll leave the whole matter to his discretion."

He handed Bill the paper. Riley and Bill thanked him for his time and left his house. While Riley drove them back to headquarters, and Bill called the name in to Morley.

*

When Riley and Bill got back to the FBI building, they found Morley pacing in agitation.

"Dr. Poole's tip didn't pan out," he said. "The man's been on vacation for two weeks, at a beach resort in Mexico. There's no

182

way he could have committed these recent murders. Of course, Dr. Poole couldn't have known that. We need to keep him in the loop in case he has any other ideas."

Morley stopped pacing and glared at Riley and Bill. He said, "It seems to me that we're no closer to closing this case than we were when you two got here."

Riley was about to snap out a reply about all the work they'd put in, but she stopped herself. She could hear Bill smother a growl. Neither of them wanted to escalate their tensions with Morley.

The buzzing of her cell phone was a welcome interruption to the silence.

She didn't recognize the number calling her, but she knew the voice on the line very well. It was Shane Hatcher, a prisoner in Sing Sing Correctional Facility who had been very helpful in their last case.

"You need to talk to me," Hatcher said. "About the case you're working on out there in Phoenix."

"Good," she replied. "I could use some fresh ideas. Fire away."

"Oh no, not over the phone. You know I've got to get something out of the deal. An in-person visit is a requirement—a prerequisite, you might say, for my expertise in matters such as this."

"That's not possible."

"I feel sure that you can make it possible, Agent Paige. I have complete confidence in your powers of persuasion. After all, you persuaded the last man you and I discussed to slit his own throat."

Riley was silent for a moment. She found it disturbing that this man who was locked away always seemed to know so much. But right now, she would welcome any source of light on this case.

"I'll see what I can do," she said, and hung up.

She realized that Morley and Bill were both looking at her in expectation.

"That was Shane Hatcher," she said.

"No kidding?" Bill said. He told Morley who Shane Hatcher was, and about Riley's unusual relationship with him.

Riley said, "He won't tell me anything over the phone. I'll have to go there."

"That's ridiculous," Morley sputtered. "Sing Sing is in Upstate New York."

"The BAU plane is still at the airport," Riley said. "That will be the fastest way for me to get there and back."

"You have work to do here," Morley exploded. "You can't just drop your job every time you get a notion to do something else."

Riley saw Morley's face redden. She knew that he had just stopped himself from saying that he wouldn't authorize the trip. She had ignored his authority before, and he wouldn't want to put himself in that position again.

"I'll get back as soon as I can," Riley said as she left the room.

Her mind was already focused on the man locked up in Sing Sing—the most dangerous man she had ever known.

If anyone could unlock this case, she knew, it would be him, with his uncanny perceptions about serial killers.

But at what price?

Chapter Thirty Six

Riley spent the next morning on the FBI jet headed for Upstate New York. The day was almost half gone by the time she walked into the little visiting room at Sing Sing Correctional Facility. She'd been here before, but hadn't expected to come here again.

It wasn't a visit she was happy to make.

And there he was—the murderer Shane Hatcher, sitting at the visiting table waiting for her. He was a middle-aged African-American, strong in body and in will, and extremely intelligent. Riley felt deep down that he was the most dangerous human being she had ever met.

Hatcher had been last night's caller, the man who had cryptically said …

"You need to talk to me."

From past experience, Riley knew that she should take him at his word.

She sat down across the table from him. As always, he was clad in a dark green jumpsuit and wearing small-framed reading glasses.

"It's been a long time," he said.

"No it hasn't," Riley said.

In fact, she'd visited him twice last month. On Mike Nevins's advice, she'd come to Hatcher for his insights into the chain killer's mind.

In his youth, Hatcher had been a ruthless gangbanger who specialized in killing with chains. After he had beaten a cop to an unrecognizable pulp and left the body on his porch for his wife and kids to find, Hatcher had been convicted and sent to Sing Sing. He'd been here ever since. He'd probably be here for the rest of his life.

That was fine with Riley. The truth was, she didn't think Hatcher deserved to live—no more than Derrick Caldwell had deserved to live. She'd even said that to his face once, to his obvious delight.

But she couldn't deny that he was a valuable resource. Over the years, he'd given himself a thorough education in criminology. In fact, he was now an acknowledged expert in the field. He'd published a number of scholarly articles, which was how he'd come to Mike Nevins's attention.

"You said you can help me," she said.

"I helped you out last time, didn't I?" Hatcher said.

Riley nodded. "How did you find out about the case?"

Hatcher shrugged and smiled.

"How do you think? Newspapers. TV. The Internet."

Riley looked at him skeptically.

"And you think you can help me, based just on media coverage?"

He didn't reply, just kept smiling at her.

"You want a favor for helping me, of course," Riley said.

"Of course."

"What do you want?"

He let out a sinister chuckle. "Merely the pleasure of your company," he said.

The words made Riley's skin crawl. Locked up though he might be, she couldn't help thinking of him as a stalker. Was he obsessed with her? Was yesterday's call just a ruse? Did he have any intention of helping her at all?

She was determined to stay focused on the matter at hand.

"There's been a new development in the case," she said. "Our killer seems to have picked up a young girl. We don't know whether she's alive."

Hatcher tilted his head with interest.

"An abduction," he said. "Interesting. Hardly his MO. Was the girl a teenage hooker?"

"We don't know. We haven't identified her. She seems to have been a runaway. The woman who saw her said she had a backpack."

Hatcher stroked his chin as if deep in thought.

"The whole prostitution thing—an ugly world, isn't it? Now, I'm all for men and women doing whatever they want. But it's all about *choice*. I've made my own choices and I'll live with them. Everybody should have that opportunity. But a kid on the streets, well ..."

He paused for a moment, then said, "There are shelters for kids like that. There are groups that help get them out of the trade. You need to check them out."

"We'll do that," Riley said.

Another silence fell. Riley felt distinctly uneasy. Had she made this trip for nothing?

"I don't have time to play games today," she said. "A girl's life might be hanging in the balance. Tell me what you know."

Again came that grim chuckle.

"No," Hatcher said. "Tell *me* what *you* know."

*

The man who called himself T.R. sat in a chair in his basement, facing the girl who was bound to another chair by duct tape. Her mouth wasn't gagged at the moment. She was too sedated to scream. She kept rolling her head and moaning.

"You shouldn't have run away from home," he said.

She tried to focus her eyes on him. He wasn't sure whether she could understand what he was saying.

"Your mother must be worried," he said. "Didn't you ever think about how worried she'd be?"

Again, she didn't reply.

He didn't like this at all. When he'd picked her up yesterday morning, he'd thought she was just another whore. It was a stupid mistake. He'd been tired, scared, and unobservant. Besides, she'd said she knew Socorro. He remembered her exact words …

"We go way back, Socorro and me."

It had only taken a few minutes for him to realize that she was lying. She was just a runaway teenager who'd say anything for a ride. But by then it was too late. The whore back on Conover Avenue had recognized him, and now the girl could identify him.

Fortunately, he'd been able to sedate her right there in the car. And now he had no choice but to kill her. He wasn't used to killing out of necessity. There was going to be nothing epicurean about this murder. It was a nasty thought, having to kill with no enjoyment.

But it couldn't be helped, and he didn't feel guilty. This was all the girl's fault, after all, for running away. And her mother's too. The girl had been calling for her mom off and on ever since he'd taken her.

"Your mother should have taken better care of you," he said. "You shouldn't have run away."

She moaned softly. She still didn't seem to understand.

He wasn't sure just why he hadn't killed her already. Keeping her alive was rather a lot of trouble. Every so often he'd coax her out of her stupor for a little food and water. A couple of times he'd even unbound her so she could use the basement bathroom. She was far too drugged to be anything but docile.

Still, killing her was inevitable, and he knew it. He seemed to be waiting for just the right moment, and that moment had not yet come. He was, after all, a civilized man who liked to do things in a civilized way.

But holding her captive was risky. He'd already had one brush with danger. Another might be his undoing. He didn't like risks. He didn't like danger.

She was moaning a bit more loudly now. She was able to focus her eyes on him. He saw fear rising in her eyes. He reached for a hypodermic needle and stabbed her arm with it. She was instantly quiet again.

*

"You're getting warm," Hatcher said with a dark smile.

Riley had no idea what he meant. What did he think this was, a childhood game of hide and seek?

A full two hours had passed without either of them moving from their chairs. They had talked incessantly. So far, Riley hadn't found the interview to be informative, but it was far from dull.

Hatcher had grilled her for specifics that even Morley or Brent Meredith wouldn't have demanded. He seemed especially intrigued by the enigmatic Garrett Holbrook, the brother of victim Nancy Holbrook. Hatcher found it odd that Holbrook had insisted that Nancy's murder become an FBI investigation, only to stay on the periphery ever since. That had struck Riley as odd too.

"What do you make of him?" he'd kept asking Riley.

Riley wished she knew. She still didn't know.

But Hatcher seemed less interested in what she'd observed or learned than in her actions and reactions—what she'd actually been doing and how it had felt, down to the last sensory detail. He demanded to know everything she had experienced since she and Bill had boarded the FBI jet bound for Phoenix last Saturday.

What had it felt like to visit an actual brothel? How had she felt when she'd pretended to be a whore? When she'd rescued a runaway teenager? Or when the suspect slipped through her fingers at the truck stop?

Then he returned to her posing as a prostitute.

He said, "That I'd really like to see."

When she made no reply, he added, "You're a good-looking woman. How are you and your partner getting along? How does he like it that there are other guys in your life?"

She ignored those questions too. Finally, he nodded and moved to another topic.

The questions had become disturbing. Hatcher's interest in Riley's inner life struck her as twisted, even voyeuristic. She felt more and more as if he were obsessed with her. Had she flown all the way out only to entertain his twisted curiosity?

Eventually, the conversation had turned toward what Riley couldn't help but regard as irrelevancies. He'd demanded to hear a full account of April's breakdown, and how Riley had defied Morley to rush back and help her.

And just now, he was grilling her about her visit to her father, of all things. He was insisting upon hearing every word of their ugly visit. To the best of her memory, she'd recited all of it.

Why? Riley kept wondering.

It was just about the last thing she wanted to talk about right now. She wanted to be through with her father once and for all. She hoped with all her heart that she'd never have to see him again.

Hatcher seemed to be toying with her. She liked it less and less by the minute.

Finally, he leaned back in his chair, his glasses resting low on the bridge of his nose.

"You're getting warm," he said again.

The words were infuriating.

"What do you mean by that?" she said

He sat there smiling in silence again.

"I like that daddy of yours," he finally said.

Riley stifled the urge to say that she didn't like him at all. She said nothing.

"He and I have got a lot in common," Hatcher said.

Now Riley had to stop herself from saying she agreed with him. Hatcher and her father were both monsters in their way. They both had done more than their share of killing—her father in Vietnam, Hatcher in the streets of his youth. They were manipulators and users of other people. And neither one of them seemed truly capable of regret.

"You don't give your daddy enough respect," Hatcher said.

Riley's anger was rising. She fought it down. He'd only enjoy it if she blew up at him.

He leaned forward toward her, peering deep into her eyes, smiling grimly.

"You're getting warm," he said. "You should listen to your daddy."

He held her gaze for a long moment. Then he turned around and called out, "Guard, I think we're through here."

He got up from his chair as the guard opened the sliding barred door.

"Is that all you've got say?" Riley asked.

"Oh, I've said a lot, honey. I've said exactly what you needed to hear. One of these days you'll thank me. Believe me, you'll thank me."

Hatcher followed the guard behind the open door. The guard slid the door shut again with a heavy iron bang.

"And we'll meet again," he said through the bars. "Mark my words, we'll meet again."

*

A little while later, Riley was in the FBI jet watching the Catskill Mountains creep along below her. Had she learned anything from Hatcher? If so, she couldn't put her finger on it. However, he'd been awfully emphatic about something …

"You should listen to your daddy."

She'd told him every word her father had said to her during their visit. He'd picked up on something. Had her father tipped her off without either of them knowing it?

Riley was tired and she closed her eyes. She slipped back into the nightmare of her captivity, the flame gleaming in the darkness. She wondered if maybe she should stay here, in this memory, in this private darkness. After all, the dark recesses of her mind had served her well in the past. She'd been able to enter into the minds of the cruelest of killers.

But then with a chill, she remembered something her father had said …

"You're not dealing with a monster. Hell, you're not even dealing with evil. You're dealing with what folks call normal.*"*

And she remembered how he'd described him …

"The opposite of me—and the opposite of you."

Perhaps—just perhaps—her father had put his finger on the very problem. Was it possible that she was finally dealing with a killer whose heart wasn't as cold and dark as her own?

With her eyes still closed, she imagined herself rising out of that captive darkness, away from the flame, up into the sunlight.

Yes, she felt closer to him now. She was on his trail. And she'd find him to be in the daylight of everyday life, in a world populated by people who weren't monsters at all. Because he himself wasn't a monster. Or at least didn't see himself as a monster.

Not like my father, she thought. *And not like me.*

Her mind was in broad daylight now. She could feel herself seeing the day through his eyes, feel the sun on his skin, the embracing comfort of a respectable life.

And yet she could also feel his apprehension and fear. Those emotions were alien to him. He didn't know how to handle them. He was accustomed only to friendship, respect, self-confidence, and even a feeling of righteousness. Even now, he didn't feel that he had done anything wrong. But he was out of his depth, and exhausted, and scared, and he'd never felt that way before.

She smiled to herself. She remembered those words that Hatcher had kept repeating.

"You're getting warm."

It was true. She was getting warm. Now she needed to touch base with Bill. She called him on her cell phone.

"Did you get any information?" Bill asked.

Riley thought for a moment. "You should check shelters for runaway kids. Start with the shelter where Jilly is. Ask if maybe the girl might have been in a shelter somewhere in Phoenix. And check on Jilly for me."

"I'll do that."

Bill paused. He seemed to have something in mind.

"Riley, I've got an idea," he said.

"What is it?" Riley asked.

Another silence fell.

"I'm still processing it," he said. "I'll tell you when you get back. Will you be back in Phoenix in time to meet me at headquarters at eight?"

"Sure," Riley said.

"Then meet me there," Bill said.

They ended the call. Riley wondered what Bill had in mind. Well, she'd find out soon enough. And in her gut, she knew that something was about to break. Tonight, in fact. She was absolutely sure of it.

Chapter Thirty Seven

Bill felt vaguely sickened as he watched the girls at the shelter for teenagers. Brenda, the resident social worker, had led him to the rec room. The girls inside were talking, watching TV, playing games on cell phones, like any teenagers would. But these kids weren't ordinary.

This damned case, he thought.

Over the years, he'd come to think that he was immune to horror. But this place disturbed him deeply. It was, after all, a halfway house for kids who'd escaped from hell—and might yet go back there someday soon.

He looked at his watch. He still had plenty of time before Riley got back. He'd make the necessary arrangements for their meeting later. He hoped that his hunch was right. He wanted to close this case as quickly as possible.

Meanwhile, there was a girl to save. A girl just like these. But for all Bill knew, she might be dead already.

He could see that a few of the girls were visibly bruised. Most of them had a wary look that he recognized as a sign of emotional bruising. All of them had been brought here because they were novice prostitutes or had been trying to become prostitutes. They'd been found wandering at the edges of a lifestyle that he and Riley had seen too much of lately. The girls had already been victims of one kind or another.

He remembered that Riley had asked him to check on one in particular.

He asked Brenda, "Which one is Jilly?"

The social worker pointed her out—a skinny, dark-skinned youngster sitting at a table with a group playing a card game. She clutched her own cards close to her chest.

"Your partner seems attached to Jilly," the social worker said.

"She is," Bill replied. Then he thought that a little explanation might be called for. "But Agent Paige has a teenager of her own who's been through some difficulties recently."

The woman nodded in understanding. Bill thought about going over and introducing himself to Jilly as Riley's partner. But he had no idea how she might react. How would she feel about being approached by a male FBI agent? It seemed best to keep his distance, at least for now. But he could report to Riley that Jilly seemed to be OK.

Brenda said, "When you called you said you wanted us to check on another girl."

"You may have heard about a serial killer we've been tracking down," Bill said.

Brenda nodded. "The one who kills prostitutes."

"That's right," Bill said. "We're afraid he's picked up a runaway, a teenage girl."

Brenda gasped. "They're so damn vulnerable. Who is the girl?"

"That's the problem. The FBI has mounted a search, but we don't even have an ID on her. Just a vague description. It might help if we knew more about her. It would be great if we could find a picture."

Brenda thought for a moment.

"Yesterday, you said? None of ours have gone missing in the past few days. But we get alerts from all the shelters. Let's go check."

Brenda led Bill straight to her office. She sat down at her computer and started to search.

"What do you know about her?" she asked Bill.

Bill remembered some details. Jewel, the prostitute who had witnessed her abduction, had given them a description.

"She's probably about fourteen," Bill said. "Five foot six, maybe a bit shorter. Blonde, blue eyes, pale skin, thin. She was wearing a backpack."

Brenda skimmed a list of names.

"Here's something from yesterday," she said. "Her name is Sandra Wuttke—Sandy, they call her. She disappeared from a center on Windermere Avenue early yesterday morning. If she was in one of our shelters, this has got to be her."

Brenda clicked the name and brought up a photo on the screen. It was a thin, blonde girl with a defiant expression. Bill nodded. It certainly looked like the girl Jewel had described.

Brenda dialed up the center and got the director on the line. She put the call on speaker.

"Claudia, I've got an FBI agent here with me," she said. "Agent Bill Jeffreys. He's worried about a girl who fits Sandy Wuttke's description. She might be in danger."

Claudia's voice sounded worried.

"What kind of danger?" she asked.

"I'm sorry to say this," Bill said. "But she may have been taken by the serial killer you may have read about lately."

"The man who's killing prostitutes?" Claudia said, her voice trembling with alarm. "But that doesn't make sense. Sandy's not really a prostitute. She's traded sex for rides or food a couple of times. Then someone steered her here. But she's been restless. I wasn't all that shocked when she took off."

Bill asked, "Was she wearing a backpack?"

"She was, according to the girls who saw her leave. But I can't believe she's been taken by that killer. Maybe she just went home. We haven't had time to check. We're so understaffed. There are so many girls."

Bill sensed that the woman was trying not to believe the worst.

"Could you get me information on her family?" he asked.

Brenda seemed to looking into her own records.

"There's only her mother," Claudia said. "Colleen Wuttke. She doesn't have a phone. I could send somebody to her house to check."

"Thank you, but it's better if I go," Bill said. "Forward everything you've got about her to the local FBI. Brenda, jot down her address for me."

Bill thanked both women, and the call ended. Then, armed with the address for Sandra's mother, he left the shelter.

His feelings were mixed. He was grateful that workers like these were here to help Jilly and other youngsters.

But why are there so many of these girls? he wondered. *Why is it so easy for predators to find prey?*

*

When Bill arrived at the address, he saw that it was a rundown apartment building. Kids were playing on the sidewalk, and some young guys sat around on the front steps. The guys glared at him, but then looked away as he passed by them and entered the building.

The dark stairs and hallways were lit only by tiny windows at each landing. Apartment 4D was at the end of the hallway on the fourth floor.

When he knocked, he heard someone stirring inside. In a few moments a woman cracked the door open a little and looked out at him.

"Oh," she said with a kind of trembling growl. "I was expecting … well, not you, anyway. Who the hell are you?"

"Are you Colleen Wuttke?" Bill asked.

"Yeah. Who wants to know?"

Bill displayed his badge through the narrow opening.

"I'm FBI Agent Bill Jeffreys. I'd like to talk to you."

Colleen Wuttke seemed undecided whether to open the door or slam it in his face. Bill moved his foot into the opening.

"Is your daughter here? Sandy?"

"Not a chance."

"Were you expecting her just now?" he asked.

"Nope. Hoping for someone else. And I don't want to talk to you. If you try to come in here, I'll scream. Some big guys live around here, and they don't like cops."

Bill certainly wasn't afraid of the guys, but it wouldn't help if she started screaming.

"I'm not here to arrest anyone," he said. "I just need some information."

Suddenly she let go of the door and backed away. She grumbled, "Hell, who am I kidding? Nobody'd pay attention if I *did* scream."

Bill pushed the door gently and it creaked open. The woman standing inside was dressed in a housecoat. She looked gaunt and weak, and her face was heavily pockmarked. Bill immediately recognized the signs of longtime meth addiction.

He studied her face. He didn't see much resemblance to the girl in the picture. But he figured she would be a blonde if she ever washed her hair.

He saw a room with a beat-up couch that obviously doubled as a bed, a rickety table, a hot plate, and a sink. A curtain hanging in a doorway was open enough to show a ratty bathroom beyond. A single bed in an alcove to one side was littered with clothes.

The woman watched him look around. "This is all there is," she said.

She plopped down on the couch and sat facing him.

Bill said, "Your daughter was staying in one of the city shelters for girls."

"Was she?"

"Yes, but she ran away."

"Did she?"

As the woman talked, Bill realized that she wasn't as old as he had first thought. Meth had ruined her appearance, but she was probably just about thirty. She must have been very young when she had her daughter.

"When did you last see your daughter?"

The woman's face went blank. Finally she said, "I have no idea when that was."

With one hand she played with the edge of her robe, pulling it open to show scrawny legs. Bill realized that she was trying to flirt with him, and he felt revolted.

"So she hasn't contacted you recently?"

"Why would she do that, anyhow?"

Bill didn't know what to say in reply.

"Sandy won't never be coming home," Colleen Wuttke said.

She picked up a pair of cheap-looking metal earrings from a table beside the sofa.

"I had a bunch of these once, pretty things, all gold-toned and shaped like flowers. I got them cheap from a guy and sold them sometimes for a little extra cash. She took a ton of them right out of my collection. I guess she's sold them all by now. They ain't worth nothing much, but she shouldn't have stole it. Is that why you're looking for her? Did she steal something else?"

Bill was about to tell her the truth—that Sandy might be in the clutches of a killer. But he was seized by a gnawing sense of futility. There was no point in it. The woman wouldn't even care that her own daughter's life was in danger.

He handed her a card.

"If she ever contacts you, call me," he said.

"Oh, I'll be sure to do that," the woman said. Bill heard a note of sarcasm in her voice.

Bill's spirits continued to sink as he walked down the apartment building's stairs. He was used to ugliness, and he was used to murder. But he was also used to being able to keep count of the victims involved. Right now, the world seemed to be positively littered with victims—if not of the killer, then of countless other tormentors and abusers.

But now was no time to let his feelings get the best of him. Riley would be back soon. And if Bill's hunch was correct, they'd be wrapping up this case this very night.

Chapter Thirty Eight

Riley hurried down the hallway of the Phoenix FBI building. It was almost eight, and Bill had said he'd meet her here. She remembered what he had said on the phone when she was still on the plane.

"Riley, I've got an idea."

She wished he'd told her what his idea was. She'd been in suspense about it for hours. Was it possible that this horrible case was going to be wrapped up soon—maybe even in the next few minutes?

She wished she could dare to hope. But she'd slept only fitfully during the plane flight back. And the truth was, she hadn't gotten properly rested since she'd been awakened at three in the morning last Friday back in Fredericksburg. She was too tired to hope.

When she arrived at the office, she was surprised to see that Bill wasn't alone.

Garrett Holbrook was sitting there, his arms crossed, staring off into space. Riley's whole body was jolted with surprise. Now she understood. Now she knew exactly what Bill had been thinking.

Sounding as stiff and aloof as ever, Holbrook said, "Can we get started now? Can you please tell me what this is all about?"

Bill looked up at Riley. She nodded. It was high time for some questions.

"Let me get right to the point," Bill said. "Agent Paige and I need to know when you last saw your sister alive."

"I told you back when you first got here," he said in a slow, sullen voice. "It was years ago. I can't remember how long exactly."

Riley's senses quickened. It was a lie. She knew it. She could hear it in his words. He could remember. He could remember the exact date, the precise time of day.

She stepped toward him.

"We need the truth, Agent Holbrook," she said.

He continued staring into space, but he grew paler, and his eyes began to glaze.

"I can't believe it," he said. "I can't believe it's taken you this long. Haven't I been acting guilty enough?"

Suddenly, as if out of nowhere, a horrible sob rose out of his throat.

"Because I am guilty," he said.

Sobs came pouring out now, one on top of another, and tears gushed from his eyes. His face was twisted with anguish. Riley could hardly believe it was the same man as before.

He calmed himself enough to speak haltingly.

"It was just two years ago. That's when I saw Nancy last. She came to my house. She was down and out. She was doing drugs. She was selling her body. She wanted my help. She said she didn't have anybody else to turn to. She wanted a place to stay. She said I could help her clean up."

He choked on a horrible sob.

"I told her to go away."

He wept for a few moments. Then he said, "Why? Why did I do that? What did I have to lose? I've never been married, I never had kids. I had room in my house, room in my life. I was selfish. I was feeling good about my career, my carefree bachelor life. She was only my half-sister, so much younger than me, I felt like I barely knew her. I didn't want that responsibility. I didn't want to be bothered."

His sobs were quieting a little.

Riley said, "So that's why you've been so distant with us. That's why you've stayed on the sidelines."

Holbrook nodded.

"Hell, I felt like I was hunting for myself. I killed her as surely as anybody did."

Bill's jaw had dropped open with shock. He stared at Riley.

She mouthed silently to him, "He's telling the truth."

Bill nodded in agreement, then patted Holbrook on the shoulder. "I'm sorry," he said. "But if you'd only told us this sooner …"

Holbrook brushed Bill's hand aside.

"I'm going home now," Holbrook said brokenly. He rose to his feet and stumbled toward the door. Then he turned back toward Riley and Bill.

With a dark chuckle of self-loathing, he said, "Well, I guess you can eliminate me as a suspect. Maybe that's progress."

He left the office. Bill and Riley sat for a moment in dumbstruck silence.

"Damn," Bill finally murmured. "I was sure. I was so sure."

"I was suspicious of him too," Riley said. "His behavior was always strange, and now we know why."

But something was starting to dawn on Riley. Those words that Holbrook had said …

"I've never been married, I never had kids."

Those words mattered somehow. But why?

Riley's intuition was in full flood now, slamming together seemingly irrelevant details. They were snapping together like pieces of a jigsaw puzzle, forming some kind of coherent whole.

She remembered those words of Hatcher's …

"You should listen to your daddy."

And what had her father said that she should listen to? Oh, she remembered all the cynical, hateful talk about monsters and madness and what vile human specimens both she and he were. But there was something else. What was it?

Then the words hit her like a lightning bolt.

"Never trust a man whose kids don't hate him."

Suddenly she was fully in the killer's mind. She was behind his eyes, staring at his next victim—a lost and terrified teenage girl. He was going to kill her. But she wasn't like the others. There'd be no joy in it. The killing would give him no pleasure.

Still, he was going to do it. It had to be done. It had to be done right now. He'd put it off too long.

She heard Hatcher's voice, repeating yet again …

"You're getting warm."

She sure didn't feel like she was getting warm. She shook her head miserably.

"We're spinning our wheels, Bill," she said.

She thought for a moment.

"I want to check in with Dr. Gordy," she said. "He only gave us one name from his list of drug-theft suspects. We need more names. Someone out of the box. I have a feeling it may be someone else on that list. Someone we wouldn't suspect. This HIV lead is the only concrete lead we have. We need to exhaust it."

She dialed the phone number she had for the doctor. An answering service began to deliver an official-sounding message. Riley turned off the message without leaving one of her own.

"We don't have time to wait for him to get back to us," she said. "Let's go over to his house right now."

Bill stared at her like she'd lost her mind.

"Jesus, Riley, it's late. It sounds to me like you're grasping at straws."

That's exactly what I'm doing, Riley thought.

But she didn't say so to Bill. She charged out the door with her partner right behind her.

Chapter Thirty Nine

When they reached Dr. Poole's front door, Riley rang the doorbell, but nobody answered for quite a long time. Riley rang again.

Finally the speaker next to the door rattled to life, and the doctor's voice called out.

"Who is it?"

Bill replied, "Doctor Gordy, it's Agents Jeffreys and Paige. Bill and Riley. We talked to you yesterday."

The voice stammered a little in confusion.

"Gosh, I—I wasn't expecting you tonight," he said. "Did I forget an appointment? I don't *think* I wrote anything down …"

"I'm so sorry to bother you, Dr. Gordy," Riley said. "This is a bit of an emergency. We'll make things as quick as we can."

"An emergency! My goodness!" the doctor said. "Of course, come in."

The door swung open, and Bill and Riley walked inside. Gordon Poole was fully dressed in casual clothes and sneakers.

"I'm sorry, did we disturb you? Were you going out?" Riley asked.

The doctor chuckled. "At this hour! Goodness, no! I'm not a night owl these days. In fact, it's getting close to my bedtime."

Riley sat down on the living room couch. Bill sat in a nearby chair. The doctor remained standing with his hands in his pockets.

"Now what may I help you with?" he asked.

Riley said, "Dr. Gordy, our killer is holding a teenage girl. A runaway, just a kid. He's had her since yesterday morning. We'd hoped to find her by now. And we're worried. We don't have any time to lose. I'm afraid we're getting a bit desperate."

"Oh, dear!" the doctor said, looking back and forth at Riley and Bill with concern.

Riley continued, "As we said when we were here before, we think the killer may be HIV positive, so he might be stealing medications. But the name you gave us didn't pan out. The man is on vacation in Mexico. We need the names you didn't give us. And any others that you think are even slight possibilities. Please don't hold back any information out of concern for a possible suspect. A girl's life is at stake."

The doctor sighed and sat down on the sofa with Riley. He said, "I really can't stand the idea of pointing an incriminating finger at innocent men."

"We need to check out all possibilities as fast as we can," Riley replied with real urgency in her voice. "That's why we're disturbing you here at home so late at night."

Dr. Gordy knitted his brow in thought for a moment.

"All right," he said. "If the killer is actually connected to the thefts, there are a limited number of people who could have access to the medications."

Riley fought down her growing sense of futility. "A limited number of people" sounded woefully unspecific.

"Do you know whether any of those people are HIV positive?"

"I'm not sure how I would be able to tell. As you probably know, HIV is a virus that attacks the immune system. When immune system cells begin to fail, the body is susceptible to a variety of infections and diseases. Generally, flu-like symptoms will turn up in the first month or two. Fatigue can be another symptom. A rash or sore throat or headaches can be signs."

Riley and Bill looked at each other with discouragement. They both knew that they couldn't go around accusing just anybody who had those symptoms.

The doctor added, "Besides, he might not *have* any symptoms. We're talking about a man who is stealing the medication he needs, who is surely taking care of himself. With someone like that, there may be no visible symptoms at all for years."

"At least you can help us narrow it down," Riley said. "If you know anyone who has those symptoms and had access to the stolen medications, that could steer us in the right direction. There can't be a lot of those."

"All right," Dr. Gordy said reluctantly. "Just let me think for a moment."

During the silence that followed, Riley sat looking around the room. She focused on the family pictures on a nearby wall. She had admired those the last time they had visited Dr. Gordy. There were a lot of photos hung in rows, all showing happy children and the parks or beaches they were enjoying, the fish they had caught, the prizes they had won.

Dr. Gordy finally said, "I can give you two names. Their duties allow them access to the medicine, and I've noticed some telltale symptoms. But I have to warn you, I find it very hard to believe that these people are guilty."

"We'll definitely keep that in mind," Bill said firmly.

Riley's attention wandered as Dr. Gordy shared names and contact information with Bill, who took notes. She couldn't help looking again at the pictures on the wall. The children looked so happy. Riley wondered why their mother had left and moved them so far away.

Then, for some reason, her father's words echoed in her mind.

"You're dealing with what folks call normal."

That was it. The photos kept drawing her attention because everything in them looked so very normal.

She realized that both Bill and Dr. Gordy were looking at her, expecting some comment on whatever they'd been discussing.

"I'm so sorry," Riley said, "I've spent too many hours on a plane today. I'm afraid I'm just tired and a little unfocused."

Bill said, "We have two more names to look into now. I've assured Dr. Gordy that we'll be very careful about making accusations."

"Oh, thank you," Riley said.

When she looked at the genial doctor, she felt as if his appearance was changing before her eyes. She started to wonder, and her heart began to beast faster.

Could this be the killer, seated before her? This perfectly normal, eloquent doctor? In this perfectly normal house and suburb? With his perfectly normal family? Could evil be so disguised?

Or was she losing her mind now for good?

She had to find out.

She tried to keep her voice steady as she chose her words carefully.

"I couldn't help admiring your photos again," she said. "Your children look so happy with you. Do you get to see them often?"

Despite herself, she heard her own voice trembling.

She watched very carefully, and her heart dropped as she caught a quick flash of anger on the doctor's face before he broke into a smile and said, "Not as often as I'd like, of course. But life doesn't always go exactly as we've planned, does it?"

Now Riley was studying the man with all her powers of observation. She didn't quite know why, but she was starting to sense that something was very wrong with this sweet-looking man sitting before her.

"I hope that my bit of professional advice was worth your driving here at this hour," Dr. Gordy said, with a tone of wanting to wrap things up.

"Of course it was," Riley said. "And thank you so much. We're sorry to have put you to any trouble," she said, her heart slamming, trying to figure out how to stall. "We'll go now, and let you get back to your evening."

She then wracked her brain for something, anything to say, as he began to sit up.

"But do you mind if I use your bathroom first?" she added.

He hesitated, then smiled reluctantly.

"Of course not," he said. Pointing down the hallway. "The guest bath is the first door on the right just down the hall."

Riley got up and hurried down the hallway. She could feel her palms sweating.

Had she lost her mind? Was she seeing things where there was nothing?

Riley poked her head into the guest bathroom that Dr. Poole had told her to use. There was a medicine cabinet above the sink and a few cabinet doors and drawers. But searching here would be waste of time. Poole wouldn't have directed her here if there was anything to find.

I don't have time to look everywhere, she thought. *I'd better get lucky.*

Trespassing deeper into his house, she passed by several other doors and went to a big fancy one at the very end of the hall. When she pushed it, the door opened into a huge master bedroom that was softly lit by two elegant fixtures.

She stepped inside and pulled the door shut behind her. There were standing wardrobes, three chests of drawers, and doors that probably led to closets.

Where should she start?

She went to check an open door on the other side of the room and found a private bathroom. She turned on the light and darted inside. The bathroom was bigger than her own bedroom. It had all the necessities, plus lots of mirrors and elegant decorative touches. She'd have to go through a whole array of drawers and cabinet doors until she found something. She threw one cabinet door open, glanced around, then reached for another.

There was nothing.

I hope Bill keeps him talking, she thought.

Bill wished Riley would hurry up. If the missing girl was still alive, they had no time to lose. And if she wasn't, they needed to nail the killer before he struck again. And they had found out everything the doctor was willing to tell them. He looked at the pictures on the wall, seeking a topic of conversation.

"So—you and your kids seem to enjoy fishing," he said. "Me, too. You folks in Arizona have got it made. So many lakes, so many places to fish."

"Yes, there are lots of lakes here, aren't there?" Dr. Poole said. "They're all artificial, you know. The products of skillful engineering, damming rivers, and filling canyons. Most of them double as reservoirs, and they're great recreational sites. Lake Mead is the biggest reservoir in the USA. We share that one with Nevada, you know."

"What kind of fish can you go for?"

"Oh, the state stocks them with trout, crappie, catfish, tilapia, and several kinds of bass. Once I caught a real trophy-size bass."

Dr. Poole was looking a little distracted. He kept glancing toward the hallway.

"I envy all the time you spend with your kids," Bill said. "I can see from the pictures how much they love you."

Dr. Poole shrugged rather absently.

"They can't possibly love me as much as I love them," he said.

"Yeah, anyone can see that."

A silence fell, and as Bill looked around, something shiny on the floor caught his eye. It was under the table right next to his chair, almost hidden in the thick shag of the carpet.

Bill got up from his chair and bent over to see it better. He picked it up, wanting to help the kind doctor.

It was a shiny metal earring—a cheap thing, shaped like a flower.

Suddenly, in his mind he heard the words of Colleen Wuttke.

"I had a bunch of these once, pretty things, all gold-toned and shaped like flowers."

This was Colleen's missing earring.

What was it doing here?

His heart slammed as it all came together at once, and he realized.

This could only mean that—

But as soon as he realized, as soon as he began to reach for his gun, suddenly, he felt a hard blow against the back of his head.

And then, everything went black.

Chapter Forty

Riley was finding nothing useful, and knew she had to give up the search soon. She had no legal reason for rummaging around in the doctor's house—nothing but her sudden intuition about him. And what if her intuition was wrong? What if her paranoid mind had her pinning the most respectable doctor that the police worked with?

Feeling her time running out, she was close to panic when she pulled open a pair of cabinet doors and heard a low humming sound. She moved a stack of toilet paper rolls aside.

Far back inside the cabinet was a little refrigerator. She opened its door and a light came on inside.

The mini-fridge was full of large white plastic bottles, not prescription vials. She reached for one bottle and poured enormous pink pills into her hand.

It was the stolen HIV medicine. She was sure of it. These bottles looked like they had come straight from a manufacturer, and she knew that some of these medications required refrigeration.

Her heart slammed in her chest, her mind reeling as all of the pieces fell into place. Her intuition had been right, and now her thoughts chased each other through brambles of confusion.

Why hadn't she suspected Poole during her first visit? Why had she let him charm her into liking him?

The answer was simple. She'd let herself be fooled by conventional wisdom. It was well understood among FBI agents that, in spite of stories about killers inserting themselves into police investigations, it very seldom actually happened. She hadn't bothered to consider the possibility.

But Shane Hatcher had considered it—based solely on what she had told him about Dr. Poole. Hatcher knew that Poole was their man. He knew that Riley had already met the killer.

She remembered his sinister grin.

"You're getting warm."

And now it made all the sense in the world. What better way for Poole to cover up his own thefts of HIV drugs? The police would never suspect the very man who was helping them—a man with a sterling reputation for honesty and integrity.

Riley heard a sound behind her, but before she could move something hard slammed into her back. She fell forward and cracked her head hard on the cabinet top. Dazed, she was aware that a knee was pressed into her back, holding her down. Then the knee moved aside and her hands were pulled behind her back and bound. She felt something being pulled over her head and face.

She thrashed and tried to turn around. But then came another brutal shove, thrusting her face against the floor. Now he was kneeling on top of her, with his weight in the small of her back, keeping himself out of her reach. He'd done this before. He knew how to do this. And he was stronger than he'd looked.

Riley struggled for air, kicking madly. She could neither inhale nor exhale. The clear plastic fogged over in front of her eyes. She was losing consciousness now. Images swam before her eyes. She expected to find herself back in the hell of Peterson's cage, seeing his face lit by the propane torch. But instead, she saw her father's face. His expression was stern and hard. He held a knife to her face.

"Let me help you out of this," he said.

Had he come to rescue her? No, Riley still had just enough presence of mind to know that she was hallucinating.

"Let me help you out of this," her father repeated.

And he pointed the knife under her chin. She knew what he was about to do. He was about to gut her from her jaw to her crotch. He was going to skin her like a squirrel—pull off her pelt as smoothly and gracefully as helping a lady out of her coat on a dinner date.

Am I going to let it end like this? she thought.

Was she going to let her father do this to her?

Was she going to let Dr. Poole do this?

Was she going to let this ugly world of abuse and exploitation strip her of everything she was, and all she hoped to be?

Riley fought her way back into defiant consciousness. She twisted her body hard and quickly. She felt Poole's weight give way as he fell to one side. She felt the hastily tied ropes on her wrists come loose, and then her hands were free.

She ripped the plastic away from her face, and her throat and lungs burned from the intake of air. She scrambled to her feet and turned around.

Dr. Gordy stood facing her, and he held a gun in both hands. It was Bill's gun.

She tried to speak, to ask him what he'd done to Bill. But after her brush with suffocation, the words couldn't force their way out of her throat.

He held the gun shakily, standing in an absurd position to fire from. She could tell at a glance that he hadn't fired a pistol in his life. But in these close quarters, that didn't make him any less dangerous than a man who went to the firing range every single day.

She lunged toward him, and he fired. But he was a split second too late, and she had already deflected his arm. She heard the bullet crash harmlessly into the bathroom tile. The gun fell from the doctor's hand and skidded across the floor.

She took a step back and slammed her fist into his belly. He lurched over with a loud groan. She brought her other fist hard against the side of his head. His head crashed against the doorframe, and he slid senselessly to the floor.

Riley shook her hand. It hurt like hell. But she didn't think it was broken. She got out her handcuffs and cuffed the doctor to a safety grip bar set into the wall, certain he wasn't going anywhere.

Picking up the gun, she staggered out of the bathroom and across the bedroom to the hallway.

Now at last, she was able to call out.

"Bill! Bill!"

There was no answer.

Riley's strength was returning. She rushed down the hallway and into the living room. Bill was lying on the carpet, bleeding from a head wound. A fireplace poker lay on the rug nearby.

Riley kneeled over her partner. He hardly seemed to be breathing, and his pulse was weak. She felt a wave of grief, of regret, of guilt. What if he died? This man she had known better than anyone on earth?

She called the FBI emergency line.

"Agent down. I need an ambulance here."

"Got you," the reply came. The voice on the phone double-checked the address.

"Hurry," Riley said, and hung up. She checked Bill again, but she knew she shouldn't try to move him. She had to wait for the ambulance.

Riley stood up and looked around the living room. She knew that if the girl was still alive, she was probably somewhere in this house. She went back into the hallway and started checking doors she had passed by in her search for medications. One opened on a landing and stairs going downward into darkness.

Riley switched on a light and hurried down the steps.

In the center of the well-furnished basement recreation room was a thin young girl, bound to a chair with duct tape. She'd overturned the chair and was lying on her side. Her mouth wasn't gagged, but Riley could tell by her eyes that she was heavily sedated.

Elation charged through Riley's body. The girl was alive.

She ran to Sandra Wuttke and began to untie her.

The girl seemed to realize what was happening. She began weeping.

"He was going to kill me," she said.

Riley held the girl and rocked her.

"It's all right now," she said. "He can't hurt you again. It's all right now."

Riley felt tears rolling down her own face. This girl was younger than April and her life had nearly been cut short. In some ways, she could not help but feel as if she were holding April, after she had just escaped from Peterson.

"He had a plastic bag," Sandra moaned. "He would have killed me."

Riley stroked her hair.

"You're a brave girl," she said. "You're going to be all right. Everything's going to be all right."

She heard sirens in the distance, the ambulance, and probably an FBI car too.

Riley only hoped that they would get here in time for Bill.

Chapter Forty One

Bill and Riley were finishing up their debriefing with Brent Meredith in his office at Quantico. Bill's head was still bandaged, and he'd suffered a slight concussion, but Riley could tell that he was doing fine now. All in all, she felt satisfied with the wrap-up of the case in Phoenix.

"Good job, you two," Meredith said. Then, with a sort of half-smile to Riley, he added, "Even Agent Morley seemed to think so."

Riley smiled back rather weakly. Yes, Morley had thanked her and Bill on the tarmac back in Phoenix before their flight back here. But there hadn't been a lot of warmth in his thanks. He had been especially chilly toward Riley. She hadn't found that surprising. And she couldn't quite blame him.

Meredith swiveled back and forth in his office chair. Riley recognized it as the chief's signal that the meeting was coming to an end. He looked at Riley and shook his head a little.

"Agent Paige, on your next case, I hope you make things easier on my end. I covered for you a lot. And for future reference, our jet is not for your private use."

Now Riley blushed a little.

"I owe you, sir," she said.

"Yes, you do," Meredith said.

Indeed, she knew that she did. She had Meredith to thank that she hadn't been kicked off the case—or kicked out of the Bureau, for that matter. What had she been thinking, going AWOL in the middle of a case?

But of course, she knew what she had been thinking. She'd been thinking about April. At that moment, her daughter had truly meant more to her than her job. Did she still feel that way?

Yes, she did.

I'm not my father, after all, she realized.

Meredith asked, "Was the second trip, the one to Sing Sing, actually useful?"

Riley considered the question for a moment. No doubt about it, Hatcher had identified the killer, even if he'd only said so in riddles. Still, the idea of having to meet him again felt intolerable to Riley.

"I don't plan to consult with him anymore," she said.

Meredith rose from his desk, a cue that the meeting was over.

Bill and Riley left the building. They said nothing for a few moments as they walked. Much of the plane trip back had been like that.

"I could drive you home," Bill said.

"It's OK, my car is here," Riley said. She had left her own car at Quantico when they had first left for Phoenix. Now it felt like that had been ages ago.

"Maybe we could stop somewhere for a drink or something to eat," Bill said.

Riley wasn't sure just what Bill was after. After his awkward pass at her last week, was he still trying to strike some romantic sparks between them? Maybe not. Maybe he really wanted nothing more than a few relaxed moments with a friend and colleague.

Either way, Riley wasn't really in the mood.

"We did some good work together in Phoenix," she said. "Let's call it a day."

Looking a bit sad, Bill said, "OK, then."

Bill started walking away.

Riley called after him. "Bill. I like working with you."

Bill called back. "The feeling's mutual."

She and Bill walked their separate ways. As Riley drove home, she wondered where things really stood between them. She was glad that they were back in the swing of things as a team again. But there was still unresolved tension between them.

The truth was, Riley now wondered how she felt about men in general. Her experiences in Phoenix had soured her. Pimps like Jaybird and rich misogynists like Calvin Rabbe didn't inspire her with a lot of trust. Neither did Garrett Holbrook, who had been so enchanted by his carefree bachelor life that he'd abandoned his own sister. Even Bill had turned Riley's stomach by getting turned on by the sight of her dressed up as a hooker.

Maybe I'm through with men for good, she thought.

*

Riley relaxed on the back deck of her townhouse, enjoying the neighborhood sights and sounds. She'd turned down Gabriela's offer of fresh lemonade, opting for soda instead. She was afraid that, for a long time to come, lemonade was going to remind her of a murderer who had at first fooled her completely.

In her mind she could still hear Dr. Gordy's *goshes* and *oh my goodnesses*, and she could still see his face when he'd attacked her.

But April and Crystal, the girl from next door, were drinking Gabriela's lemonade. They were sitting down in the yard watching a movie on April's laptop. They kept laughing and pointing to the screen.

Even without the lemonade, Dr. Gordy kept pushing his way into Riley's mind. Luckily, the man was in jail and the case against him was solid. He would never be free again. In fact, Arizona had the death penalty for those convicted of multiple homicides, so Dr. Gordy's arrogance would eventually come to a complete end.

Unfortunately, neither his incarceration nor his death would do anything for the three women he'd killed. Maybe it would be helpful to the two others he had terrorized, and it would certainly benefit those he'd never gotten a chance to take.

Riley briefly wondered if Socorro had gone back to prostitution or had found some better way to support her kids. There were organizations in Phoenix that would help her make a lifestyle change if she wanted to do it.

April came up the stairs to the deck and interrupted her ruminations. She poured herself more lemonade from the pitcher that Gabriela had left on the table. Her friend Crystal was still down in the yard, glued to the computer.

"Are you thinking about your case?" April asked.

Riley managed to smile a little. "Please don't worry about me, sweetie. Go back and watch your movie."

"Hey, after all we've been through together, you can tell me about it."

Then April shrugged.

"Besides, it's a stupid movie," she said, sitting down next to Riley.

Riley sighed.

"I can't help wondering what will become of some of the people I met. Especially the young girls."

"Like the one you rescued from the killer?"

"Yes. At least Sandy is back in a shelter now."

"From what you've told me, she for sure won't run away again."

Riley didn't reply. She hoped April was right. But April hadn't seen all that she'd seen lately—the hopeless faces of women like Chrissy, who simply couldn't comprehend a better life, and the vacant stares of much younger girls who were already starting to lose all hope. She fell quiet for a few moments.

"There was another girl," Riley said. "I took her from a truck stop to a shelter. Her name's Jilly, and she never had a decent break in her life up until now. Thank goodness, she's getting the best help anyone could give her. Both Jilly and Sandy will need some time, but they'll have a chance now. They'll have a choice."

She could hear Shane Hatcher's words again.

"It's all about choice."

Her own choice, she decided, was to never call on Hatcher's help again. There was no denying that he had helped her find her way through puzzling crimes, but his advice sprang from a darker place than she had ever encountered. She didn't want to go there ever again.

Her thoughts were interrupted by the doorbell ringing. She heard Gabriela answer the door and tell somebody, "They're out back."

April stood up to see who had come in.

She then looked back at Riley, looking deflated.

"It's Dad," she said in a flat, emotionless voice.

Riley felt like fleeing the scene, but she didn't move. How dare he show up now, after ignoring April when she'd needed him so badly?

When Ryan came out onto the deck, she stared coldly up at him and said, "What the hell do you want?"

Ryan put one arm around April and said, "I'm so glad you're OK, honey."

He turned to Riley and added, "I'm sorry, Riley. I know I was being rotten when you called me."

When Riley made no reply, he added, "It seems like you never want to talk to me unless you need something."

Riley replied, "Your daughter needed something."

"I know. I hope you both can forgive me."

April ducked out from under his arm and went back down to the yard to join Crystal.

Without being invited, Ryan turned the empty chair and sat down facing Riley. Riley was studiously ignoring him.

"You've got a nice place here," he said. "I'm glad you got out of that little dump in the country where you lived before."

Riley knew that he was reminding her that she had him to thank. And it was true. She had been able to buy this townhouse that she and April and Gabriela all loved because Ryan was being generous with child support. Her ex-husband wasn't stingy with his money— just with himself.

"Yes," she said reluctantly. "We're all happy here. Now I have an easy drive to Quantico and April has no problem getting to school."

Riley finally looked directly at him. She realized that Ryan looked good. He was as handsome as ever.

He leaned forward and spoke earnestly. "I miss you both. I think we should see more of each other. After all, we were together for a long time. We're still a family."

Riley could hardly believe what she was hearing.

"What happened to …" Riley couldn't remember the name of the woman Ryan had been seeing.

"It wasn't the same with her."

Riley's jaw dropped a little.

He wants me back, she realized.

Didn't he have any idea how through with him she was?

"Well," she said, "I'm sure you'll find the right woman someday."

Now Ryan looked hurt. But Riley was determined not to show him any sympathy.

She said, "You say we're still a family. But we were never a family—at least not all three of us. You were never there."

"I can change," Ryan said.

"Face facts, Ryan. You're never going to change. April and I both gave you every chance, for years and years. It's not going to happen."

She sensed that her bitterness showed in her face.

Ryan looked out over the backyard.

"I guess you're probably enjoying your freedom," he said.

Riley groaned. That was him all over, reducing her motives to his own level. She had a world of reasons not to get back together with him, but he had to believe that this was the most important one. Still, he wasn't entirely wrong.

She said, "As a matter of fact, I *am* enjoying my freedom. And you're not going to be part of it."

Before Ryan could reply, the doorbell rang again. In a few moments, Gabriela appeared, joined by their next-door neighbor, Blaine Hildreth—Crystal's father.

Gabriela's eyes were gleaming. Unable to suppress a giggle, she turned and hurried away.

Blaine took one look at Ryan and Riley and stopped in his tracks.

"Oh," he said. "I didn't mean to interrupt."

"Actually, you are," Ryan said gruffly.

Oh Jesus, Riley thought. *Is this going to turn into a testosterone-fueled pissing contest?*

Ryan was the taller of the two, and the better dressed in his expensive, casual clothes. But Riley didn't find him the least bit attractive at the moment. Blaine was younger, and he seemed livelier, more engaged with the world. And at the moment, he was showing much better manners.

"Actually, you're not," Riley told Blaine. "Ryan was just leaving."

Ryan glared at her, looking completely defeated, and a smoldering rage forming behind those eyes. A look meant to intimidate.

Riley, though, was through being intimidated. She remembered how she'd blocked her father's punch and had finally stood up to him. The memory stuck with her, and it was oddly empowering. After all these years, Ryan still had no idea who he was dealing with, what she was capable of.

She held his gaze and glared back.

She repeated in a commanding voice, "*Weren't* you, Ryan?"

From the look on his face, Riley was pretty sure he'd gotten the message. Without a word, he stood up and stalked back through the house. She heard the front door close behind him.

"Well, I guess I've just met your ex," Blaine said.

Riley laughed a little. "That was him."

Blaine chuckled as well. "How did things go in Arizona? Any new stories to tell?"

"Not yet," she said. "I've got a lot of processing to do before I can talk about it."

"I understand."

The sounds of giggling girls' voices were coming up from the yard. Riley was sure the giggling was all about what had been going on among the adults.

Blaine got up and walked to the deck rail and called down to Crystal.

"There you are! I've been looking all over for you!"

Crystal rolled her eyes, grinning from ear to ear.

"Come on, Dad. That's so lame. We all know who you really came over to see."

Blaine flushed, thoroughly embarrassed.

Riley was amused. Crystal had called the situation perfectly.

For a second, she was reminded of her father's words.

"Never trust a man whose kids don't hate him."

She smiled inwardly. She guessed that this made Blaine trustworthy.

Blaine turned to her and still clearly embarrassed, took a deep breath and said, "Now that you're back, I was wondering if you wanted to all have dinner together at the Grill. The four of us."

Riley smiled, outwardly this time. It had been a long time since she'd been asked out on a formal date. It felt good. And being with Blaine, even though she barely knew him, felt good, too.

"I'd like that," she said. "I'd like that very much."

COMING SOON!

Book #4 in the Riley Paige mystery series!

BOOKS BY BLAKE PIERCE

RILEY PAIGE MYSTERY SERIES
ONCE GONE (Book #1)
ONCE TAKEN (Book #2)
ONCE CRAVED (Book #3)

MACKENZIE WHITE MYSTERY SERIES
BEFORE HE KILLS (Book #1)

Blake Pierce

Blake Pierce is author of the bestselling RILEY PAGE mystery series, which include the mystery suspense thrillers ONCE GONE (book #1), ONCE TAKEN (book #2) and ONCE CRAVED (#3). Blake Pierce is also the author of the MACKENZIE WHITE mystery series.

An avid reader and lifelong fan of the mystery and thriller genres, Blake loves to hear from you, so please feel free to visit www.blakepierceauthor.com to learn more and stay in touch.

Heritage Point HOA
44 Heritage Point Blvd
Barnegat, NJ 08005

97273896R00124

Made in the USA
Columbia, SC
08 June 2018